The Gunsmith

by
Norman Kerr

Order this book online at www.trafford.com
or email orders@trafford.com

Most Trafford titles are also available at major online book retailers.

Note for Librarians: A cataloguing record for this book is available from Library
and Archives Canada at www.collectionscanada.ca/amicus/index-e.html

Printed in Victoria, BC, Canada.

ISBN: 9781-4269-136-8-6 (soft cover)
ISBN: 9781-4269-136-9-3 (hard cover)
Library of Congress Control Number: 2009931999

*Our mission is to efficiently provide the world's finest, most comprehensive
book publishing service, enabling every author to experience success.
To find out how to publish your book, your way, and have it available
worldwide, visit us online at www.trafford.com*

North America & international
toll-free: 1 888 232 4444 (USA & Canada)
phone: 250 383 6864 ♦ fax: 812 355 4082

For Tarryn and Amy and their cousins Christopher and Craig.
A special thank you to Lorraine and Boetie Ramsauer for their help
in launching "The Gunsmith"

Chapter One

The estate was magnificent. The surrounding farm and woodlands too were magnificent. That they all belonged to the same owner was obvious from the elaborate security precautions common to both. The overall beauty of the vast area which the Estate was part of was an area of planned wilderness where the woods and forest were set off by small irregular cultivated fields and meadows, surrounded by dense hedges and shrubbery.

A landscape artist of genius and superb good taste had laid down the design some seventy years before when the International Banker, Lord Montdrago's grand father, had bought the vast acreages. The new owner had decreed that a habitat perfect for the sustainability of wildlife and which could also support an annual shoot of a quality that even royalty would covet, be established without regard to cost.

A rail link to London existed within ten miles of the estate and the express train delivered a person into the heart of the city within an hour. Initially, in those far off days, all London's rich and famous attended the shoots and parties which banker Montdrago held but gradually, as the bank grew and prospered, the invitations became fewer and more selective until eventually when Montdrago's grandson, Lord Montdrago was the sole survivor of the Montdrago family, few invitations were ever extended to anyone by the enormously rich and powerful and mysterious Lord Montdrago.

The family mansion was built at the same time as the estate's landscape was laid out but it differed in that no famous architect was commissioned to effect the design, old Montdrago insisted that he alone would design and supervise the building of the new family home. Another strange and unorthodox procedure was adopted to construct the massive and lavish mansion; there was to be not one master builder engaged but rather several small builders were to be utilized. The small building contractors were all recruited from remote areas in Scotland and Ireland and security was tight whilst the building was in progress.

Sightseers were not permitted and the plans submitted to the authorities were deemed ridiculous. The walls surrounding the main working rooms were over six feet thick, the banker explaining to the amused authorities that he wanted to emulate the old designs of medieval England; it was his money so they humored him and approved his plans. Secretly, subtle modifications not in the plans were incorporated in those thick walls, secret passages and other secret refinements which the disjointed small building contractors soon forgot about when they returned home to their remote towns and villages hundreds of miles away.

The building however was superb and showed that old Montdrago had studied the designs of the finest country houses and mansions of England. Good taste, perfect proportion and avoidance of any modern innovation or deviation of authentic line, produced a country house as beautiful as any in the country.

Most Victorian grand houses on estates or farms had gunrooms where not only were the guns, rifles and ammunition kept but usually they were large enough to accommodate work benches, tool cupboards, cartridge loading equipment and sometimes even a lathe and other small machine tools. The gunroom in the Montdrago house was in a specially designed basement room which included a short, soundproofed shooting tunnel where guns were fired to both test and calibrate, especially the double express rifles that Montdrago owned and which he took with him on his frequent hunting trips around the world. His grandson, Lord Montdrago had fitted the latest tool makers' lathe and milling machine and other sophisticated tools and instruments when he became the master of the grand house.

It was a Montdrago tradition that guns were never sent out for maintenance or post season cleaning and oiling, gunsmiths came in to do the work which was always checked by the owner himself before allowing those craftsmen to depart back to their London headquarters until summoned again. All the Montdragos had excelled at shooting, a skill always cherished by the true lover of fine guns.

Another tradition concerned staff, they were kept to a bare minimum in contrast to most grand houses where there were far more servants than were needed. A servant's wages were very low in the founder's time, a condition that encouraged lavish servitude. An aristocrat had boasted at a shoot one day that he could have his gun smothered in the finest engraving, the most expensive art in gun making, for a guinea. Lord Montdrago's father, in keeping with tradition, had also kept the staff complement low and introduced all sorts of rules and restrictions as to how the staff must conduct themselves. These laws were eagerly embraced as the wages paid at the mansion had become extravagant and the staff were handsomely treated as long as they conformed.

Lord Mondrago's father, who had handled the banks affairs in Eastern Europe, married a woman from those parts whose father was equally as rich as Montdrago and whose main bank controlled many of the financial institutions situated in the surrounding cities. The new bride was plain and sickly and had a young woman constantly attending her, a position the young woman had held for a number of years. The young woman, Margaret, was not from Eastern Europe but from Scotland and had been selected by the father because of her education and a recommendation from a business associate who had said that Margaret had proved to be very closemouthed in his dealings with her and was neither a mixer or a gossiper.

After a year at Montdrago's estate, it was announced that the wife was with child and would be going back to Europe to await the birth at her father's home. Margaret accompanied her as usual and after a year the wife returned with her new son and was sicklier than ever. Despite the finest medical expertise and the best of nursing care the young bride died barely three months after returning to the Montdrago estate.

Very few attended the funeral and the young woman was interred in the family burial ground alongside the founder and his wife.

Margaret took complete control of the infant and became a super nanny in the custom of the times. Tutors were engaged as they were needed and the future Lord Montdrago received the finest of private educations. The child spent long hours cloistered in the main room with his father where the arcane skills of international banking were instilled in him. Margaret and the other staff noticed that as these secret sessions progressed the boy's character slowly changed. A suppressed arrogance and a barely disguised attitude of complete superiority developed; the superiority was disguised with good manners and a ready smile, the disguise gradually being enhanced by a natural attractive demeanor of consideration for all those he came into contact with. The entire staff gradually grew from liking the young banker to adoring him.

Margaret, a canny Scot with the highlander's distrust of anything English was never fooled for one split second and knew that the cunning and ruthlessness of the international banker had become second nature to the developing young man.

Margaret had joined the Montdrago household after a few years in an Edinburgh bank where she had first worked when leaving the small Scottish village where she was born. She had been a beautiful young girl who dressed plainly and endeavored to smother her beauty with plain clothes and an old fashioned hairdo which she complemented with an austere manner and an abrupt style of conversation. She succeeded as well as Lord Montdrago did in creating a false impression of the person within. The real person was a young woman of deep intelligence who was aware of the unfairness of life and who had trained herself to accept what life had bestowed upon her and not to plan too far ahead; as she grew older the mask she adopted became impenetrable and the austere middle aged lady that she became and Lord Montdrago barely tolerated one another.

Lord Montdrago's title was bestowed upon him after he had arranged and profitably put into motion, an international plan which was of great benefit to the nation. His lifestyle did not change with his elevation to the House of Lords, if anything he became more remote and secretive.

Many meetings were held in the main "Conference" room of his great manor house with the senior staff of his many banks and finance houses. The pre-meeting ritual never varied. First a team of technical experts would sweep the room for electronic listening devices immediately before the meeting commenced and again after the meeting ended. This precaution proved to be prudent when after one meeting a device was found. The miscreant was identified and severely dealt with and thereafter every delegate to a meeting had to pass through an electronic detection barrier at the entrance to the "Room."

Margaret, having observed these precautions over the years, decided that international banking and those who practiced the dangerous craft were a thoroughly evil lot and her dislike of her master grew. She remembered that some of the old staff who had served Grandfather Montdrago had told of the security that had prevailed in his time and of a curious feature of his way of conducting business. He never attended the meetings in person but always seemed to know of everything that was said or done in those meetings. Many thought that he always ensured that one or maybe two of those attending were his "spies" who told him of everything that had been discussed and of the potential disloyalty of any member in attendance. His son, Margaret observed, always attended every meeting as did his grandson, Lord Montdrago, who had instituted the electronic searches of the modern age. But, according to the original retainers, he, the founder of the bank, had never attended a meeting in the "Room."

One day, after Lord Montdrago and two of the banks senior executives had concluded a shoot on the estate, Lord Montdrago summoned Margaret.

"Margaret, when you were working in Edinburgh did you ever come into contact with anyone from the gun making firms?"

"Yes, Sir, I handled the account of one small gunsmith whose premises were in a village just outside the city. The proprietor took care of the guns of the local gentry including the bank manager's weapons; the manager attended most shoots in Scotland. I don't think he was a genuine enthusiast but rather he thought it was good for business." Margaret replied.

"The shoot this morning was marred by the malfunction of one of my guns. I intend to engage a gunsmith on a permanent basis who will live on the estate. The candidate must be highly skilled and young and not from the London firms, they gossip far too much. I would like you to go up to Edinburgh and if that firm you attended to is still in operation or if any of its staff can be located I want you to arrange for a young Gunsmith to come to the estate to be interviewed and inspected."

Margaret did not like the term "inspected" but knowing the Lord Montdrago behind the mask she knew it was a natural precaution of his training which his father had instilled in him all those years ago.

"I do not know anything about guns or gunsmithing, Sir."

"So much the better. I shall give you some notes to guide you in your dealings with the Edinburgh firm and I would like you to complete this task as soon as possible."

"Yes, sir, I shall leave for Edinburgh tomorrow morning." Margaret said.

"Good, is there anyone you would like to visit while you are there, family, perhaps? If so, feel free to spend a day or two and enjoy yourself. Thank you, Margaret." He said and with a nod, he dismissed her.

Chapter Two.

The train trip to Edinburgh was pleasant and Margaret had time to think without the pressures and cares of her daily routine. She was an only child that had been born to elderly parents who adored her and ensured she had a loving, sheltered and secure childhood in the small cottage they owned set in a lovely, small garden. The village where the cottage was situated had just sufficient small shops in the high street to meet the needs of the few villagers and the small farming community upon which the economy of the village depended.

Margaret had a happy childhood and as she grew older she realized how fortunate she was to have been born so healthy considering the age of her parents. She instinctively prepared herself for their deaths which followed in due time, as old age and not ill health, ended the earthly years allotted to them. Each passed over within a year of one another and Margaret's mourning was as intense as it was sensible; her maturity for a seventeen year old was remarkable and after placing the cottage which she had inherited in the hands of an agent to oversee the tenants whom she had leased the property to, she traveled up to Edinburgh and secured a position with a bank, impressing the senior staff with her no-nonsense efficiency and her integrity. She did not mix socially with her fellow workers and kept her thoughts to herself.

During her second year at the bank, Margaret fell in love. Two soldiers came into the bank one day, one of whom wanted to open an account. He was tall, in his early twenties and as Margaret assisted him in filling in the various application forms, he informed her that he was being posted abroad in two weeks time and would she care to have dinner with him that evening.

"You are a very forward young man, and no, I shall not have dinner with you. Please sign each form at the bottom and at the side next to the date." said Margaret primly, with a grin.

"My regiment, the Black Watch, trains all its men to be verry careful of strangers and as a canny Scot I cannot leave my money in the care of someone I don't know, so as a loyal employee of the bank, do your duty otherwise the bank may lose an important client. Incidentally, despite what those forms indicate, I am known as Big Jock so please stop calling me Mr. McBride, even Corporal McBride is not good enough. If you won't grant me an immediate overdraft, I'll dig into me sporran and scrape together a few pennies and we will go to a wee restaurant I know. You must promise, of course that as a representative of a Scottish bank with high Scottish standards, you'll not eat extravagantly and stick to oatmeal and haggis." concluded Jock with a laughing grin.

" No, one, you cannot have an overdraft and two I'll glutton out on caviar and cake and, three, will your wee friend chaperone me?" asked Margaret with a smile.

"I never go anywhere without Wee Willie and don't let his size and reticence fool you, Willie is my best friend and he hardly speaks to me either, but he is a bonny fella and tis I, I think, that needs the chaperone. They say that bankers always take advantage of underpaid soldiers and sneak in an extra percentage or two of interest when they can." Jock signed the last form with a flourish and asked,

"Where shall we meet?"

The arrangements were concluded and Margaret could hardly wait for the day to end.

Two wonderful weeks sped by and her happiness was complete when with a bursting hymen she entered into joyous womanhood one night in her small furnished flat. The lovemaking went on through the night and only ended when a pensive subdued Jock told her that earlier that day his regiment had been posted urgently overseas and that he would be leaving within a day or two and that because of the seriousness and the urgency, all soldiers would be confined to barracks until their departure. Margaret wept silently and held him close. He said he would write as soon as was permitted and that he was sure the emergency would be over presently. They declared their love for one another quietly and sadly and at dawn, Jock left with a gentle embrace and a promise to come back and marry Margaret and to love and cherish her forever.

The days dragged on to weeks and then months and there was no word from Jock. Margaret slowly came to the realization that she would never hear from Jock again and with the bitterness of the betrayed woman became unhappy and indignant that she, of all women had been so easily seduced.

One morning she was sent to an interview cubicle where the clients were attended to and was both surprised and angered to see Wee Willie sitting in the booth.

"Jock asked me to give you a note; I have it in my wallet."

"How very considerate, did he say anything to go with the note?" she asked with a tight voice dripping with bitterness.

"No, the bullet tore out his throat so he couldna speak but after he had given the note to me he made a gesture of holding someone to his bosom and then fixed his bayonet and jumping out of the dugout attacked the enemy position all on his own. The action took place barely twenty yards from where I crouched and it was glorious to see how he killed three of the enemy who tried to stop him reaching their dugout and how he threw the grenades in and how he stood his ground when a machinegun got his range and the bullets tore out chunks of his body while he continued fighting until he fell."

With that, Willie withdrew the badly black red stained note from his wallet and gave it to her.

Margaret unfolded the splotchy stained paper and was barely able to discern

" I love Thee." written on it. The dark pall of bitterness that had become part of her life lifted and the silent tears washed away the remnants of it.

"I'm so verry, verry sorry Lass." Said Willie softly, "I'll leave you now with him."

Willie struggled up out of the chair and Margaret saw that he had an artificial leg;

"It was a bloody battle." Willie said as he leant across and kissed her on the forehead and then turned around and walked away.

Margaret resigned an hour after she had received the note and worked out her notice without divulging her grief stricken motivation for leaving the banks employ.

Within a few days of serving her notice, an employment agency had placed her with an Eastern European Banking house as a companion to the proprietor's daughter.

The outskirts of the Scottish capital were unattractive, Margaret noticed, as the train sped past. Lord Montdrago had instructed the bank to book her into a five star hotel and to provide her with a car and chauffer during her stay in Edinburgh.

The following day an appointment was made to see the manager of the gun building firm at the workshop's offices, which were still situated where they had been when Margaret had dealt with them all those years ago.

Chapter Three

The sign above the office door stated boldly "David McAlpine, Gun Maker".

The young secretary showed Margaret into the office,

"Here is the lady who made the appointment to see you." She led the lady into the room.

"Good morning madam, my name is David McAlpine, and I own this firm." David stood up and extended his hand.

"Good morning, my name is Margaret and I represent Lord Montdrago who has a proposition for you; it concerns a very well paid position to take control of His Lordship's guns and gunroom on the estate which has one of the finest driven bird shoots in the country. Many years ago, I dealt with your family when I worked for your bankers. As I recall Mr. McAlpine senior had three sons and I think that after his retirement, two of those sons ran the business although I don't think they were gunsmiths, more to do with sales as I recall."

"Yes, unlike me who served a seven year apprenticeship in the gun trade, they whiled away their time hobnobbing with the gentry drumming up sales at the various shoots they attended." David replied.

"Well, very few people are gifted with the aptitude to master the art of sculpting beautiful guns out of a solid block of steel that work perfectly and never wear out. Would it be rude to ask about your training and your aims in the craft?" asked Margaret.

"Of course not, although I must make it clear at the outset that I am considering going into partnership with my leading gunmaker artisan and when the contract is signed I intend to go back to Africa where I worked as a professional hunter after a three year apprenticeship with a safari firm which has branches in a number of African countries.

When my two uncles were killed in a car crash I returned from Africa to manage this firm which I inherited. The hobnobbing with the gentry, kissing backsides to enhance sales, did not appeal to me although kissing backsides on a ladies day shoot had me never missing an event. Well Africa calls and although the pay is not good, I dream of the bush and the smells of those distant places. I regret to have to decline his lordships offer." David replied, "But while you're here, have a look at the workshop and I'll introduce you to one of the apprentices that completes his training in a few months time and may find his lordship's offer just what he needs."

David steered Margaret past his desk to a large glass panel that overlooked the workshop. The glass was tinted so that those in the office could observe but could not be seen. There were two young men and a middle aged man standing directly below the glass, leaning against a work bench talking and laughing and eating their lunchtime sandwiches. They could be clearly heard discussing the latest James Bond film.

"Sean Connery is the greatest actor in the world and he is Scottish too." said one of the young apprentices in a broad Scottish accent.

"His fame rests on his Scots accent," explained the journeyman, "His film "Goldfinger" has a female lead named "Pussy Galore" and people around the world, after hearing Mr. Connery's pronunciation of her name, will never forget her. Even a Texan Vice President tried to ape his accent when enquiring after his remote President's recent amours,

"Who's Jack's pussy?" he would ask the President's aids."

The older craftsman laughed and continued,

. "The vice president being a Texan pronounced Mr Connery's "Pooohsie" as "Posse", leaving the terrified aides wondering which one was about to be lynched and who the sheriff was." concluded the craftsman as the apprentices hooted with laughter and shouted "Pooooohsie" over and over again.

David took Margaret's arm and, steering her to a chair in front of his desk, asked her if she would like some tea. He was embarrassed and wondered what the lady with the beautiful smile was thinking.

"Yes please, I'd love a cup with milk and sugar." Margaret had made up her mind. These men were so like Jock, they were Jock's people and she was determined to ensure that David came to the estate.

"Lord Montdrago is an experienced hunter and goes on Safari twice a year to various countries all around Africa and the master of the guns will always have to accompany him and Lord Montdrago is a generous man and the gunsmith will, of course have all the licenses he needs to participate equally in the hunting."

David's eyes lit up as he asked,

"Can you confirm that?"

Within a month David had settled in on the estate and was waiting to meet His Lordship to be formally instructed as to his duties and to be given the keys and the authority to completely control all aspects of the "Gun Room" operations.

During the first weekend spent in his new home, the suite of rooms he had been allocated in the servants' quarter, were re-arranged to his satisfaction by the cleaning staff under Margaret's personal supervision. She noted with approval David's collection of books, many technical, pertaining to his craft but also some works of poetry and fine literature.

The pictures of wildlife in Africa and some prints of the De Jonghe's, both father and son, magnificent paintings of the mountains of the Cape Province in South Africa were hung tastefully. With their shadows painted within shadows, a depiction of the beauty of the blue tinted mountains which the casual observer might miss when visiting that paradise, was emphasized. The paintings were hung so as not to dazzle but to insidiously establish an atmosphere of wellbeing in that room so far away from Africa.

"I am sure you will be comfortable, David, and if there is anything you need ask me and I shall see that it is provided." said Margaret.

"Thank you. I am to present myself to His Lordship at nine am on Monday morning in the conference working room. Do you think I could wander around the estate and familiarize myself with his shooting grounds or are there parts which are out of bounds?"

"Provided you carry a special pass which I shall arrange for you, there should be no problem should you bump into any of the security staff which constantly patrols our estate." Margaret said.

"Why the elaborate security?" asked David.

"Lord Montdrago is one of the world's great bankers and financiers and with all the terrorism based in those parts of the world where he does business, prudence is very necessary; you will notice too that very few visitors attend the shoots which are solely for his own passionate pursuit of the art of wing shooting. He is a banker's banker, almost invisible and is never photographed, his bodyguards see to that." Margaret said with a strange look which David couldn't fathom, a look of disguised dislike of the man she was describing, perhaps?

Margaret was as good as her word and David had the security pass within a few minutes of her leaving his room.

David left the mansion by a side door through the kitchen and as he walked around the house to the front entrance he was greeted by a stunning panorama. There was an artificial lake of massive proportions, of irregular shape and cunningly crafted to give the appearance of complete naturalness, surrounded on one side by a forest and on the other by banks, lawns and shrubbery right to the waters edge. There were two islands with patches of bulrushes to provide shelter and habitat for the numerous water fowl and birds. David had been told that water fowl were strictly protected on the estate and rare migrants arrived every winter from Central Europe to over winter and breed in the well protected, food rich haven. David had arrived at night and had missed the full impact of Lord Montdrago's magnificent estate.

After the long walk around the lake, David climbed a slight rise and before entering the woods he looked back at the lake and the mansion and noticed that a certain amount of subtle military planning as to fields of fire from the mansion coupled with secure approaches were evident to a trained hunter such as himself who was a master at using natural cover to approach prey. To get close to the mansion unobserved would be impossible so David assumed that he was under surveillance at that very moment; this influenced his ambling stroll causing an unnecessary pause here and there to show the watchers that he was unaware of them as he enjoyed the shrubbery and the view.

Lord Montdrago must deal with some very dangerous people and this must have been from the beginning when the bank commenced its international dealings in His Lordships grandfather's time, thought David. Perhaps the landscape artist worked under certain restrictions as to the overall design that prevented him from creating a far lovelier estate than he had, if that was at all possible.

David, the hunter was now very aware and alert as he strolled through the lovely forest and it was soon evident to him that artfully placed and hidden in the high branches of the surrounding trees were surveillance cameras. The elaborate security system told David that somewhere there was a well staffed security centre and that the interior of the mansion would also be riddled with surveillance devices;. was Margaret aware of this? It seemed certain that she must be after nearly forty five years with the house of Montdrago. He would not tell her of his discoveries just yet but wait and see what the first few months with his new employer yielded.

The hours sped by and David was reminded that he would lunch with Margaret in her sumptuous apartment that was well separated from the other staff, as were his own living quarters. The walk back was hurried, although the beauty and loveliness continued to impress and delight the Gunsmith.

At lunch, David enthused over his walk and mentioned that he was not approached by any security personnel; in fact, he had not even seen a guard.

"You are always under surveillance everywhere on this estate as is proper, with the home of an international banker of Lord Montdrago's stature, being a target for villains who burgle and steal when those criminals become aware of His Lordships great wealth."

David took in the nuances of Margaret's statement, one being to warn him and another to placate the listeners who probably had devices in her suite of rooms; thank God for the canniness of the Scots.

"I am looking forward to my interview with His Lordship tomorrow and to being shown the gunroom. Do you know Margaret, that during my career as a professional hunter, I developed a feel for the type of rifle that a hunter chose to hunt with. As a banker of Lord Montdrago's caliber I don't think he would have chosen the calibers and types of weapons without a great deal of thought especially, as you say he is very experienced in the field. The number of newly rich industrialists that I have guided in Africa who could not even select the correct hunting boots, let alone rifles, was depressing. It will be very pleasant to hunt with an experienced hunter." David concluded.

"Always remember one thing. Never ever lie to His Lordship, as an astute banker he can smell a lie from a thousand miles away." Margaret warned with a strange look on her face indicating to David that she was assisting him with the surveyors and listeners to establish his bona fides so that should he have to lie, he would have a better chance of concealing it if he did it properly.

"Margaret, as a gunsmith and a professional hunter I have to be blunt and not varnish the truth with a lot of false embellishments. I was once removed from a hunt when the client complained about me. I had berated him for attempting a shot with a rifle that was not up to the standard that his quarry demanded. It did not give me joy when I heard that later, during a buffalo hunt, he had got a horn up his ass. When I go hunting with his Lordship and I think great danger threatens, I will insist, no order him back while I attend to the matter. There is no greater disgrace amongst the professional hunting fraternity than to have a client injured." said David sincerely.

The lunch ended and they both knew that a rapport and a sort of comradeship had been established between the two of them. David retired to his rooms and his poetry and his gun smithing manuals.

Chapter Four

Promptly at nine am the doors to the "Room" were opened and David was ushered in. Lord Montdrago rose from his desk, extended his hand and said,

"Welcome, David, please sit down. Would you like a cup of tea or coffee?"

"Yes, My Lord, I would like a cup of coffee, thank you." replied David.

"Please dispense with my title whilst on the estate, a plain Sir will suffice; the title is only used off the estate in the presence of others."

"Yes, Sir," said David.

"Let us not beat about the bush, your duties will comprise of the care and maintenance of all my fire arms and also to see that my very valuable collection of historical pistols and rifles which are kept in the gunroom, are inspected regularly and kept free of rust or any other form of deterioration. That is not to mean that any stains or dents of historical significance are to be removed, they are as valuable as the firearm itself. In particular, don't try and improve on the original metal finish or any other original deficiency; the key to maintaining the weapon's value is to prevent deterioration and not to in any way disturb anything original. The glass door cases are carefully maintained at a precise humidity which the experts say ensures optimum storage and the humidity controlling air conditioning equipment, must be kept in perfect condition at all times.

Because of the dangerous times we live in, only yourself and I will have the keys to open the gunroom door from the outside and I insist that whenever you are in the gunroom, you keep the door locked from the inside. My outside key can still unlock the door but I never carry my gunroom key on my person, it is kept in another safe in my bedroom. Furthermore, there is a personal weapon which you are expected to carry concealed on you at all times and you must use it if you must to prevent any unauthorized entry into the gun room. If I call out for you, from the outside, to open up, it will always be under duress no matter what I may say. Is that clear?" asked Lord Montdrago in a stern voice.

"Yes, Sir, perfectly." David replied equally firmly.

The banker smiled and picked up the phone and ordered the coffee.

"Just bear with me for a minute while I complete perusing these documents, and then, after the coffee, I will take you down to the gunroom and introduce you to its mysteries."

David was ignored whilst the banker attended to his papers and he was able to closely examine the grand, sumptuous room which had an air of long accustomed comfort but nonetheless, the atmosphere reeked of authority and absolute control. Behind the large leather covered desk the wall was paneled with expensive wood and a series of narrow glass doors enclosed a slim wall hung cabinet which seemed to house bound files. Above the wall paneling, a beautifully carved panel stretched right around the room and extended, close fitted, up to the ceiling. This was decorated with various moldings of subdued perfection, yet of a design that could only have been effected by a great artist. The other walls were tastefully fitted with photographs of hunts in Africa and large bags of birds taken on the estate; a lovely Persian carpet hung on the wall to break the pattern of the hanging pictures. All the chairs, cabinets and other furniture in the room was the work of various masters but the style was not out of conformity with any other piece in the room.

There was a knock at the door and at His Lordships beckoning call, the door opened and a most beautiful woman entered carrying the coffee tray. She glanced at David, and, as she placed the tray on the table, Lord Montdrago said to David,

"David this is my personal assistant Miss Jones, Debra meet David McAlpine the new, in house, Gunsmith."

The beautiful woman's high cheek bones and slightly slanting large blue eyes betrayed her Russian origins and the fiction of her surname; the lustrous wheat colored hair confirmed David's accurate assessment.

"Pleased to meet you," she said in a soft pleasant voice and without waiting to be dismissed, turned and slipped out the "Room."

They drank their coffee silently and David surreptitiously observed his new employer who had his head bent down as he fingered the documents before him and signed one or two.

The banker was a man of average height with a prominent forehead and thinning hair and about forty years of age. His eyes were pale blue and seemed to David to be cold and without feeling, despite his considerate manner and infectious smile. A bankers stock in trade, thought David, ruthlessness combined with an air designed to lull one into the false perception that one was in the hands of integrity and

kindness. A well trained, well disciplined, untrustworthy bastard David concluded, not to be meddled with, despite his frail appearance and lack of physical bulk.

"Well, now that we have finished our coffee, let me introduce you to your little kingdom where you will, I am sure, spend many a happy hour. I have both the keys of the gunroom with me so I shall give you yours now. As I said earlier, always ensure the absolute security of this key." With that Lord Montdrago handed David a smart card to open the electronic lock and a small leather wallet to keep it in together with a piece of stiff paper with the code PIN number printed on it.

"Until you have memorized the PIN number, keep it in your personal safe which you'll find behind the mirror in your suite's bathroom. The safe's combination is also on the on the same cardboard as the gunroom's PIN number. I suggest you make a separate copy of the safe combination and keep it on your person until the number is burned in your memory. Banking and secure safes are still wedded firmly together despite the electronic age we live in. Incidentally you can keep your personal firearm and ammunition in your safe as well when necessary." With that the banker strode out of the "Room" with David following.

They turned right and walked a short way along the wide passageway until they reached an unobtrusive door on their right which His Lordship opened and they both walked down a short flight of stairs to basement level and stopped before another plain door.

"This small ante room, as you shall see, has a small table where any thing you may have ordered is left such as a food tray or maybe a barrel length of steel and some other engineering material, also, there is an intercom on the wall should anyone wish to advise you of the delivery of your food or order. The very important point is that no one except me or you must ever enter that gunroom.

The gunroom will of course be swept from time to time by a technician to uncover listening devices which may have been cunningly introduced on a tea tray when the device would fall off and attach itself magnetically to the metal of a doorframe or work bench. You must always keep the technician under intense surveillance while he is sweeping. It is not unknown for a sweeping technician to plant a bug or two before he leaves.

Lastly, there are interlocks on the ante room door so that you can hear it open and close, and that interlock has a memory in order that you may know if it has been breached. The spy hole in the main gunroom door should always be used before you open the door or when goods are delivered."

"Won't the surveillance cameras in the gun room record a technician planting a bug, sir?"

"There are no surveillance cameras in the gun room, or in the main conference room, for it is too easy for others apart from ourselves to see what is in there or what transpires in there." Said Lord Montdrago with a mysterious smile, "There may be a machine pistol or a sub machine gun on the bench being checked by you which should never be recorded on a surveillance camera as well as other things which is nobody else's business." The banker looked at David with raised eyebrows and an expression inviting a query about his last statement. David said nothing, which together with a look of complete acceptance, satisfied his employer.

They passed through the ante room and His Lordship opened the main door and they entered the Gunroom. An amazed feeling of joy and excitement surged through David as he looked around the room.

Against the right hand wall a row of finely made glass fronted gun cabinets where expensive hand made rifles and shot guns of "London Best Grade" quality were standing in racks behind the glass. Right in the center of the row of cabinets, incongruously, stood a beautiful old fashioned cabinet made of oak which could be plainly seen to have been bolted to the wall, this cabinet housed the antique collection of firearms of great historical interest and some photographs of the men and incidents that had ensured their fame. As David stared at the oak cabinet, Lord Montdrago said with pride,

"My grandfather placed that fine, valuable cabinet there and had it bolted to that six foot thick wall. Yes, would you believe, that wall built by my grandfather is six feet thick as are several others in our family home. The old man strived for old English authenticity, which is also seen in the layout of the house's surrounding grounds; "Capability" Brown was the originator of that landscape style and very lovely it is too." The banker explained.

There was an office at the far end of the room with a washroom and toilet facilities adjacent. A glass fronted area which had the glass extending up from a lower hip high wooden panel to the ceiling could be seen to house a heat treatment furnace not much larger than a large domestic oven with its precise electronic temperature controls.

"The glass fronted cubical is to ensure that any noxious fumes and other rust forming gases cannot penetrate the area where the guns are. Please see that the extractor fans are always on and should they fail, don't use the cubicle and keep the door closed until repairs can be effected." said His Lordship sternly.

The left hand wall had the work benches and the lathe and other essential machines lined up and a cupboard for hand tools which David could see, through the glass doors of the cupboard, were hung from clips along the back of the cabinet and were magnificent; all the best that money could buy and many gems that David's own shop could never afford.

The banker pointed to a steel door near the benches.

"Through that door you will find the shooting tunnel, a shooting range to test and calibrate my guns and for you to practice with your own personal weapon. A side door just inside the tunnel houses the reloading equipment and all the loaded cartridges, keep the tunnel doors locked when not in use." and then, with a flourish the banker produced a Browning Hi-Power, the superb 9mm self loading "automatic" hand gun with a long record of reliability that had been proved by many police forces around the world; armed forces too preferred them.

"The holster is in the drawer beneath the main bench. Practice regularly and like other consumables, such as files and cutting tools and machine tools, ammunition should not be spared but used lavishly to attain proficiency. Make a list of anything further that you might need to know and anything else you need and give it to my personal assistant, the lady who brought you your coffee this morning." instructed the banker, and without another word, turned and left the gunroom, closing the door behind him.

An entranced David stood in the middle of his new empire and thrilled to the moment. After what seemed to be a long time David walked over to his new office and sat down, noticing a shotgun on his office desk with a label attached to the trigger guard which had written on it "This gun is malfunctioning" and initialed with an ornate "M" an initial he would come to know very well.

The day was magic. David inspected everything. One of the rifles in the "special" cabinet had the well known photograph of Lee Harvey Oswald holding that very rifle positioned next to it. As had been remarked on by many an astute journalist, the shadows of the man's face and those thrown by the rifle he was holding, seemed to have been made by two different suns, a morning sun and an afternoon sun. David realized that he was looking at a photo of the only innocent man in that twisted, tainted, Warren Commissioned fabrication of the murder of a President.

Another weapon, displayed in the cabinet, was a cheap point two two revolver, with the supposed ability to shoot several more bullets than the cylinder could ever accommodate. It was known as the magic gun that killed Robert Kennedy and complemented the magic bullet used in the older brother's murder.

The magnificent world shattering achievements of the citizens of America, contradicted the view that Americans of the Warren Commission era, were stupid and would swallow anything.

David went back to his office and picked up the delinquent shotgun and took it to the workbench where he intended to study it before stripping and examining it with the practiced eye of a master gunsmith. He couldn't help thinking whether those historical weapons were the genuine artifacts, while other collectors, elsewhere in the world, thought that they had the originals which in fact were cunning copies substituted by the all powerful wealth of a master manipulator who had purloined the actual weapons used in those historical events; did this explain the total banning of all surveillance of the Gunroom.

David further speculated on the bankers unhealthy concentrating on certain specific events as he had also noticed the pathologists report on the autopsy of the Lindbergh baby, who was found some time after the kidnapping and who the famous flier secretly knew was not his child, pinned up next to the historical collection of firearms.

International bankers and financers must know a history of the world far different to the history taught at universities and written about by scholars hoping for a Nobel prize; do the secret money manipulators ever yearn for a Nobel prize to adorn their collections of weapons that had killed and changed the course of human history, David wondered, and was the brilliant Henry Ford prompted to utter his much ridiculed phrase "History is Bunk" by his knowledge of the evils of international finance? David stopped thinking of ignoble matters and concentrated on the malfunctioning, but noble, weapon before him.

The shot gun was a side lock; an action some thought was superior to a box lock. It certainly was more expensive to make and to repair but David preferred a box lock for its robustness even if it did not present those roomy side plates usually smothered with too much tasteless engraving. David had seen a classic which had been sent into his Edinburgh shop for repair by an eccentric, or mad, Scottish Laird. The scene engraved depicted Custer's scout's report of the famous last stand at Little Big Horn.

The side plate showed a large ellipse encircled by a sort of garland, which on close inspection with a magnifying glass, consisted of many naked, intertwined Red Indians, fornicating enthusiastically and in the center of the interesting ellipse of fornicating Indians was a dinner plate with a large fish on it, adorned with a halo above it and the last immortal words of Custer's scout engraved below,

"Holy Mackerel, what a lot of fucking Indians."

David dissembled the magnificent gun, carefully, pausing to examine each part and component as he removed it from the perfect inletting and also from the delicate, riffler filed metal enclosure sunk into the action which housed the bridle and the safety catches. The action had two triggers and as he was stripping the powerful springs out, the bridle support plate accidentally sprang open and a vital link was flung out as the spring broke loose. David's eyes followed the links progress through the air and across the room until it hit the floor in front of the "old" cabinet and slid underneath where there was a small narrow gap which straddled the distance between the two front carved ball and claw feet upon which the beautiful oak cabinet stood.

David stood still, as he always did when some thought was needed before plunging in, like a bull in a china shop, which always made matters worse. He could make another link which took much time and whose accuracy was essential to maintain the actions timing, so that the many movements, which were inter related when a fine shot gun's breech was opened, would interact perfectly. But it would take time to familiarize himself with the electronic controls of the heat treatment equipment. No, he decided, he would first try and feel beneath the cabinet where he could just reach and put his hand under.

David lay down full length in front of the cabinet like an ancient worshipper of some heathen idol and felt underneath. As he ran his hand under the base of the cabinet, he discovered not one, but two little concealed levers that seemed to have some movement. They were quite stiff and each sprang back after they were released.

David got onto his knees and as a toolmaker, he knew that many levers were meant to be moved together, like the operating control of a powerful press, to ensure that both the operator's hands were safely out of the way when the mighty press's ram crushed down.

David, on his knees reached under with both hands spread apart and pressed in both levers and instinctively pulling on the cabinet, was surprised when the large, heavy, oak cabinet silently glided forward. In amazement he continued sliding it forward until it stopped. He got up and looked on the floor to find the link. Not only did he find his link but to his utter astonishment he saw that he had uncovered a doorway which led into the thick wall.

David again stood stock still while he thought of what this all meant. The banker could come back at any time and he was certain that the banker was unaware of the secret doorway and he was equally certain that the tale Margaret had told him of the founder never having attended an important meeting but had nevertheless known of all that had transpired at that meeting, had not depended on human spies that could mislead but had somehow observed everything from the secret chamber behind the oak cabinet.

No he would return it to its position, tell no one and wait till he was sure that Lord Montdrago was abroad for a few days which he frequently was. David noticed that the architrave that surrounded the cabinet with its wall fixing bolts all moved as a unit in an undetectable, well thought out, deception. He would use the trained gunsmith's patience to wait for the day when he could determine the old founders carefully concealed and planned tool of the bankers rise to great wealth; David slid the cabinet back against the wall.

The rest of David's week was spent attending to the malfunctioning shot gun. Although David had brought his own specialized tools with him, he decided to leave them in his room ready packed so that when an African safari cropped up, he would be saved the trouble of repacking his tools. With all the guns lock parts clean and laid out on the bench, he went to the Gunroom's tool cabinet and selected a head band mounted, adjustable, magnifier with two lenses, one for each eye. He grinned as he remembered the difficulty he had experienced when trying to source one in Edinburgh.

He was strolling down Princes Street one day when he passed a medical supply shop which displayed many of a doctor's essential instruments, and there in the window was a headband mounted magnifier. He rushed in and asked the lovely young lass behind the counter if he could have the magnifier.

"What do doctors use it for?" he asked.

"Gynecologists use them." She said, blushing to the roots of her hair.

David couldn't resist it and replied,

"That's a coincidence; I've just got married and need one too."

The young girl looked at David and blushing furiously enquired

"You're a male virgin then?"

"No, I have an insatiable curiosity and my new wife encourages me. She says that I am bound to improve with a little knowledge."

The young lass fled to the back of the shop as soon as she had given David his change.

Under the magnifier, it was clearly evident that the sear of one of the shotgun's triggers had lost its sharp edge and was not engaging the tumbler adequately which allowed it to slip out of engagement under the force of the recoil of the other barrel, causing a dangerous double discharge. David re-cut both sears with a small file then re-hardened them, using a small hand held gas torch and then he stoned the hard steel to a perfect engagement. The reassembled gun was taken to the tunnel and test fired against a patterning board which revealed nice dense patterns attesting to the skill of the guns original makers.

The refurbished gun was returned to its cabinet and placed in the appropriate rack and David wrote a detailed report of the repairs in a special book he had acquired for that purpose. Later he wrote a report for His Lordship detailing what repairs had been done and went to find His Lordships personal assistant to ask her to deliver it.

David went first to Margaret's office and told her what he had done and asked for directions to the lovely Debra's office.

"His Lordship has flown over to the USA for a week, to attend some important meetings. Sit down and have a cup of tea with me." Margaret managed to brush her lips with a warning finger to impress on David the surveillance was active.

"When you have some time I would like to show you the estate's gardens, they really are spectacular and give one a feeling of complete freedom." said Margaret with a penetrating, knowing look which implied, without surveillance.

"I'd love to, there is so much that I would like to ask you about the flowers and shrubbery, do you know that the shrubbery influences the quality of a shoot. Do you think His Lordship would be amenable to suggestions on how to improve the shoot?" David replied with an equally knowing look and could see that they understood one another, perfectly.

"Well, toddle along to Debra's office, it's easy to find, it is opposite the conference room. After, you have concluded your business with her, I will meet you at the side entrance in, say, thirty minutes." said Margaret.

David found Debra sitting at her desk staring pensively at a calendar on the wall.

"Hello Debra, I've completed that task His Lordship gave me and here is the report on the repairs carried out. Would you please give it to him when you get the opportunity?" David said.

"Yes, I will. Please call me Miss Jones as I would prefer to keep our dealings on a formal basis." said the beautiful girl.

"Certainly, my name is McAlpine, don't forget the mister." said David with a good natured grin. He turned and left the office and slowly made his way to the side entrance. The passages on the way were impressive, antique chairs and tables were placed tastefully where appropriate and oil painted portraits of great men and important European battles and lovely landscapes by Constable adorned the walls.

Shortly after he arrived at the side door Margaret approached wearing a scarf and a cashmere jacket and was wearing Scottish brogues, those sturdy walking shoes favored by the sensible. They strolled together, Margaret leading the way towards the back of the mansion.

"He is not what he seems" she said quietly, "he is cold, ruthless and regards all people as expendable tools to be made use of and discarded if their usefulness ceases."

"Are you not vulnerable?" David asked.

"No, his father knew him well so he had an unbreakable trust drawn up for me which covers all my needs until death and there is also a delightful cottage nearby, furnished to the highest standards which I never use but it is always available. That is also for my exclusive use."

"What am I in for, Margaret?" David asked ruefully.

"You will be alright and please don't think of leaving, you're the only one here who I can talk to and can help me if I need it. He told me that he was going to Africa on business in about a month's time and he is taking you with for the hunt he has planned after the conclusion of his business. He only travels on his private jet which has a range that spans continents and is fully equipped with emergency medical equipment and is manned by two medical men, a physician and a surgeon.

He always has his legal advisor with him although it is rumored that he is as good as any when it comes to law in various countries.

Apart from you there will also be an expert taxidermist to prevent the loss or degradation of any trophies; it is a large, fast executive aircraft with two of the best pilots that money can hire."

"I suppose that I must not let on that you have told me of the trip?" asked David.

"That is correct. In our environment prudence in all we do and say is very necessary." Margaret said.

As they walked Margaret pointed out some of the estates unique plants and shrubs, many brought from all over the world, surprising many a botanist with their hardy adaptation to a foreign land but, of course, Lord Montdrago had the finest horticulturists and foresters in the land living on the estate.

"His Lordship's Personal assistant chided me and ordered me to keep any business with her on a formal footing and I addressed her as Miss Jones as requested. Is the Russian lady the banker's mistress?"

"You're very observant David, I think she is of Russian origin too but she is not his mistress. He will never permit himself to be vulnerable. As to his sexual needs, high class whores are flown in from distant places and his lust is serviced up in the air in another untraceable jet that he owns." Said Margaret bitterly, "From a loveable child whom I loved and nursed he has transformed into an evil man." said Margaret, with a sob.

"How much, if any, time is the staff given to prepare for his arrival at the estate after his arrival at the airport?" asked David.

"That's a strange question," Margaret said "Usually the security staff and the chauffeur on duty are notified of the jets E.T.A. and a car is waiting at the airport in good time for his arrival. When he goes to the City it's any bodies guess when he will return."

"When a meeting in the conference room begins is there some one posted at the door and is it possible to know when the meeting is over?" David asked Margaret urgently.

"Your questions arouse my curiosity; I hope you are not planning to steal the priceless Historical Weapons which I believe he stores there."

"Of course not but I want to inspect all the equipment in the room and I don't want him to walk into the gunroom when all his guns and equipment are strewn about." David replied weakly.

"He is unpredictable so if you are planning anything, be careful, he has ways of retaliating that are both cunning and terrible. He is an evil man, as I've said before.

Let us go and inspect the nursery up there ahead as I see a security guard approachingand he is bound to speak to us, we have been chatting too long in one place and that is suspicious to them." Margaret said quickly as she moved on.

"My God, is it always like this?"

"Yes, I'm afraid; your employer is the most suspicious, cautious man alive."

The guard approached and greeted them.

"Good day, Margaret, conducting a tour are we?" he asked pleasantly.

"Yes, showing our new resident gunsmith our flowers and the nursery. Your name is Mr. Smith, is it not? Meet Mr. David McAlpine."

"What an unusual name." David said with a grin as he extended his hand to the muscular, military man who looked foreign.

The guard shook David's hand and said,

"I saw you wandering around the lake and walking in the woods yesterday, are you interested in horticulture?"

"Yes I am interested in the environment as I shall be directly involved in His Lordship's shoots and do not wish to look foolish when he discusses the terrain." David said earnestly.

"You should meet the game keeper then, his name too is unusual, Mr. Brown and he is attached to the security department."

"Are the security personnel all color coded then when they've not adopted the more obscure Anglo Saxon names?" David joked.

The guard ignored the jest, touched his cap and walked off stiffly at a military pace.

"The security personnel never fraternize or encourage the other staff to mingle with them, they are a suspicious lot and keep meticulous records of everything that occurs on the estate, and I assure you, all are perused by His Lordship."

After a pleasant and instructive spell in the nursery and the large hot houses and meeting the chief horticultural officer, they strolled back to the mansion and David went up to his room to shower and change before meeting Margaret in her dining room for supper.

Chapter Five

David's day began after he had had a solid English breakfast with Margaret and had hurried down to the gunroom after drinking his coffee and taking his leave of the lovely, middle aged lady. Before he had gone to sleep the previous evening, he had memorized both the gunroom pin number and the combination of the safe behind the bathroom mirror. The imprinting of the numbers had been achieved by constantly repeating them over and over again and writing them down over and over again until he had printed them indelibly on his brain and he knew that they would be there forever.

He entered the gunroom and secured the door behind him. His excitement was intense as he crouched down and released the secret levers and pulled the old oak cabinet forward to give access to what lay behind the wall. As he entered the doorway, he noticed that all surfaces, including the back of the cabinet were covered and lined with thick sound absorbing felt or wool. He checked very carefully the closing and opening of the cabinet from inside the chamber; the locking levers worked the same way as those on the underside of the cabinet and were clearly accessible. It would never do to close the chamber after he had entered and then not be able to get back out again, he thought; he also searched successfully for a peephole to look back into the gunroom with the cabinet closed and up against the wall. The observation point was a thin slot, which gave a panoramic view of the entire gunroom, including a few yards into the shooting tunnel, which was set up high above the cabinet and easy to reach.

Immediately one entered the narrow chamber, a stairway about two and a half feet wide, sloped up, attached to the inside of the gunroom wall so that the position reached at the top of the stairway was above the gunroom ceiling and high enough up the opposite wall to give the watcher a perfect position to peer down and look into every hook and cranny of the main "Conference Room" Every surface was covered in the same soundproof material.

With the cabinet closed, there was a dim eerie light that took a few moments for David's eyes to become accustomed to. As he climbed the stairs the silence was absolute and the musty smell told of the long disuse of the cunning deception. How the old bastard, the founder, with his money lender's instincts, must have gloried in his cleverness, thought David, as he observed and listened to his underling's disparaging remarks about their master before they were dealt with in many unpleasant and malicious ways, some days later.

David walked along the gallery which extended from one end of the "Room" to the other, taking note of the way the observation was undertaken, astounded by the thoroughness of the planning and execution of the devices that ensured the security and the impossibility of detection. There were several large boxes, about twelve Inches Square with the words "Cough Box" painted on their sides. The boxes had a large foam lined hole in the top where one's face could be placed tightly to smother a sneeze or a cough. What a master of deception the founder was, but, thought David, how did one smother a healthy fart.

The spy holes were ingenious; these, too, were slots high up, both through the "room's" paneling and through the decorated panels above, closed off with lever operated strips that could be opened or closed silently, like a Venetian blind, when necessary. David opened a section of the observation slots right above the Bankers desk and was surprised to see some open documents relating to arms shipments, legitimate shipments to some of Britain's friends. What about the illegitimate ones? David wondered.

David closed up and carefully, in the semi-darkness, crept down the stairs, establishing a routine of intensely surveying the gunroom before opening the concealed doorway and entering the gunroom.

After sliding back the cabinet, David went into his office and sat down thinking furiously. He phoned through to the kitchen and asked for a tea tray with some biscuits to be sent down. The tea soon arrived and David was told it was in the ante room over the intercom.

Drinking his tea and munching on the biscuits calmed David down as he considered all the implications of his discovery. There was certain to be another access to the secret room. There were other six foot thick walls; did they also have secret passages and rooms? Were there bedrooms adjacent to the other secret observation passages? Was the founder a secret voyeur who discovered secrets unrelated to banking and finance; everything was related to money, David knew, as Oscar Wilde had observed "Money was the only Aphrodisiac that never failed"

One thing was certain; David must never reveal his secret to another living soul both for his own personal safety and his own personal power. The founder had not even revealed the observation passages to his own son; was he spying on him too?

The conclusion that David came to was that he would have to spend the few remaining days before Lord Montdrago returned, exploring the secret chamber and, with the aid of a small flashlight, map out and pace every passage and any other passages that may fork or branch off the main passageway.

The map would have to be both cryptic and obtuse so that should another see it, the lines and figures obtained from his pacing would mean nothing, but would reveal a lot to David as he walked about the mansions premises. He would now have to pace out the distances between his rooms and Margaret's rooms and the kitchen and any other rooms that he could safely wander past, or through, without drawing attention to himself.

Pacing in a measured way would attract attention so he would have to measure distances surreptitiously and write them down unobserved. Once he had the ground floor layout down on paper, he would start on the second floor and finally the third floor. He was sure that the thick walls would all contain secrets but it was going to take a long time to record every thing without detection or the raising of suspicion. Every foray of his proposed mapping strategy would be preceded by a carefully contrived, well thought out series of explanations as to why and what he was doing in that part of the house. The explanations would have to be plausibly perfect with supporting evidence and logical realities.

Why was he doing all this?Did the knowledge he would acquire justify the risks? To what end? David knew it was more than just the very human weakness to poke his nose into someone else's business, someone's very dangerous business. No, there was a mystery here and a man who exuded evil, needed to be investigated, and of course it may profit David somehow, a motive that no Scotsman could seriously ignore.

Lord Montdrago returned in high spirits, the staff noticed, and David received a note thanking him for his report and the prompt restoration of his favorite gun to its old perfect self. He had urgent business in Africa and he would be leaving in two weeks time and he informed David of his wish that David would accompany him as there would be hunting trips in each of the countries that were to be visited. They were Zambia, the Democratic Republic of the Congo and the Republic of South Africa. Would David kindly recommend a battery of weapons for each of them bearing in mind that Big, thick skinned game and Dangerous game would be hunted and so too would Game, that would be taken at long range, in the R.S.A. on the vast plains of the Karoo.

Liaise with our physician Dr. Cohen, he instructed, and give him the benefit of your hunting experience as to tropical diseases that may be encountered and injuries that may be sustained in encounters with the big five. Dr. Cohen's rooms are on the third floor of the house. The final departure date would be known after his meeting with certain heads of state in the regions that were to be visited.The familiar initials were neatly inscribed at the end of the note.

David was overjoyed but realized that he must rapidly complete the secret layouts and try and find out when the meeting would take place with the African officials. Debra would almost certainly know and his visit to Dr. Cohen's rooms would finally and hopefully allow him to pace and measure the top floor of the mansion.

David worked late in the gunroom office correlating the floor plan with the secret chamber plan and slowly the layout of the secret observation points as they related to each room became clear. Tomorrow, he thought, he should be able to finalize the second floor plans but in the meantime he would make a start on the compilation of the coming safari's requirements. His professional hunting experience allowed him to rapidly plan the task and fortunately there was a ledger in the drawer of the office desk, which listed out all the weapons in the gunroom in great detail such as their calibers, serial numbers, telescopic sights attached and the ammunition in stock for each weapon.

The next morning, after a quick breakfast, David made his way to the office of the beautiful Miss Jones.

"Good morning Miss Jones and how does Miss Jones feel this morning?" David wondered if he could incorporate a hundred more "Miss Jones" in the conversation but decided that he was being petty.

"I'm very well thank you and very busy, how can I help you?" Debra replied.

"I received this memo from Lord Montdrago yesterday and it would help if I knew just when he is having his meeting with the African dignitaries, as the deadline for the completion of the equipment lists that he wants could be ascertained and I shall know if I must work late for a night or two to meet that deadline?" asked David, handing the memo to the lovely lass. Debra read the memo, and satisfied replied,

"The meeting is scheduled for the day after tomorrow at ten am and is expected to last most of the day so you should have a departure date for the African trip the day after the meeting is adjourned." Debra said and indicated with a stare and a gathering of papers on her desk that David should leave unless there was anything else.

"Thank you Miss Jones, good day." David turned and left the office.

Now for the third floor to visit Doctor Cohen, David decided, but he would go via the second floor and if asked would explain that he was looking for the doctors chambers.

The house was vast and like the ground floor, was laid out with beautiful furniture and with oil paintings in ornate frames hung everywhere, with small low intensity lamps fixed across the top of each frame so that regardless of the light in a room or passage, the paintings were displayed to their best advantage. Within ten minutes the inevitable security guard approached David, with the inevitable query as to his purpose and intentions in that part of the house and when David had convinced him of his need to visit the doctor, backing his explanation with His Lordships written instructions, the guard became almost friendly and said that he would escort him up to the third floor to the doctor's chambers. When they reached the third floor, David was told that the entire South wing of that floor, which faced the lake and the front of the building, was composed of the living quarters of Lord Montdrago and was strictly out of bounds. Furthermore, the suite of rooms situated beyond and down the passage from the doctor's rooms served as security's control center and it too was out of bounds. Arriving at the doctor's rooms, the guard knocked and when the doctor's nurse opened the door, he left.

"Good morning, I am David McAlpine, the in-house gunsmith based in the gunroom, may I see Dr. Cohen?" With a pleasant smile the attractive nurse bade David enter and said.

"We have been expecting you. It's about the African trip, is it not?" she asked.

"Yes." answered the gunsmith, with a cheery smile. David was shown in to the doctor's office and Dr. Cohen, a jolly little man with an open face wrinkled with an engaging smile said,"Good morning David, I'm Bernie, and be careful what you say," he paused to see that the nurse was out the room and the door closed before continuing, "Those fucking security guards have us under surveillance." He pointed to the camera,

"And don't fart, they have listening devices too." He was blunt and his irreverent good humor was infectious and David laughed outright.

"Must you examine me in the toilet? Or are my sexually transmittable diseases to be disclosed to the entire staff?"

"No, after my female patients complained to His Lordship, the surgery with the examination table was declared a no go area for the cameras and the bugs, which, I suspect, removed one of the major incentives promoting diligence amongst those randy bastards behind the surveillance monitors. But to escape the uncertainty, it has to be the toilet." explained the laughing medic. David now understood why the officers in the Israeli Army, although ferocious with the enemy were reputed to be pussy cats when confronted by their own men.

"I was told that you were a professional hunter in Africa for a few years and would liaise with me on the preparations for the safari next month." Bernie stated, "This will be my first trip together with my colleague, the surgeon Douglas Hamilton, a Scot like you."

"The only extra necessities are several snakebite kits and the usual anti malaria prophylactics which should be started now, at least a few weeks before entering the malaria zones. As the parasite is constantly adapting to the drugs, a specialist in African diseases should be contacted for the latest bad news; I am told that some specialists recommend a cocktail of anti malarial drugs, but I am sure you will get the answers."

"What about injuries sustained during the hunt?" Bernie asked, now deadly serious.

"I will be preparing the list of weapons that we are taking. Most incidents are provoked by inexperience when hunters use unsuitable weapons for their quarry.

However accidents happen, and, in my opinion the filth and rotting meat in a predator's claws and mouth when some one is mauled pose the greatest challenge to the doctor and worst of all, is when the doctor is hurt, who is going to attend to him. As there will be two medical men that wont apply on this safari." David concluded.

"Well that takes care of the medical side, but, I shall take a few boxes of condoms in case His Lordship includes a member of our security services, those randy bastards will screw anything with hair on it, even the barber shop floor." Bernie made a rude gesture to the watching camera.

"Condoms are useful to wrap over the muzzle of a rifle in rainy weather." David volunteered.

"Do you fuck them?" asked Bernie.

The nurse entered the room as Bernie passed the last remark.

"Mr. McAlpine is such an innocent gunsmith, must you Bernie?" the nurse queried.

David left the surgery a relieved man, the intelligence in the joking, irreverent doctor's eyes indicated that this ex Israeli army doctor was more than competent, thought David; what else could be expected, the banker only hired the very best.

David meandered down, back to the gunroom pacing and paying attention to the location of the security headquarters. He would take note of the dimensions of the outside of the magnificent building when he got the opportunity.

Once in the gunroom, the latest measurements and observations were transferred to the plan and David gradually got a feel for the layout and wondered if he had the strength to desist from peering into the lovely Debra's bedroom and bathroom. No, he hadn't.

A list of suitable firearms was drawn up. David chose only one double barreled rifle for His Lordships battery, A Holland and Holland in 470 caliber, this to handle the dangerous animals. He supplemented the double with another large caliber, a bolt actioned 458 Winchester magnum, a controversial cartridge that had in its early developmental days, suffered some set backs now, happily corrected. The rifles chosen for lighter game and long range hunting were a 300 magnum and a well made 30-06 by Rigby. The Shotgun he had recently repaired completed His Lordship's battery and David then spent a happy few hours in the tunnel behind closed doors testing the weapons with ear protection and a complete disregard for the amount of ammunition used, which was very expensive in the larger calibers.

The rest of the afternoon was spent practicing with the 9mm pistol. It pleasantly surprised David how quickly he returned to his old deadly self with the speed and accuracy he had always had with a handgun. He quickly blanked out the memories of other times when he had used a handgun to kill in the service of the Crown, a long, long time ago.

After supper that night, in the quietness of his room, fully aware of his watchers, he completed the inventory of all the other equipment needed for the coming trip to Africa, taking care to duplicate those items vulnerable to damage or malfunction. The open list he left at his bedside, wondering if the surveillance cameras could zoom in and capture the contents to forewarn the banker who may then hint at changes. He made a note that the telescopic sights would be sighted in just before the hunt, as was customary, to take care of any bumps and jarring they had suffered in transit. Before falling asleep, he contemplated his spying in the chamber the next day, with a shiver of both apprehension and excitement. Yes he would be a much wiser man tomorrow night.

Chapter Six

David woke up before sunrise, his brain in turmoil. What if he was caught, could he claim that he had only just discovered the chamber after the banker was in conference and shut behind closed doors and unable to be contacted and that he was bumbling around in the dark not knowing what he was doing? That was what he would claim, if the worst came to the worst. He had learned that immediately after the first meeting, the banker was having another with some of his close banking associates, David knew that when both meetings were over, he would have a good insight into the arcane workings of high finance; and so his thoughts whirled round in his head.

He got up and showered, dressed in dark colored clothes and made sure that there was nothing to rattle around in his pockets. He checked his wristwatch to ensure its accuracy and then slowly strolled down to Margaret's quarters to greet the surprised lady, who exclaimed,

"My but you are early this morning, are you that hungry. Would you like an extra sausage and egg and two extra slices of toast?"

"No, just the usual, but a coffee to begin with would be appreciated." David said. He told her of his meeting with Bernie and the reason for the visit and the shooting in the Gunroom tunnel and the compiling of the list of equipment and his reasons for his choice of weapons and, and,--. David knew that he was waffling, his sense of guilt at what he was about to do, coupled with the excitement caused him to behave out of character. Margaret, ever mindful of the listeners and watchers, interrupted to slow David down and her eyes warned him to be aware.

"I am so excited about the safari; forgive me for going on and on." He said trying to retrieve the situation. Margaret was puzzled as her young friend was certainly agitated and knowing of his professional hunting career thought that his explanation was a lame one so quickly changed the subject.

"Now that you are getting to know the house, what do you think of it?"

"It is stunningly beautiful but difficult to really take everything in as whenever I stopped to admire a painting or a piece of furniture, a guard appeared from nowhere and moved me on." David complained.

"When you get the opportunity, ask Lord Montdrago if I can show you around. I know the history of many of the paintings and the furniture, the Montdrago bankers, from the beginning displayed a great appreciation and knowledge of the many works of art presently in the house and some pieces could only be acquired after years of patient waiting. But the house of Montdrago is never deterred by difficulties and always prevails when great works of art are at stake." Margaret declared not without genuine admiration.

David excused himself and thanking Margaret, hurried down to the gunroom. Once securely inside, he reviewed his planning. He would phone Debra and ask if he could hand over the safari documents personally as there were a few important decisions to be made and time was short. He was sure that she would point out to him when the meeting was to start and the impossibility of seeing him as the following meeting would commence shortly after his African guests had departed at the conclusion of first meeting. David would then say alright he would leave it until she notified him of an appropriate time; his spying activities could now be synchronized with the happenings in the conference room. He prayed that the ghost of grandfather Montdrago would guide him and perhaps enjoy the deceitfulness of the gunsmith's disloyalty together with him.

The phone call to Debra followed the desired course and David thanked her and he now knew that he had just an hour before the conference doors closed on the group. The hour passed slowly and the tension built up as David prepared to enter the soundproofed secret chamber. As a last sudden thought, he took a note book with him and a ball pen that he had just briefly used and which wrote perfectly.

The old oak cabinet slid open smoothly and David entered, closing the entrance when he was safely inside and had made a final inspection of the gunroom.

Slowly climbing the thickly covered stairs, the silence was unnerving and David was straining not to break it. Standing next to a "cough box" he slowly and carefully opened a slat which covered a spy slit just above the banker's desk. The immediate noise of the talking and joking of the African delegates shattered the silence and David watched enthralled as the meeting commenced with His Lordship holding up his hand for silence.

"Gentlemen, we are here to discuss the aid packages that have just been allocated to your countries. The amounts are large and the agency who distributes the funds is under the jurisdiction of, and is assisted by, a consortium of which my group is the senior executive authority. Your good selves have put in a great deal of work to secure the packages and as you all know, my group handles all your personal banking needs, and both advises and implements your investment portfolios, in great secrecy while keeping the donors satisfied that their donations provided by their countries tax payers are efficiently used. I know, although the agency doesn't, that your sterling work must be adequately rewarded and I have always attended to your personal remuneration." Lord Montdrago paused and let the implications of the blatant defalcation sink in, to the avaricious Africans obvious delight.

"The mechanics of the placing of funds into personal accounts is well known to you, however I must warn that no one, no one, must know of your hidden accounts, not your wives or your children or your relatives and especially your fellow politicians; if they find out, the international aid agencies will demand repayment and if your fellow politicians or family members find out, your life is in danger." said the banker sternly.

"Now, President Imbongi, do you know who is behind the rebel movements in the east of the Democratic Republic of the Congo, or DRC as it is generally known?" asked His Lordship.

"No, the money and arms are supplied by the Russians, we suspect, perhaps even a large mining conglomerate. We just don't know. Those rebels are basically conducting tribal warfare that is why they kill even children of tribes not affiliated to them. The only way to stop this internecine warfare is to cut off the supply of arms." said the president sadly.

"Well gentlemen, let us adjourn until we meet again in your own countries in a few weeks time. I hope that there will be no impediment to the hunting for myself and my staff."

"Of course not." said one of the others.

"President Mbongi please stay behind, I regret to inform you that the British Internal Revenue service is investigating some of your accounts and share holdings and it is imperative that we discuss your personal financial affairs so that my banks legal advisors can prepare a strategy to fend off those greedy officials. Please sit down as I show my other friends to the door and ensure that they are escorted back to London." the International banker said.

David could discern dark scowls of suspicion on the faces of the departing two officials as if they suspected that their colleague was getting money that they should share in. Lord Montdrago returned to the room and faced his client.

"Don't worry, that story of tax evasion was untrue, I wish to make you an offer that only you and me will know of. I offer you the sum of fifty thousand pounds sterling if you will complete a task for me. I want you to have a man removed permanently and I want independent confirmation that his body has been seen and positively identified by Western officials or Western Journalists and then, only then, will the money be deposited in your account. The man's name is Kowolski and he will be in your capital in two days time and will be seeking an audience with you," said the English Lord pleasantly, and he continued "If knowledge of our deal is leaked out, I will see that knowledge of all your bank accounts and financial holdings become public knowledge. Do we have a deal?"

"Bwana your Lordship, have I ever let you down. Kowolski will be dead within hours of entering Kinshasa." declared the African President.

"Well our business is over; my security staff will escort you to the airport where my private jet is waiting to take you back to Kinshasa. Have a pleasant trip." smiled the banker, extending his hand in a farewell handshake.

David was stunned. What next?His Lordship reached for the phone,

"When the DRC president has left, show in our other guests; make sure they do not see the departing African gentleman."

Shortly after Mbongi had left, David saw three other men ushered in. The banker jumped up and walked over eagerly to the men, extending both hands and glowing with goodwill and bonhomie.

"My dear Kowolski it is such a pleasure to see you again," said Lord Montdrago reaching for Kowolski's hand and placing his other hand on the shoulder of his friend,

"How is the family, I hear that your daughter has presented you with a lovely grandchild. Your first?" he asked delightedly.

"Yes" beamed Kowolski.

"Well gentlemen, let us begin. My schedule is tight, I am leaving first thing in the morning for two days and want to clear up any misunderstandings that have arisen," his Lordship said with a jolly smile.

"Lord Montdrago" began Kowolski, "I am quite distressed; I understood that my share of our last venture in the DRC was to be ten million dollars but I have only received five million. Is there a problem?" he asked plaintively.

"Of course not." beamed the banker "as soon as you return from Kinshasa, which I believe will be next week, the other five million will be deposited. There was an exchange control hiccup." explained the banker to a visibly relieved Kowolski.

David was flabbergasted and completely appalled at what had transpired.

This evil, horrible man seemed impervious to any human feeling, with not an ethic or a decent feeling in his soul. Was this a genetic evil or was he carefully trained by his banking family? Could he ever be redeemed or should he be destroyed. Were there others like him? Did some world leaders behave in this way? Did the ends justify the means?

"Gentlemen, let us be brief. Is the military equipment getting to the Rebels in the DRC timeously? Has the rebel leader informed our people out there when the coup will take place?" asked Lord Montdrago.

"Yes any day now" answered Kowolski.

"My orders were not before you had a day or two or maybe a week to meet with President Mbongi and discuss the new aid package with him. Please radio the military advisors to hold back the rebels for a week and to ensure that Mbongi does not survive the coup. We do not want a repetition of the Moise Shombe affair where mercenaries had to entice him into an aircraft where they could strangle him between refueling touchdowns." said the banker with a look of one who knows that his underlings were grossly inefficient.

David stood open mouthed at the smiling, beaming man's audacity in directing a man who he had just ordered to be murdered, to facilitate his own killing.

"Gentlemen, I must get good nights sleep tonight as I will be leaving early tomorrow and I still have things to do in preparation for my trip."

They all rose and the visitors left followed by a calm, happy banker.

David closed the observation slot and hurried down and after re entering the gun room closed the entrance and walked over to his office, his mind reeling at the evil he had witnessed. He knew that as a matter of urgency, he must make a silencer for his pistol, a task he had done many times for his estate owning customers in Edinburgh, who had to shoot vermin in their barns and fields; the silencer was absolutely essential and urgent, now that he had gauged the timbre of his opposition.

David was late for lunch and missed Margaret which he was grateful for as he doubted that he could have contained himself and it would be unwise to enlighten anyone as to the business methods of the grand English Lord.

After lunch, David returned to the gunroom and took a bar of heat treated, aircraft grade aluminium from the materials cupboard and went to the lathe and roughed it down to the correct diameter. He then removed it from the chuck and went to select a pistol from the armory cupboard where he knew there were several handguns stored.

Most people thought that a silencer could silence any weapon but David knew better. He had served a seven year apprenticeship as a gunsmith and then had served for three years in the Special Air Services, an elite sub section of the British army, where he specialized in weapons and the use of them and, finally, hunted professionally in Africa where weapons were the tools of his trade.

A bullet that left the muzzle of a pistol at over the speed of sound, which is just over 1100 feet per second, made a very loud "crack" sound as it broke the sound barrier, that couldn't be silenced, although the noise of the explosion of the cartridge could. David selected a pistol of point 45 caliber, a 45ACP which had a heavy 200 grain bullet, with excellent killing and knock down power, that exited the barrel at around 900 feet per second, well below the sound barrier and without the tell tale "crack".

He removed the barrel and mounted it in the lathe, centering it with an accuracy that only a well trained man could. He cut the appropriate fine thread and then removed it from the lathe and replaced the aluminium in the chuck. The rest was a cakewalk for the gunsmith's skills. The baffles within the silencer were of his own design which he had improved upon from the specialized baffles the SAS used; the finished silencer was screwed onto the barrel.

David phoned Margaret and knowing full well that his phone, and all phones except Lord Montdragos were tapped, he explained that he would be working late preparing all the rifles for the African hunt and that it would stain his reputation should a weapon fail in some Godforsaken jungle when His Lordship had a world class trophy in his sights. He asked her to notify security if she thought it necessary. He finished and tested the silencer just after seven pm, it was perfect even the "Plop" was nearly inaudible and would not be heard except by a dog or a child whose hearing was exceptional.

David decided, with the confidence that his silenced pistol now imbued him with, to enter the secret labyrinth and spy on the master himself. He had noticed when he had explored the secret passages that every room, including the main conference room, and the bedrooms too, had a secret door that enabled a person to enter those rooms. Of course, David knew that with the surveillance of such a high standard in every room except the conference room and the bankers living suite of rooms, an entrance would be noticed immediately. So the bank founder had had access from most rooms and could disappear if he heard someone approaching whilst he was about his evil ways.

David had come well prepared for his mission, a pair of snug fitting gloves so that no fingerprints would be left if he decided to enter any room. He slid open the oak cabinet, entered the chamber and closed the entrance. The layout of the secret walkways and their relationship to the various rooms was imprinted on his mind and as he crept along towards the masters suite, he wondered what would be revealed, a naked obscene English Lord preparing for his nights sleep, if so, would he ever be able to regard him with the awe that his fully clothed person usually commanded?

When in position, David slowly opened the spy slot hole to reveal His Lordship berating a tearful Brenda. My God thought David, she is his sexual plaything after all. He was now shouting at her.

"You will do as you are told, you are my daughter, illegitimate or otherwise, and as my daughter, you will, I repeat, you will obey me."

"Please let me go home, please let me go back to Russia to my own people" she sobbed.

"Let me explain again your predicament. I have many dangerous enemies, ruthless men, dangerous men, which places you as a pawn for those men to use against me. You have no idea what these types of men will do to you if it enables them to get at me. For your safety and my protection, you must stay at the estate where my security staff can watch over you and protect you. Only the head of security knows that you are my daughter and his special task is to protect you, for which he is paid a great deal of money," his voice softened and became almost pleading, "so please be patient it will not be for more than another year or two and then you can go back to Russia and live a magnificent life, having anything you want, anything." he concluded.

"Can't I go up to London occasionally to spend a day or two, free of those tiresome security men?"

"Katinka, we have been through this before. Anything you want to make your life happier, you can have, it can be brought to you regardless of the cost but you cannot leave the estate. What ever you want can be brought here to the estate, anything, anything." Lord Montdrago pleaded.

"May I return to my room now?" She asked.

"Yes, use the back passage which is not under surveillance and remember that after I leave tomorrow for my two day trip, try to be happy." His Lordship ordered.

Katinka or Debra walked out of the reception room through a simple, unadorned small door. The banker walked through to his bedroom and David, mind reeling, decided he had as much as he could digest for the moment and returned to the gunroom, ritually scrutinizing the gunroom carefully through the spy hole before sliding the oak cabinet open.

There was a message on the intercom. Margaret wanted him to try and make supper which she would delay until she heard from him. He phoned her, saying that he had been in the testing tunnel so had missed her call but he would be packing up and after he had returned the rifles to their cabinets he would wash up, lock up and repair to her dining room, say thirty minutes. That should satisfy the phone tapping bastards, thought David.

The supper was excellent and David was ravenous.

"Was your day interesting?" Margaret enquired.

"Routine. Testing His Lordships rifles and preparing for the African trip."

"What about your own rifles?" Margaret asked.

"I must check with security, I had made arrangements for my partner at the gunmaking workshop to send my personal rifles here to me, perhaps they're already here in securities office. If they don't know about the impending African safari with His Lordship, they're probably wondering what I need the rifles for. I shall be happier when they're locked up in the gunroom. I hope you will excuse me, Margaret; I have had a tiring day and must go to bed early as I have a great deal to do tomorrow. I shall be in the shooting tunnel most of the day regulating and testing His Lordships guns, so don't be surprised if I don't answer the intercom, just leave a message." That should satisfy those listening sods, thought David as he took his leave of Margaret.

David's pre-sleep thinking was spent mulling over the incredible information that he had overheard in the secret passage. That beautiful, lovely girl, could she be a product of that monster's loins? Unbelievable but true. Or had a Russian milkman been responsible? Wondered David

David wrestled with his conscience and won; having defeated the conscience of a decent Scottish gunsmith, he would spy on the lovely Russian tomorrow and what he observed may reverse the dilemma of his rapidly falling in love with her, he thought.

He hardly knew her and yet he was falling in love with her. There had been other women, beautiful desirable women of great accomplishments, some of them; but not one of them had aroused the feeling of love which he felt for the poor Russian butterfly pinned to a dangerous board of which she had no chance of extricating herself without a gunsmith who loved her. He drifted off to sleep in a haze of lovely thoughts about her.

Shortly after entering the gunroom, security called on the intercom and the chief of that despised body informed David that there was a crate of rifles for him that had just been delivered at the main gate of the estate, he personally would accompany his men and help them to carry it into the gunroom.

"No." David replied, "His Lordship's express orders were that all goods must be left in the ante room and that no one was permitted to enter the gunroom."

"The crate is very heavy." grumbled the security chief.

"I will manage, just leave it in the ante room and notify me when it is there"

"It is unsafe to leave it unattended." persisted the chief.

"I shall mention to His Lordship that the surveillance equipment both within and without the ante room is malfunctioning and I am sure he will get the technicians in."

The chief slammed down the phone and David wondered why he was not surprised at the rifles being delivered so promptly after his conversation with Margaret the previous evening.

Chapter Seven

David spent his day practicing, alternating between the Browning Hi-Power and the silenced 45. He had to modify the shoulder holster drastically to accommodate both handguns, but by mid afternoon he was satisfied that either pistol could be drawn fast, very, very fast and fired accurately,. He knew that should anybody, in the house of evil, threaten him in the secret burrow he would kill them, as all who might threaten him would certainly kill him when they had extracted information from him that would reveal his unauthorized spying. He thought of the banker issuing orders for the murder of Kowolski.

David entered the chamber, clad in black with his silenced pistol securely held in the shoulder holster and his black gloves snugly fitted, feeling as natural as the skin on his hands.

He crept soundlessly along until he reached the spy slot which covered Katinka's main living room adjacent to her bed room; there were secret access doors to both. The lovely girl was sitting paging through a Russian magazine, looking sad and wan. From time to time, she would pause; put the magazine down and stare with her lovely face straight ahead, thinking without expression. David's feelings were intense. How to get close to her and let her know how he felt and how he would do anything to remove her from the terrible situation she found herself in. He been observing her for about half an hour, his love growing stronger by the minute, when there was a firm knocking at the door. Katinka got up and went to the door and as she opened it, two men David hadn't seen before rushed in and one of them grabbed her by the shoulders and said,

"Pack a bag with some clothes and anything else you will need for a few days, and make it fast."

"You are under surveillance by security cameras and the guards will be here within seconds." Katinka gasped in a frightened voice. One of the men drew a gun and said,

"Forget about it, the chief of security and one of his men are in with us and they are the only two on duty, the cameras and bugs are switched off. It was planned this way. Let's make this a nice clean kidnapping and you will come to no harm. Your father is our target, go and pack your bag now, and don't bother to use the phone, it has been disabled." With that he pushed her roughly towards the bedroom.

"I must collect my toiletries from the bathroom first." She said and ran into the bathroom.

"Don't let me have to come and fetch you, you have three minutes to do anything you have to." The man said. David slid noiselessly through the secret door behind the men,

"And you have an eternity to do anything you want to." David said as he shot him through the head followed by an instantly placed second shot which took his companion too in the head. They collapsed as the bullets struck and David dashed past into the bedroom, tore the covers off the bed and ran back to place the covers under the dead men's heads to prevent blood from saturating the carpets. As he knelt over the corpses, lifting the remains of their heads to push the covers under them, he felt a presence behind him and spun around, gun in hand in the gun fighters crouch.

Katinka stood in the bathroom door way staring at him intently

"Who are you? did my father instruct you to watch over me?" she asked.

"I am a gunsmith Miss Jones and no, your father is totally unaware of the secret entrance to your room, Miss Jones, or the myriad of secret passages and spy holes which his Grandfather built into this house secretly, the knowledge of which he took to his grave, Miss Jones, not divulging those secret passages to anyone, Miss Jones. You see, Miss Jones, I stumbled onto an entrance in the gunroom—."

Katinka interrupted him with a smile.

"You have had your formalized formal joke Mr. McAlpine. My name is Katinka, David, and thank you."

"After I had discovered the secret chambers I did spy on your father in the conference room. I listened to some evil things including instructions to President Mbongi to murder Kowolski when he arrives in the Congo in a few days time. I also spied on you and your father arguing about you wanting to go to London. Today I must confess I spied on you because I have fallen in love with you and just wanted to be near you. We had better move quickly before the surveillance equipment is re-activated or those two traitors come around to check." David said to a dumbfounded Katinka who was blushing furiously.

David dragged the bodies into the secret chamber and took the blood stained cover with him.

"There are just a few blood stains on the carpet, try to remove them quickly, I will wait by the observation point until you are finished and stay there for a while. Go and visit Margaret when you are finished and I will meet you there for supper. Margaret does not know of my discovery, nobody does and nobody must ever know, and you must never admit to witnessing the death of the two men in fact deny anything to do with the kidnapping attempt, especially to your father. Remember when the cameras come on, so do the listening devices, therefore be quick and do not call out to me or talk to me while I watch over you. Never let on, never." With that David went into the chamber and closed the door behind him.

David observed Katinka clean up the few blood stains, tidy up and then, after putting on a jacket, leave her suite to go and visit Margaret.

David carried the bodies, one by one down to the end of the passage above the stairs that led down to the oak cabinet concealed entrance. He checked the gunroom through the spy hole and then entered, closing up the entrance and securing the cabinet in place. He noticed that the red light on the intercom was on and he listened to the recorded messages. One to notify him that the crate of rifles was in the ante room and the other from Margaret to tell him that Debra had surprised her with a visit and would be staying for supper.

When David entered Margaret's dining room, Katinka was seated next to Margaret having a glass of wine.

"Ah, there you are, look who we have for dinner." Margaret enthused.

"Good evening Miss Jones." David greeted the lovely girl

"Off duty, you may drop the formalities and call me Debra." Katinka said.

"Do you know, His Lordship's expensive doubled barreled rifle needed regulating, it must have received a bump on his last safari? Regulating can be a very difficult job sometimes but on this weapon it was much easier as certain cunning, modern adjusting devices had been built into the rifle. I am so looking forward to the African trip." David said stupidly. They were both looking at one another in a way that betrayed their feelings for one another to Margaret who said.

"David, remember when I showed you around the estates nursery, I forgot to point out the shrub that provides the most important drying oil which gunsmiths value highly for finishing fine walnut gun stocks, "Aleurties Fordii," the Tung Oil plant. I have a few minutes spare tomorrow first thing, meet me as before, after breakfast and let us stroll up to the nursery and I'll show it to you, it may even have nuts on it at this time of the year and I am sure that His Lordship would not mind if you picked a few."

"Thank you, Margaret, that's magic and it will be the first time that I have actually seen the tree that produces Tung oil, an oil which I favor above all others for my stocks." David knew that Margaret wanted to talk to him urgently out of range of those infernal cameras.

The dinner was memorable if only for the two young people desperately trying to hide their feelings for one another. They all chatted about various things, Katinka displaying a wide knowledge of music and the ballet, her Russian heritage, David thought; should he quote Robbie Burns and the recipe for highland haggis and enlighten her of the advanced culture of the Scots?

Katinka eventually excused herself and said that she must go and David left about ten minutes later and noticed the intense look that Margaret gave him as he left.

"See you at the side door in the morning." David said acknowledging the stare.

In the morning as they strolled towards the nursery, Margaret said,

"Your love for each other is very obvious and I hope the cameras didn't pick it up. When did this all come about then?" queried Margaret

"What I am about to tell you must never be repeated, even to the lovely Miss Jones, promise?" asked David.

"We who live in this horrible atmosphere must trust each other; I mean you and me especially. Does that reassure you?"

"Yes, Margaret, I fell in love with her shortly after I killed two intruders in her room who were trying to kidnap her before supper last night." David said to a stunned Margaret

"She is Lord Montdrago's illegitimate Russian daughter." He stated bluntly.

Margaret stopped walking and covered her mouth with both hands in a gesture of shock.

"Are you sure?"

"Yes, completely sure and she knows that I know."

"How-." Margaret began when David interrupted

"No how's, you promised."

They continued walking in silence; Margaret was obviously deep in thought.

"This alters everything." She said softly, almost to herself.

"He keeps her here against her will and although she can have anything she wants, he will not let her go back to her home, he says that he has ruthless enemies and that they would do anything to get at him and that the only place where she can be safe is here under the protection of his security services, but he is wrong." said David.

"There are the two corpses of the kidnappers hidden in the gunroom and before His Lordship gets home tomorrow, there has to be two more. The chief of security and one other security guard who were in with the kidnappers and facilitated their entrance to Debra's suite while the surveillance was switched off." He continued.

"If allowed to live, they may silence Debra, suspecting that she has had something to do with their two fellow conspirator's disappearance."

"As you will not tell me how you accomplished all this, can you tell me if you will be able to neutralize the threat without getting help from Montdrago?" Margaret asked.

"Yes Margaret, I am going to kill them today. How me no how's." David requested.

"That bush over there is the tung nut tree and that sweating, hurrying man coming up behind you is a security guard." said Margaret pointing at a shiny leaved bush.

They turned and walked past the guard on their way down to the Mansion.

As they reached the side door, David said,

"Make your way back to your office; I am going straight to the gunroom. I have two very important tasks to attend to before His Lordship returns tomorrow."

"God bless you." whispered Margaret fervently, as he walked off purposely.

In the gunroom, David strapped on the shoulder holster, refilled the 45's magazine, put on his gloves and his dark jacket. A plan was forming in his mind. He would carry the two bodies up to the observation points at the security surveillance room with its monitors and tape recorders. He would leave them there and then enter the security chief's office when he was out and wait for him. He was pretty sure that the chiefs own office would be neither bugged or under camera surveillance Hopefully he would discover who the other security guard was. He would leave all the bodies in the chief's office secure in the knowledge that the staff that discovered them would be scared shitless and would run to His Lordship when he got home tomorrow morning. Lord Montdrago would immediately institute the finger printing of the corpses and would soon know a great deal about them and would also dispose of the bodies. Everybody on the estate would be under suspicion except the gunsmith cloistered in his gunroom.

David carefully followed procedure in entering and closing the cabinet, climbed up the stairs and carried the bodies, one by one up to the security chiefs secret observation position, opened the spy holes and waited. The chief was already in his office and was seated at his desk. David didn't have long to wait, as a guard entered the office and sat down opposite the chief who had been sitting waiting for him

"Where the hell are our two friends?" the chief asked the other security guard.

"I don't know, I waited for them at the back entrance as arranged and when they didn't arrive, I came back to the surveillance room and searched through the mansion with the cameras. The target was not in her room but I found her in Margaret's room, sitting with the old lady having a drink. I picked up the gunsmith leaving the gunroom and followed his progress up to Margaret's suite where he had supper with the two women."

"Let's sit tight and see what happens, perhaps our two left before you got to the rear entrance and went back to London. We will hear soon."

David watched intently. Only the chief had his back to the secret door, the guard faced obliquely away. David held the gun up at the correct angle and height to align and shoot the guard instantly, and silently opened the door and fired almost immediately. The guard slumped forward.

"What's the matter with you, are you drunk?" were the chief's last words before he too slumped to the floor. David didn't touch them but hurriedly dragged and carried the other two bodies in and beat a hasty retreat, closing the secret door behind him. He sat quietly at the spy holes, breathing deeply and thinking. He felt no remorse, he was in a nest of vipers and they were evil vipers too, some beyond the law, their wealth and power guaranteed their immunity. After about fifteen minutes and continuous knocking at the chief's door, two men broke in. One, the senior of the two barked out,

"Alert all the staff and man all the monitors. Maximum alert."

Marvelous, thought David, I'll give the monitor something to look at and hurried back to the gunroom, exercising maximum caution and observing the ritual spy hole pre-entry precautions. David took off his gloves, stashed away the pistol in the armory and walked out to the ante room and made a great show of dragging and lifting his rifle crate that had been there for some considerable time. He was sure the cameras had recorded every single, muscle straining, second of it. David was late for lunch again and he hoped that Margaret would forgive him. At lunch, he apologized for his lack of punctuality saying he had to finish off two important jobs. Margaret understood and looked very relieved.

"His Lordship returns tomorrow morning and I am sure it will be a relief to be back home where he can relax and enjoy some peace and quiet" said David with an enigmatic smile. "I'm getting into the routine of things and the work is becoming less stressful." Margaret choked slightly and David said

"Margaret you must masticate your food thoroughly otherwise you risk digestive problems that always follow a warning choke or two, I have heard of men dying suddenly for want of thorough mastication, usually when they have bitten off more than they can chew."

"Please stop." Margaret whispered.

Chapter Eight

David spent the afternoon checking his own rifles and one shotgun. Unlike the traditionalists who attended the "Grand" shoots" his shotgun was an over and under, not a side by side which the snobs used. Having the barrels stacked one above the other, made for a stiffer action and, if the results of the clay pigeon competitions were anything to go by, improved one's shooting. His rifles were all well used, showing the scratches and small dings on the stocks which spoke of Africa. There were three rifles in his battery, a large 458 Lott, a medium,375 Holland and Holland magnum caliber and a 7mm by 57mm Mauser. All rifles were made by the famous factory in Brno in Czechoslovakia, CZ, and all had only aperture sights and were not fitted with scopes. The rifles were inexpensive but Africa had proved them reliable and David liked several of the features of their actions which, as a gunsmith, he knew were the only genuine improvements of the Mauser 98 action, an action so well designed that a hundred years after Paul Mauser designed it, it was still the standard that all other actions were judged by.The choice of calibers had been dictated by a professional hunters needs and the two main calibers were both based on the same cartridge case so that with hand loading equipment, an ammunition supply glitch in the bush need not be a tragedy, furthermore the ammunition was obtainable freely in most African territories.

After he had checked his weapons, he placed them back in the purpose built crate and went into the office and ordered tea over the intercom and started thinking.

He must locate the surveillance cameras in his room and the listening devices and must somehow frustrate them without alarming the watchers and spurring them into remedial action. His suite was fitted with both a large screen TV and a radio and CD hi-fi set. Although he seldom watched TV he had brought his small collection of CD's which he played at times. Perhaps he could frustrate the bugs with a loud symphony or a Pavarotti high C or two? Maybe he could place something in front of the cameras which security could hardly ask him to move and re-site. First he must locate the little buggers. That would be tonight's task because as soon as he could accomplish this he could access the secret chambers through his room. The ante room intercom buzzed, his tea had arrived.

Thinking and drinking tea, an English pastime, David thought, as he considered security's surveillance of the staff's bedrooms. It was morally and ethically indefensible but the pay and conditions were superb and the staff accepted it, so if he placed something in front of the camera, not something that could be construed as a deliberate attempt to block surveillance but something that could be perceived as an improvement to his living conditions, such as moving the TV set up high on a stand or bracket so as to watch it while he was lying down. Would His Lord Ship or security chastise him for blocking their surveillance of him? Of course not. Maybe the bodies that they were panicking about at this very moment, he thought, could be attributed, they might think, to an unhappy staff member who could not have a sexual interlude with another staff member, unobserved. The tea certainly stimulated thought, David mused.

David locked the gunroom early as he went up to his living quarters and started a nonchalant search. He knew he would be under surveillance so he pretended to be pacing the suite making notes with a pad and pencil in his hands. Tomorrow when Lord Montdrago returned, there would be some interesting developments in the mansion.

David knew the position of the secret door and once he had located the camera or cameras, he could plan his tactics. Because of his subterfuge, the search was long and difficult, but eventually, he had located two, one in the living room and one in the bedroom where the chamber access door was. Yes, a bracket with the TV mounted on it would enable him to watch while lying on his bed and block the surveillance camera and allow him to use the secret door unobserved. He would make up a bracket tomorrow, if the inevitable trouble that would occur when His Lordship was informed of the four bodies discovered in the surveillance chiefs office, did not involve him. Certainly, all the security staff would be suspect and there might be changes.

David was late again for supper and Margaret's worried look dissolved into a smile of relief as he walked in.

"What is for supper, I could eat a horse and chase the rider" he said hungrily

"Steak, egg and chips with scotch broth to start and milk custard with fruit to finish" Margaret said.

"When I lived in Edinburgh I developed bad habits such as lying in bed and watching TV and as you can't teach an old dog to break old habits, I'm going to arrange to watch TV from my bed." he declared.

"I don't see the harm in that" she replied.

"Is there a handy man who maintains the estates buildings?" he asked.

"Yes, he lives in a cottage behind the nursery" she replied.

"Could I ask him to fit a wee bracket for the TV or do I need permission from someone?"

"No, for minor things, the handy man decides whether permission is necessary. Would you like me to give him a ring and you can speak to him?" she asked.

"Please." David said gratefully.

When Margaret got Mr. Evans on the phone, David spoke to him and described what he wanted and arranged to meet him in his suite at seven thirty the next morning; Mr. Evans said that he had a standard fixture for just such an application.

After supper, David took his leave and retired to his suite, well pleased with the way events were unfolding. Security would be so busy tomorrow morning, he surmised, that it would be a day or two before they noticed his surveillance camera was giving them superb details of his TV's backside.

Mr. Evans was as good as his word and had the stand fixed to the wall by eight thirty and the TV in position and connected up within ten minutes. David thanked him and, late again, went for breakfast. Margaret wasn't in her suite but left a note saying that His Lordship had summoned her shortly after he had arrived back at the house.

David ate a hurried breakfast and walked briskly down to the gunroom. David had locked the silenced pistol in his bathroom's safe but on second thoughts had taken it down to the gunroom having left the browning in his safe. If the silenced pistol was found, the game would be up. After locking the gunrooms door behind him, he placed the silenced 45 on the stairway behind the oak cabinet in the secret chamber and resealed it with the oak cabinet. He busied himself completing the inventory of the equipment needed for Africa and waited, expecting to be summoned to the conference room. As the day wore on and he prepared to break for lunch, he realized that there would be no summons as the surveillance monitors would show that he had spent all his time in the locked gunroom when the bodies were found yesterday.

Margaret was pale and worried and said very little during lunch but her stare warned David not, even in an oblique way, to say anything that an equally oblique thinker, like the banker, could interpret.

"Have you seen His Lordship and how is he?" David enquired.

"Yes, I spoke to him this morning. He is well but very busy and will be fully occupied for the next few days and will not be available to anyone," she replied,

"I am just waiting to be told when the African trip will commence," he said.

"Oh, I nearly forgot, here is the list of names of the estates game keepers and the foresters and horticulturists who plan the shoots and drives. You mentioned that you would have to meet them sometime," the list was passed over to David, who stuffed it in his pocket and said,

"Thank you Margaret, please excuse me I must go down to the gunroom and finish oiling the guns that we will be taking to Africa," with that, David left the room and hurried back to the gunroom burning to read Margaret's note.

Once inside the gunroom, David sat at his office desk and unfolded Margaret's note. There were two pages, one listed out the names he had asked for and the other was a hurriedly written message,

"Be very careful and aware. He is very angry and very alarmed, even scared, some new body guards are being brought in and he is bringing forward the departure date for the African trip and he is taking Debra with him to Africa. Blood is thicker than water and he is worried about her safety here. He didn't mention why but he said that security had been breached and there were to be changes whilst he was in Africa. Take care. Burn this note." David's heart had leapt when he had read that Katinka was to accompany the Banker to Africa and this decided him to somehow smuggle the silenced 45 with him to Africa and the Browning too. He destroyed the note.

The phone rang, it was Katinka or formally Miss Jones.

"Good morning Mr. McAlpine, would you be so kind as to present yourself to His Lordship immediately?"

"Of course, Miss Jones, I shall go up to the conference room immediately, er, er, nearly forgot, Miss Jones" he replied, emphasizing the final Miss Jones.

When David reached the conference room, Katinka was waiting at the door to usher him in. The Banker looked worried, the easy self confidence was gone and David could detect a hint of fear about him.

"Good afternoon, David, I shall be brief, we leave for Africa in three days time so have everything ready. I have an overriding lock on my card for the gunroom which allows me to lock the door from the inside which prevents your card from functioning. I shall be going over my collection tomorrow morning so don't bother to go to the gunroom before midday, after lunch will be perfect. I prefer to be alone when I work with my collection of valuable artifacts."

"Yes Sir, I will not be down before lunch, but one question, Sir, can I have the various custom and firearm import forms for our African trip to fill in?" asked the gunsmith

"They are not necessary, my Executive Jet and its entourage do not have to pass through customs, only immigration. We land and alight in an area well away from the main buildings where our transport will be waiting. By the way, Debra will be accompanying me to Africa," he replied. "You may go"

David returned to the gunroom elated that Katinka would be with him in Africa. His joy was tempered with the realization that he was going to kill her father sooner or later and that his own life was at risk in the dangerous world he now lived in, far more dangerous than when he was in the SAS or following up a dangerous animal that a client had wounded out in Africa. He tidied up the gunroom and made his way up to Bernie's rooms to discuss the change of dates and if Bernie had all the medical equipment and supplies to hand.

Bernie answered his knock and greeted David with a worried look on his face, bade him enter,

"Go straight through to the examination room, I've been told that we are leaving for Africa in three days time, so I better stick my finger up your ass and check your prostate, and you can cough at the same time as I hold your balls for a good old fashioned medical examination." Bernie followed David into the room and closed the door after him.

"I don't know if you have been told and I have been instructed not to tell anybody of the events of last night but, fuck them, I must discuss it with somebody or I will go mad. I was rushed into the chief security officer's office to try and revive him and a guard and two other men. Their bodies were lying on the floor all efficiently dispatched by someone who an amateur, he is not," Bernie was being very Jewish, "the two strangers had been dead a few hours but our lot had just been killed. It was pure disorganized panic in the room and fear too. I suggested that the police are informed but the assistant chief vetoed the idea and insisted that we wait until Montdrago returned the next morning. Montdrago summoned me this morning early and said that he had reported the matter to the chief constable and that we were all to keep our mouths shut. He said that I could phone the Chief Constable if I wished to confirm his instructions. The cunning old bastard has everyone in his pocket, including the Chief Constable. What should I do?"

"Margaret once told me that whenever there is a bad crisis, security prevents anybody from leaving the estate until it's over and the outside phone lines are closed down, but His Lordship has the crises brought rapidly under control and things return to normal quickly. I suggest we concentrate on the Africa trip. I was working as a professional hunter in Africa for a few years recently and I guarantee you the experience of a lifetime, and who knows you may have to declare the old bastard dead one happy day," said David with a grin.

"You must start taking the anti-Malaria pills, they're the latest on the market and are very effective but they do have side effects. You become as randy as a little pig and if the user's pecker didn't turn yellow and drop off after three months, it would supplant Viagra," said Bernie.

"When I hunted in a remote area of the Congo, I could not help noticing the peckers of the scantily clad tribesmen of those parts. Their appendages were long, full bodied like a good wine and robust and it was rumored that they could withstand much abuse. I asked the Congolese chief if he could help me to have one like his and he showed me the secret. He tied a cord tightly around the base of my tassel and hung a heavy stone from it which I concealed down my trouser leg. When I went back to him the next day and we inspected it he was overjoyed, it was just like his. It had turned black," David concluded seriously.

"Yes, a large part of my practice in the Israeli army was treating high ranking officers for erectile dysfunction but fortunately I possessed an old secret Jewish traditional remedy for the affliction, a three to one injection," said Bernie seriously.

"Is it based on desert herbs?" asked David equally seriously,

"No, three stone, two sand and one cement," replied Bernie with the self satisfied conceit of the master physician "Take your pills and go and have a good nights rest. Don't repeat what I have told you," Bernie said.

"Before I leave; a question. Where are your living quarters?" asked David.

"I have a beautiful house allocated to me on a rise, overlooking the lake, with a beautiful garden surrounded by lovely trees about half a mile beyond the nursery. The horticulturist and the forester live nearby. My lovely wife is very happy here as the splendid furniture supplied by the estate is kept clean, together with the rest of the house by a maid also supplied by the estate. I neutralized all the bugs and surveillance equipment and it has not been restored," Bernie replied.

Bernie showed David to the door and he left.

At a few minutes before eight the following morning, David locked both his apartment's doors, his main entrance door and then locked himself in his bedroom. After checking to reassure himself that the TV, high up on it's new bracket, obscured the surveillance camera's prying eye, David slid through the secret door and hurried down to the staircase behind the oak cabinet, perching comfortable where he could observe the interior of the gunroom. He strapped on his shoulder holster and with the comforting weight of the silenced 45 beneath his left arm, he waited. He had taken the precaution of unclipping a cough box and had placed it in easy reach. After about twenty minutes, the gunroom door opened and His Lordship walked in, closing the door behind him and using a smart card, of a different color to that of David's, inserted it into a slot at the side of the door handle. Ha, thought David, that's the way to freeze the lock mechanism so that it cannot be opened from the outside with my smart card.

The banker walked into the tunnel and as he moved deeper in, he was out of view from David's high vantage point. After five minutes, he re-emerged carrying a heavy aluminium box. He placed the box on the nearest bench and opened it. The box opened, revealing many small linen bags. Lord Montdrago took out a bag and untied the drawstring and carefully poured out a stream of glittering diamonds, cut, not uncut, gems, most of which were large magnificent stones. He ran them through his fingers, fondling them with an enraptured, glazed look on his face. After a while, he put the diamonds back into the bag and then removed all the other bags, not opening them but carefully counting each bag.

My God thought a spellbound David, this is unbelievable; no wonder there is no surveillance of this room. He now realized why he had been given the Browning Hi Power automatic. He was the keeper of the Privy Purse.

The banker closed the box after carefully replacing the bags, and carried it back into the tunnel only to re-emerge with a larger, lighter box. He opened the box to reveal files and files of certificates. Large denomination bearer bonds thought David, as he strained his eyes to see. The banker carefully counted the certificates.

.David realized with certainty, that the finding of four unexplained corpses in the heart of the mansions security complex had the banker thinking that maybe his treasure trove had been the target and had been breached. A visibly relieved Lord Montdrago returned the box back into the recesses of the tunnel.

When he came out of the tunnel, he stood deep in thought and then, after dusting his trousers down with his hand, he straightened and started to walk to the gunroom door and stopped, clapping his hand to his head and saying audibly,

"Re-set the alarm, you bloody fool," and turning walked back into the tunnel. He emerged from the tunnel and walked straight to the gunroom door, letting himself out and closing the door behind him.

David picked up the cough box, returned it to its position then took off his holster and placed it together with the 45 on top of the cough box and rapidly returned to his bedroom, where a quick inspection showed all was well.

Chapter Nine

David went down to the gunroom after an interval of time. He phoned Margaret and said that as the hunting trips departure time had been advanced, he would have to start packing the weapons and ammunition ready for transport to the airport the next day, therefore he would skip lunch. Margaret said she would prepare a tray and have it delivered to the ante room.

Before walking down the tunnel to the side cubicle where the ammunition and reloading tools were kept, David carefully, on his knees, tracked His Lordships foot prints along the tunnel's dusty floor. They went right up to the bullet back stop at the extreme end of the tunnel and seemed to continue on into the sand bags stacked against the final steel wall. He retreated back to the ammunition cubicle and started taking out and stacking on the workbench all the ammunition and accoutrements that would be necessary for the coming trip. He also took to the bench the superb hand crafted aluminium rifle cases, one each per rifle and one for the shotgun which made up His Lordships Battery. David's crate, which accommodated all three of his rifles and his shotgun, had long extra compartments built down each side against the inner walls of the crate. These accommodated the ammunition for his rifles and a basic, well thought out, set of tools for emergencies; there was enough space to pack both handguns. Two benches were needed to stack the equipment, whereas only part of one had been needed to hold millions of dollars, thought David ruefully.

The intercom buzzed indicating that the tray was in the ante room.

Sitting in his office and enjoying the sandwiches He opened a paper napkin to wipe his lips. Clearly written was "I love you. K" David did not wipe his lips with the napkin, he kissed it repeatedly.

The phone rang, it was Miss Jones

"I was going to convey your instructions from His Lordship personally and I bumped into a servant bringing you a tray to the ante room so I took it from her and delivered it myself. As I went into the ante room I remembered that there was to be an important meeting with some visitors from the USA this morning so I left your tray in the ante room, buzzed the intercom and hurried back to my office as the visitors are due any minute now. Did you get your tray?"

"Yes, Miss Jones, I've been wiping my lips with the napkin repeatedly, thank you,"

" I noticed the napkins, the Kitchen is very thoughtful. His Lordship's instructions are to be ready with all the weapons and equipment as the transport staff will be picking it up at seven tomorrow morning to take it to the airport. Arrangements have been made to load everything, without having it checked by officials, but all the people traveling with His Lordship's party still have to go through emigration at this end, so don't forget your passport. I must hang up, Mr. McAlpine, the visitors have arrived and I must show them in to the conference room."

Time to enter the secret world of high finance David decided as he cautiously crept up to the observation slots servicing the conference room.

Snugly in position, David observed the meeting beneath him in the conference room. There were three middle aged men; judging from their accents, one was from the USA and one was from France and one was from Germany. They all spoke impeccable English except the American who slurred his words, whilst brutalizing the Queen's English, with obvious relish.

"Word has reached me this morning that the threat posed by Kowolski has been eliminated. Apparently he was murdered in his hotel room last night, so the mutiny can commence. Immediately after I received the news, I instructed our man at the British Broadcasting Corporation to arrange for that agricultural program on the "containment of tropical plant diseases" to be broadcast on the BBC's Africa service. That was the pre-arranged signal for the rebels to attack was it not?" Lord Montdrago asked.

"Yes," slurred the American "and the content of the program can be a great help to the subsistence farmers of the Congo too."

"Good, we are not averse to the practice of philanthropy, provided it's not over done, a practice, which experience has shown, smothers enterprise and true development." said the banker earnestly, without a smile.

David could hardly believe what he was hearing.

"Gentlemen," continued His Lordship "Our small band of brothers, since my father's time, has seldom exceeded ten men, usually less and occasionally more, but never more than twelve. Ever since it's creation, we have avoided trivialities and our members, all men with vast holdings in the business world or high positions in the governments of the great Western Powers, have based all their actions and strategies on the distilled and refined essence of pure basic intelligence, or facts, if you will.

All our vast enterprises have armies of accountants, auditors and analysts in the various filtering and verification sections, manned by men of deep intelligence and knowledge; thus is the essence of pure intelligence refined to its ultimate, and that essence dictates our actions and directives. Should someone in one of our enterprises steal one hundred million dollars, that information would be refined out of the intelligence passed up to us, as a triviality. Those lower down in our empire have the power to deal with the miscreant. However should the same miscreant not steal money but interfere with a secret directive to the world's media which we control, even innocently, and frustrate a long term goal, this would be passed on up to us to deal with. Even the most intelligent of our servants, who perceive a barely perceptible rattle from our tail, and do not correct their actions promptly, will uncoil our strength and feel the bite of retribution; a sometimes fatal bite as did Kowolski," concluded Lord Montdrago. His Lordship slowly stared from face to face ominously, his eyes like those of the serpent with the soft rattle.

"The money, over a billion at last count, which President Imbomgi siphoned off the Aid disbursements with our help, and which is invested and held by us on behalf of the now deceased President, is untraceable and is now in our Africa account. It is all accountable. The arming and financing of the coup which killed Mbongi was from that account," smiled the banker with obvious glee.

"Tomorrow I leave for Africa; our intelligence essence from there has become diluted and adulterated with misinformation. I refer to the mining and granting of mining rights in the Congo, Zambia and the Republic of South Africa, in particular Gold, Platinum and Copper. Since the advent of Black Democracy in those countries, any third rate nation or conglomerate with the audacity to bribe every petty president or his cabinet, thinks they can usurp what is rightfully ours. I intend to personally put a stop to these irritations, with extreme prejudice if necessary. We have very competent men recruited from the best regiments of the armies of the West stationed in Africa for just such an eventuality," said His Lordship with an exaggerated sniff of indignation.

"The Safari Company that I have engaged to outfit a hunt in Zambia, has a white hunter on its staff who has carried out certain work for our organization in those parts in the past. I have instructed him to remove a member of our group which is accompanying me. I have heard a rumor that he may work for Mossad."

David was spellbound, who could the Mossad agent be and why? So these men were part of the conspiracy that many hinted at and which governments denied. David had never seen a rattle snake but its African cousin, the deadly Puff Adder and even the more dangerous Gaboon Viper were known to him; neither was as deadly as Lord Montdrago.

"Yep, Montdrago, you don't get into a pissing contest with a skunk, you stomp on it and fuck it," said the Texas Billionaire. His Lordship's nose wrinkled with distaste at his colleague's crudeness.

"Gentlemen, as I have to prepare for my trip tomorrow, let us adjourn and I shall keep you fully informed of both my findings and my actions in Africa," Lord Montdrago said as he stood up and ushered his guests to the door.

A stunned and horrified David got ready to go back to the gunroom but paused before shutting the spy slot when he heard the banker say over the phone to Katinka to show the three new body guards into the room and then to summon David to the conference room. David dashed back to the gunroom quickly observing the usual precautions and had barely placed the oak cabinet back into position when the phone in his office rang. He hurriedly went to the office and picked the phone up.

"McAlpine," he answered.

"His Lordship wishes you to come up to the conference room immediately," said the lovely Miss Jones.

"I will come up right away, Miss Jones," David could not keep the love out of his voice.

David was shown in to the "Room," by the very feminine and beautiful Debra.

There were three large men seated in front of the banker's desk. Three very well trained and disciplined men who did not acknowledge or show any sign of recognition of David. David was taken aback with surprise to see them.

"David, let me introduce you to my three new body guards who will accompany us to Africa tomorrow. They are all former members of the SAS and have only recently left the British Army. This is ex sergeant Jock Hamilton and he will introduce you to his two colleagues,"

David stretched out his hand and said,

"David McAlpine, resident gunsmith,"

"Well gentlemen, leave now and repair to the staff dining room where you can get to know one another over tea and cake. David, lead the way," ordered His Lordship.

They marched out of the room.

As soon as they were seated in the dining room and the serving maid had brought their tea and a huge plate of various cakes and tidbits, David said quietly, barely moving his lips like a ventriloquist,

"Everywhere is bugged and there are surveillance cameras,"

"Lang may your lum reek," said Jock. David smiled as he remembered when he was their commanding officer in the SAS, Jock had asked him what that Scottish saying meant when David had used it. David explained that in olden times in poverty stricken rural Scotland, if a humble cottage's lum or chimney was smoking and smelling of smoke, that is reeking, it denoted prosperity as it meant that the inhabitants of that cottage could afford fuel to keep themselves warm through the bitter winters of that harsh but beautiful land.

"What did you say your companion's names were again?" asked David. The two men had been silent, in awe of their former commanding officer who had left the SAS with a splash after an action of terrible destruction conducted solely on his own without any backup and a long way from the help of his men.

"That's Hamish and that's Scottie," said Jock with a smile and restraining the natural inclination to end the sentence with a "Sir" David shook their hands with pleasure, it had been a long time.

"Before you go back to your quarters to prepare for the trip to Africa tomorrow, I'll take you to meet a Fellow Scot, a lovely elderly lady who has been with His Lordship for all his life here in the mansion." With that, they finished their tea and left the table, David leading, to go and meet Margaret. David managed to whisper to Jock as they walked through the dining room towards the door.

"Guard the beautiful lassie with your life, she's my woman."

Jock looked intently into David's eyes and nodded very slowly; he had pledged his life, David knew.

The last thing David did as he left his bedroom the next morning to go with his luggage down to the waiting minibus that was to convey them to the airport, was to lock his bedroom door and place three of his own hairs across the door gap where it closed against the frame. He had brought some colorless light glue from the gunroom for that purpose, so that the hairs could not just fall off but they would have to be sheared off by the opening of the door. The hairs were placed a long way apart to avoid detection of all three; maybe one or maybe two but not all three. He did the same to the secret door.

Lord Montdrago's personal jet was the fastest and largest of the corporate jets available and was fitted out with a small, elaborately equipped, surgical facility capable of dealing with any medical problem and sustaining life until a hospital could be reached. The sophisticated modern hospitals of Johannesburg were just a few hours away from most the Central African territories using His Lordships jet. There was a luxurious suit in the front of the aircraft which the banker, his legal advisor and his P.A. Miss Jones used, the other seven men, David, the taxidermist, the two doctors and the three bodyguards, shared the main cabin. The two doctors, Bernie and the surgeon spent a great deal of the trip discussing medical matters and David spoke to both the taxidermist and the bodyguards from time to time. It was a relief to be in an atmosphere without the constant surveillance although David kept up the pretense of not knowing Jock and his companions before they had met the previous day.

It was a long flight and as soon as they landed at Ndola, a small town with an airport large enough for most commercial aircraft that served the vast Copperbelt with its large mines, Lord Montdrago and his bodyguards were whisked off by a convoy of Government vehicles. His Lordship had told David and the others, including Miss Jones that a Hunting Safari Outfitting company would take them to a hotel for the night and then off to the hunting camp in the Luangwa Valley the next day where he would join them in three days time.

As the convoy sped off, a luxury minibus drew up next to the aircraft with two men dressed in the usual hunting jackets and kahki trousers. One of them walked over to David and greeted him warmly,

"Hullo David, what the hell does your party need me for, have you forgotten how to hunt?" he asked laughingly.

"Jimmy, you old reprobate, do they still use you as bait to attract the man eaters?" David asked, stretching out his hand and shaking Jimmy's vigorously.

"Meet my companions." There were introductions all round.

"After you have unloaded your personal luggage, I will take you to your hotel, together with your pilots. The safari equipment and firearms will be perfectly safe locked in the jet for the night,"

At David's invitation the safari men joined His Lordship's people for dinner and David held and squeezed Katinka's hand whenever possible under the table like a love stricken schoolboy.

"Lord Montdago is a regular client, very aloof and unapproachable but an excellent shot and unafraid of the scratchers, biters and horners. In fact on his last hunt with us he held his ground and withstood a charge from a very angry lion. He was not fazed," related Jimmy "But he is completely divorced from the other joys which the bush provides, the sunsets and the beauty of the surroundings of our most exclusive and seldom used "Special" camp reserved for only the well heeled and important clients. He has no empathy with the animals he hunts and is sometimes cruel," Jimmy said to David, although the others must have overheard.

"I look forward to tomorrow and as soon as supper is over, I am going to hit the sack, I am sure the others will want to do the same," David hid his bitter disappointment when he learned that Katinka had been booked into the luxury suite far, far away from where the others were accommodated. Jimmy told them all of the arrangements for their departure on the morrow before he left the hotel.

In the past when Zambia was known as Northern Rhodesia and ruled by the colonial authorities, the game laws had been carefully thought out and ruthlessly enforced. Usually, the hunting areas surrounded the large reserves, many covering hundreds of square miles. The idea was to encourage game to stay in the reserves. The hunting was rigorously controlled and the hunting areas were split up into areas of different hunting quality, the best adjacent to the completely protected reserves and the less desirable areas further away. Lord Montdrago's hunting area was a choice one with a large variety of game. The Luangwa river, a tributary of the mighty Zambezi, ran through both the reserve and the hunting area. After Zambia gained its Independence poaching and the slaughtering of game was wide spread, unhindered by the new black government. Large syndicates usually with politicians and government ministers sharing in the spoils while protecting the butchers, nearly wiped out the game altogether but concerned conservationists world wide had slowly forced successive black politicians to see the wisdom of protecting the remaining game not without, it was rumored, many bribes and other inducements; all this was discussed around the campfire the first night in camp.

The camp was set out on some high ground overlooking the river where the thick forests and the many open areas near the river could be viewed. The game was not as visible as in the protected reserve; it seemed as if the hunting area was treated with alert caution by the animals.

David was sitting with Bernie a little apart from the others who were clustered around Katinka regaling her with tales of Africa and hunting and tribal mysteries.

"When are you going to become the banker's son in law?" Bernie asked. David nearly fell out of his camp chair in astonishment.

"How did you know Debra was his daughter?" David asked.

"Mossad knows a great deal about the evil lord and that his lovely illegitimate daughter, Katinka, is being kept at the estate against her will," Bernie replied.

Of course, a man of Bernie's skills and especially a man of his strong character would not tolerate surveillance for one split second unless he was on a mission, David reasoned.

"We also know of a SAS captain who disobeyed his superiors and single handedly attacked a terrorist camp to avenge the deaths of some of his men caught in an unexpected ambush by terrorists whom his superiors now referred to as freedom fighters and had been ordered to protect if necessary against retaliatory attacks from those whose villages they had plundered with much slaughter. We of Mossad understand your actions as we are ignorant fellows, unschooled in the niceties of the English language. To us, a terrorist is a terrorist; what the fuck is a freedom fighter? The dishonorable discharge that you suffered in consequence has been to your advantage. How else could you have met the beautiful maiden in distress?" smiled Bernie.

"Freedom fighters are men, usually based in London, heavily protected by the British authorities, where the British press laud their objectives whilst laying down a solid base of blatant lies about the freedom fighters so that British historians could continue to influence future generations about their, the terrorists, lily white activities in Africa. I daresay that those worthy Scandinavians who provided Hitler with his iron ore and other commodities during the last war would have awarded Hitler the Nobel peace prize had he survived. I say this because I know of one black freedom fighter who took to the church after his country had been democratized, who was awarded a Nobel Peace prize. He had been recorded exhorting rioting mobs to "Kill the Whites" when he was younger" said David bitterly. "Do leopards change their spots?"

"Let's face it, every country in the world uses the media to influence the masses into supporting the most terrible events; bloody, cruel, unjust events which the masses would never condone, let alone enthusiastically join in the slaughter, if they knew the truth. As a reasonable devout Jew, I have often thought that editors and some journalists would have a lot to answer for on judgment day up there in heaven kneeling before God,"

Katinka had strolled over to where they were sitting,

"Why the gloomy faces on such a magnificent night with the stars hanging so low that you could reach up to them, and the glow of the fire magically turning all of us into golden hued Gods. I am so happy that I can't bear anyone to be unhappy so please smile or laugh," she said with joy; she bent down and kissed David on the forehead.

"Now the cat is out the bag," said David not displeased.

"Doctor Cohen has a wise and interesting face, and as a doctor, knows how to keep secrets," Katinka wrinkled her nose and laughed and strolled back to the other men, a hunter, a surgeon and a taxidermist; men with different skills and, slightly drunk, with different thoughts about the great adventure of life.

"My mission is to monitor and gain intelligence of our evil lord's activities and who visits him and how often. We suspect that he is supplying arms to certain enemies of ours which does not over concern us but if he is meeting physicists then we are concerned. Jews are very wise and I wonder who is going to kill him, us or you? That same wisdom would advise you not to; as many years down the line your wife would resent you if the deed surfaced, as the best of well kept secrets tend to do. We would appreciate any intelligence that you could give us should you discover anything. Mossad is worried that His Lordship may know of my status and has warned me to exercise great care," said Bernie quietly.

David now knew who was to be eliminated. Should he tell him? David was pleased that the first thing he had done when he had unpacked and taken his rifles out of the crate, was to take the holster and the silenced 45 and strap it under his hunting jacket; a loose fitting jacket with cartridge loops across the chest which completely disguised the shoulder holster and the gun. When he went to bed at night, he would keep the holster on after removing the jacket.

"Well, Bernie, let us finish our drinks and go to our tents. And yes, I will help you in any way I can."

As they stood up, Jimmy came over,

"I am shooting for the pot tomorrow, would Dr. Cohen like to join me?" Jimmy asked.

"We will both join you," David interjected "Bernie, I insist that you come, you will thoroughly enjoy the hunt and you asked if I could help you with the hunting of dangerous quarry and although hunting for the pot is not dangerous, it's a start."

"Great," said Bernie.

"I am glad you're coming David, You can help me to carry the meat back. I cannot spare a tracker tomorrow morning as the entire staff is preparing for the main hunt which we'll commence after the midday heat is past. We will be hunting a buffalo and it will be the last decent hunt we can have before His Lordship arrives in camp; He will be hunting every day for the following three days before you all fly off to the Congo where His Lordship has further business to attend to," Jimmy said "We will leave camp at sunrise,"

The day dawned as only a day can dawn in Africa; the early morning light, the smells of the dew drenched grass drying and the subtle sounds of the bush emerging from night. David had brought his own 7mm Mauser for Bernie. Low on recoil and with enough power and penetration for the light skinned small buck they were after. They soon reached the river and walked softly along the high bank. Jimmy had slowed down and was a few steps behind them when he called out stop. David didn't see any game and he and Bernie turned to see what Jimmy had seen.

Jimmy had his rifle pointed at them and said

"I am sorry David but if you interfere with what Lord Montdrago has ordered me to do, my instructions are to shoot you after I have killed Dr. Cohen but His Lordship is a good judge of men and he knows all about your dishonorable discharge from the SAS and your killing spree and he assures me that if you co-operate there will be a very generous bonus for you. Doctor Cohen will be taken by the crocs which the Luangwa is notorious for. Are you going to co-operate?"

"Definitely, I am an anti-Semite but I suggest that you dump the body at that small beach over there," David pointed over Jimmy's shoulder and as he turned his head to see where David was pointing, David drew the silenced 45 and with a slight "Pop" shot Jimmy behind the ear.

"Not a bad shot for an anti-Semite. You knew didn't you?" asked a relieved looking Bernie.

"Only after you had revealed your connection with Mossad. We must carry his body to that small sandy shore back there and stage a croc attack and then obliterate our tracks from here and then get our story right, it must even convince the banker. I must not jeopardize my bonus, so strive to pay attention, Bernie," David re- holstered the 45.

They carried Jimmy to the edge of the river and David removed his boots and socks and rolled up his trouser legs. David took his hunting knife and slit open his stomach, taking care not to spill any of its contents and then threw the body into the river. He placed the socks and boots next to a rock which stretched out into the river and said to Bernie,

"He was paddling and dangling his legs in the water from the edge of that rock when a huge croc leapt out and caught his legs and pulled him under the water. Note, the body is already being attacked," David pointed to the floating body which was being savaged by several crocodiles "an open belly is irresistible to our scaly friends,"

They sat quietly for a while and Bernie asked,

"Who are you?"

"I am a gunsmith, quickly help me to find the ejected empty cartridge case and brush away our tracks which we left when carrying down the body to the river," David asked as he broke off a small branch to use to brush away the tracks. Bernie found the brass case and threw it into the river.

"You are not a very cost conscious Jew, I could have reloaded that case," David complained.

"Fuck off, I am a doctor and only re-use blunt hypodermic needles if I can derive joy from the screams of my patients as I plunge the recycled needles in," said a serious Dr. Cohen.

"Ready, steady, go," said Bernie and they both started to run and trot back to the camp where they arrived panting and sweating and shouting to all the others that there had been a terrible accident, explaining how the giant croc had ambushed Jimmy and taken him under the water. They said that they had seen several crocs tearing at the body lower down stream as the body briefly surfaced. There was a great deal of panic and Jimmy's assistant got on the radio to notify the safari company's and ask for instructions; David asked the Safari company to contact Lord Montdrago and to ask for their instructions.

Swiftly and efficiently the safari company had the situation under control and said that their senior hunter/manager would fly into the airstrip about twenty miles from their camp where the camp staff must collect him and bring him to the camp. He would contact His Lordship and take instructions.

Within four hours the Safari company manager arrived at the camp together with two officials from the department of Game and Fisheries. All went down to the river to inspect the scene and took statements from both David and Dr. Cohen. It was abundantly clear that the deceased had foolishly taken of his boots and socks and cooled off his feet in the river. The more the investigating party milled around trampling away any evidence of a body being carried, the happier David became.

The men returned to the camp and prepared to leave for the airstrip,

"What were Lord Montdrago's instructions?" David enquired.

"There has been a military coup in the Congo and his Lordship advises that the hunting may continue for the next two days and he will contact you on the camp radio with instructions when the situation in the Congo becomes clearer," The Safari Company manager said.

The investigators were anxious to go back to the airstrip as there was just enough daylight left to facilitate a safe return flight. They said their goodbyes and left.

Chapter Ten

The buffalo hunt was postponed to the next day and they all sat around the campfire and had an early sundowner.

"It has been an eventful day," said the surgeon Douglas Hamilton.

"Yes Africa does its best to fascinate," mused David.

"You knew Jimmy well?" asked Jimmy's assistant, now the groups new Professional Hunter, Charlie by name.

"Not as well as I thought," replied David "I never figured him as a careless man who would dip his toes into the Luangwa," David said.

"He had become very foolhardy and often did not pay the dangerous animals the respect they demanded. He felt himself indestructible and often flirted with buffalo to impress the ladies on safari," the shocked Charlie recounted.

"'I hope you insist that the report sent to Lord Montdrago contains that information as His Lordship may blame me as an experienced hunter for allowing Jimmy to do such a foolish thing although, as I recall, I did ask him not to take such a foolish risk, didn't I Bernie?" asked David,

"You did indeed and even I, who Jimmy warned only yesterday about the dangers of crocs, thought he was being foolhardy," said Bernie.

"Well, it is over and done with, let us drink a toast to Jimmy's memory and then talk of Africa and its glory's. What can I pour you to drink Debra? All of you just help yourselves" Charlie was cheering up as all men do at sundowner time.

The group broke up with Charlie and the surgeon and the taxidermist clustering around Debra who was looking ravishing in a Safari outfit with a jacket with cartridge loops and long kahki trousers. Bernie and David sat somewhat apart from the group where they could chat quietly without being overheard.

"How did you know Jimmy was going to try?" asked Bernie.

"I didn't know it was Jimmy but I did know there was going to be an attempt on a suspected Mossad agent. I didn't warn you as I felt, that no matter how hard you tried, you would be unable to act normally and this would have alerted the assassin and then he would have been very cunning and pre-emptive. As it turned out, Jimmy let his confidence exceed his ability. That His Lordship had thought that I would play

along, if true, requires some thought on my part and it does not bode well," David answered.

"You haven't answered my question, how did you know?" repeated Bernie.

"Margaret was standing just inside the door of Debra's empty office, unobserved when the bankers three guests left, and overheard the Frenchman say that he wondered what nasty surprise Montdrago had arranged for the Mossad member of the group going to Africa with him. Margaret told me, perhaps she thinks I am linked to Mossad too." David lied hoping it would satisfy Bernie. David might have told Bernie of his discovery of the secret passages, but after seeing the banker's treasure trove, he knew if Mossad knew of secret chambers, they would tear the place apart at the first opportunity, and find the banker's cache.

"Bernie, do you know how to use a Browning Hi-Power?" asked David,

"Yes, I trained with one," Bernie replied,

"I have one in my gun case unfortunately I haven't a holster for it," David said,

"That's alright, I will keep it in my waistband, I prefer a cross draw,"

"That's what I'm afraid of; you might blow the head off your circumcised organ when you draw fast in an emergency," David said,

"I should be so lucky," said Bernie in a lisping, exaggerated Yiddish accent, "the Rabbi who attended to me after I was born, was a malicious old bastard and used Pinking shears. I am known by my Mossad colleagues as Frilly Willie and in my departmental record lists under, "Identifying Marks" the fact that I have bite marks where I shouldn't,"

"That's good," David laughed.

"You should be so lucky to hear "Frilly Willie" in Hebrew," Bernie lisped.

David stood up and called to the others that he was going to show Bernie the other rifles in his gun case and with Bernie following he went to his tent.

David gave the Browning to Bernie and could see by the way he checked it that he was an expert.

They drew their chairs around the campfire with the others after they got back from David's tent. David sat next to Katinka and said

"Are you happy?"

She looked at him, the glow from the fire accentuating the intense blue of her slanting Russian eyes and her high cheek bones and her voluptuous lips, radiant and in the golden light so obviously in love that David knew that this fact would be reported back to the evil lord and this would bring him closer to the day when David would have to kill him, if only for the children that he and Katinka would one day have.

Katinka lent over and whispered in his ear,

"I desire to make love to you to express my deep love for you,"

David felt Bernie staring at him and turned to Bernie who said quietly

"Do not throw God's gift back into his face; after we have all eaten, excuse yourself and go back to your tent, I will bring your heaven sent bride to you later without anyone knowing,"

They had a few after dinner drinks, then David excused himself and went to his tent. All the tents were separated and Bernie's was the closest to Katinka's

After a half hour of talking and drinking, Bernie stood up and said to Katrinka,

"Come, I'll walk you to your tent and check that there are no scorpions or other beasties in your tent before you enter," With that, he held out his hand and led Katrinka off to her tent.

David watched through a slit in the tent's front laced up canvas, as Bernie danced back to the group sitting around the camp fire, describing a wide circle as he jigged and danced; the men at the fire were laughing at his antics and following his circular progress towards them as he burst into some Hebrew song and contorted his way from a direction almost opposite from the direction of Katinka's tent.

David slipped out under the rear covering of his tent and moved back well out of the light, and then circled round until Katinka's tent was directly in line with the campfire and he crouched and moved to the back of her tent. He called softly out to her and she called softly back. David crawled under the back flap and stood up to be greeted by the sight of Katinka, naked and beautiful standing in front of him with her arms outstretched.

"Be gentle, I am a virgin and nothing must spoil the magic of this coming together with the man I love,"

They didn't speak again until it was time for David to leave when he said,

"This is forever, you know,"

"Yes," she replied.

As he made his way to his tent in the darkness before the pre-dawn light subtly stole across the magnificent bush, David noticed one of the trackers standing between the tents observing him. David went up to him and asked quietly,

"Why are you watching me?"

"Bwana, I have been instructed to by Bwana manager," he answered.

"Will you report back what you have seen?"

"No Bwana, some years ago when Bwana was hunting in Africa, my father was Bwana's tracker, Mikalashi, and I as a small boy used to help around the camp and make Bwana's tea, my name is Dickson. Bwana was very good to me and my father and I know you. I stood so that Bwana would see me,"

"Good lord Dickson you have become a fine man, I remember the little Dickson who would play with my old guitar," David said with pleasure.

"I will watch over Bwana and tell the manager nothing. I heard the manager say that two white men will join the camp tomorrow. He told the radio that he would help them to fix you and the Bwana Doctari," related Dickson.

"The manager, do you mean Bwana Charlie?" asked David.

"Yes, Bwana," replied the tracker.

"Thank you Dickson, Come with me and Doctari when we hunt today,"

"Yes, Bwana, I go now," said Dickson as he turned and walked off.

The sun was still rising and the sky was full of color when David put on his hunting jacket after strapping on the shoulder holster. The holster with the 45 and silencer fitted so well, that David knew the rig would not interfere with or hamper his rifle when mounting it in a hurry should the hunt require a quick shot. He strolled over to Bernie's tent and called out,

"Wake up, you lazy old man, I come bearing glad tidings,"

"Make my day, make my day," said a smiling Bernie as he emerged from his tent, dressed in fresh hunting gear with a floppy hat with a wide brim and wearing the fake leopard skin hat band around his neck like a woman's choker. David burst out laughing,

"Are you advertising your professional hunter's status?" asked a bemused David,

"No, like Marilyn Monroe, who when asked if she slept naked indignantly retorted that she always wore her choker in bed, I too have a sense of propriety," said the little Jew who, David suspected by the way he handled the Browning automatic, was as skilled at taking life as he was at saving it.

"And furthermore, in nine months time I will deliver your child for free, free do you hear, in fact my very Jewish instincts will be suppressed to deliver it free gratis and for nothing. Don't take advantage of me; I'll only do it once in repayment for delivering me from the nasty Jimmy, now, the glad tidings, speak," Bernie commanded.

David became serious.

"Before first light as I was going back to my tent, a tracker allowed me to see him watching my movements; he didn't have to. I approached him and asked him why he was watching me. First he identified himself as the son of my old tracker, Mikalashi, who was with me throughout my professional hunting career in Africa and said his name was Dickson. I then remembered him as a child who played in my camp and who I had let play with my guitar that I had. He said that Jimmy's assistant Charlie had ordered him to keep me under surveillance and that he had heard Charlie speaking on the radio to some one saying that two men were coming to the camp today who would fix me and the Doctari. Has that made your day, Doctari?" asked David concernedly.

"The evil lord's largesse in insisting we continue enjoying our hunt until the day after tomorrow had the purpose of keeping us here in a situation where we could be attended to without anyone else's knowledge and his black government cronies would arrange for complete secrecy and the none intervention of the police," Bernie said.

"We cannot plan until Charlie informs us of his intentions and when the heavies will arrive and under what guise," David said.

The camp staff was building up the camp fire and the smell of coffee was pungent in the cold African morning air. Katinka had emerged from her tent looking radiant and was strolling towards them.

"May I join you for coffee around the campfire?" she asked,

"Of course," Bernie replied and they all walked towards the fire,

"Is it not a beautiful morning?" David asked, of no one in particular,

"The best in my life," said Katinka with a radiant smile.

Dickson, the tracker, brought three steaming cups of coffee to them with a large smile and a cheery greeting. Behind him, a surly, hung over Charlie approached,

"Good morning, we will have to rearrange our hunting plans for today, I was advised by radio last night that I must collect two new clients who are to join our camp this morning so I will have to go to the airstrip to fetch them; they are due to arrive at about ten O'clock. I'll leave in the mini-bus at nine. Could you, David, take the others on a hunt today? I will take the new clients on the buffalo hunt when we get back as this is what head office has instructed," Charlie asked,

"Sure, that's perfect, I'll take the Land rover, it's the long wheelbase model so it will easily manage our party and a skinner and tracker. Is that OK?" David asked,

"That's fine; I'll tell the staff to prepare the vehicle; most the hunting is done within fifteen miles of the camp. I must tell my man Dickson to clean my rifle and those for the new clients so that we can leave when we get back from the strip. There is a large herd of buffalo nearby, with a trophy bull that I've yearned for, it was for Lord Montdrago and the licence has been endorsed over to me at his instruction," Charlie was beaming in anticipation.

The taxidermist and the surgeon had joined them around the fire and the staff served breakfast. Charlie repeated his story and the group were keyed up in anticipation and every one was excited and happy. After a leisurely breakfast, Charlie went off to his tent where the radio was kept and all the others except David and Bernie returned to their tents to prepare for the hunt. David and Bernie continued to stand around the campfire and David motioned to Dickson to bring two more cups of coffee. As Dickson gave them the steaming cups David asked him,

"When you clean the rifles for Bwana manager and after he has left camp for the airstrip, call me I want to inspect his rifle but no one must know?"

"Yes bwana I do as you say," Dickson smiled and went away.

"What have you in mind, David?" asked Bernie.

"The three baddies obviously want to be away from camp where they can plan without being overheard and also to establish the fiction that theirs is a genuine hunting trip should there be any questions after we have been disposed of. The taxidermist and Dr. Hamilton and Katinka will certainly be curious as how two people had met with an accident. We must assume that the hit men are competent and have a plan, as I'm sure that they have done this before, His Lordship would only hire the best.

Always on a guided hunt, the clients shoot first and only after their licenses have been fulfilled, does the professional do his private hunting, if he has the licence to do so. If the clients are not experienced hunters, they're almost certain to wound an animal and in the follow up, the professional has to take over. Hopefully this will happen so I intend to break off the tip of Charlie's rifle's firing pin ensuring a misfire and if the wounded buffalo behaves as wounded buffalo always behave, we will have an incident which will confuse their plans,"

"If you have a certificate to prove you have been circumcised, there is a bright future for you with Mossad. If we should be so lucky, the Safari Company will go down in history as the only outfitter to lose both its professional hunters to wild animals within a few days of commencing a hunt. The Safari Company will certainly not attract any Jewish clients to hunt with them in the future. It is an excellent plan," said Bernie with approval.

Shortly after Charlie had left camp, Dickson called David who first went to his own rifle storage crate and selected some tools from his field tool kit and followed Dickson to where he was cleaning the rifles. Dickson pointed out Charlie's personal rifle. It was a 505 Gibbs built on a 98 Mauser long action. David removed the bolt which he dissembled in a few seconds. He held the firing pin near the tip with the small pin vise and about a sixteenth of an inch back from the tip, nicked it with his small diamond coated file and then with a slight tap from the small ball peen hammer, broke off the tip and reassembled the bolt.

"You know those bad men have been sent to kill us, so I want you to accompany their hunt for the buffalo and when the strangers wound one and bwana Charlie has to follow up, lead the men into danger. Remember, Bwana Charlie's rifle cannot fire, so be careful and be prepared to climb a tree if the buffalo charges," David instructed,

"You are my father Bwana. It shall be done," Dickson said.

David marshaled the others; saw that those who wanted to shoot, each had a rifle. Bernie wanted to hunt and David lent him his own Brno 375 HH magnum, the taxidermist had his own weapon. The group, Katinka, Bernie and the taxidermist but not the surgeon, who preferred to stay in camp, and a skinner and a tracker made up the party. They headed off with the tracker directing them to area known to produce some excellent trophies.

They had traveled along a barely discernable track for about ten miles, bumping slowly through the bush when they were flagged down by two tribesmen.

The tribesmen were in a highly excitable state and after speaking rapidly to the tracker, pointed in a direction slightly off the track.

"They say Bwana," the tracker said in response to David's query, "that two men from their village were taken by a lion and that the lion is still feeding on them just down over there," the tracker pointed ahead. David knew that man eaters had caused havoc up near Mpika, a small settlement near the top of the escarpment bordering the Luangwa valley; one had seized a schoolchild at the school near the Crested Crane, an hotel on the Great North Road, and eaten it on the long verandah along the front of the mission school about fifty years before. There had been many other attacks in the Northern Province of Zambia, some fairly recently. David's dilemma was, should he send the others back before he attended to the problem or should he proceed now while the lion was available without the need for a long follow up hunt after the lion had left his kill which may prove unsuccessful.

David decided to proceed cautiously. He asked Bernie to load his rifle and as soon as they were close, to follow him and make sure the safety of his rifle was off. The eager excitement in Bernie's eyes gave David the assurance that the back up would be rock solid. He told Katinka to sit tight and not to leave the vehicle under any circumstances. The taxidermist, an experienced hunter was asked to stay in the vehicle and protect Katinka if necessary.

The vehicle crept slowly forward in the direction the tribesmen pointed and within half a mile, there was a break in the trees and they came up to a depression on their left, with an open space not more than a hundred yards across, devoid of all trees or bush. The trees on the opposite side of the grassy opening were dense and thick and there, near the dense trees, were the remains of the two tribesmen. One partially eaten and the other nearly completely consumed except for his feet and skull. The lion was not at the kill.

David stopped the vehicle and slowly slid out, releasing the safety catch of his rifle and saying softly to Bernie,

"Stay up here and shoot if the lion appears and you have a clear shot but be careful in the excitement not to shoot in my direction, don't even point the rifle in my direction, I'll handle the beast if he appears close to me; are you alright with that Bernie?"

"Yes, I am a Jew and lions only eat Christians."

"Release your safety catch now," David said as he slowly walked down the slight embankment into the clearing and the grass; he had loaded the Brno with premium cartridges with Barnes expanding bullets renowned for their terminal performance on lion.

Slowly as he approached the bodies David carefully looked around them in every direction, imprinting on his mind to place his shot precisely and then immediately reload for a finishing follow up shot, necessary or not. Slightly to the left of the corpses David noticed the thick stem of a small plant sticking up above the waist high grass and as it appeared to wave slightly from side to side in the windless grassy opening, David knew with certainty and mounted his rifle very quickly, just as the lion stiffened his waving tail and launched his charge. David paused for a moment to allow the lion to close in so as to present a larger closer target, a tactic he had used in the past; it was a mistake.

David fired when it was about thirty feet away as it crouched down before its final spring; at the shot, another lion launched his charge from the right of the bodies. The first lion somersaulted as the heavy bullet struck him with tremendous force and David worked the rifles bolt, ejecting the empty case and feeding in a fresh cartridge faster than a heartbeat but was unable to mount the rifle back onto shoulder before the second lion sprang and was airborne. It was only ten feet away and in midair when the bullet fired from the hip hit it in the chest. David saw that the lion had gone all loose and floppy, a sure sign of instant death but could not avoid the knockdown impact momentum of the five hundred pound beast as it struck him and bowled him over. In that instant when time stood still, he heard a terrible scream from the top of the bank which thrilled him, she cared, she really cared.

Bernie was running down to David as he staggered to his feet and said,

"I am alright, thank God you didn't shoot, they were too close and you might have shot me,"

"I thought you were in for a mauling," Bernie replied, helping the winded and bruised gunsmith to his feet. A stumbling, running, beautiful, woman was crashing towards them and reaching out, flung herself at David, sobbing and calling his name over and over again. David with the help of Bernie and Katinka hobbled towards the jubilant tribesmen and David's two men, the tracker and the skinner, who were excitedly waving their arms about and singing

"Please supervise the skinner, I would like the heads mounted too, attached to the skins if that is possible?" David asked the taxidermist.

"Is this the sort of life you lived when you were hunting professionally?" Bernie asked.

"Yes, sometimes lion, sometimes wounded buffalo, always interesting, never dull,"

"Well" said Bernie "The Roman games went on for over five hundred years and you Christians have an inbred genetic desire to fight with wild animals and those that didn't have those genes, were culled out by the Romans, crucified on those six thousand crosses alongside the Appian way, the ancient Roman road from Rome to Brindisi" said Bernie facetiously.

The skinning took time and David, Bernie and Katinka sat under the trees as the taxidermist drove the remains of the lion's victims back to the tribesmen's village with the tribesmen. He took the skins and heads with him to reassure the villagers that the threat had passed.

They sat quietly under the trees, talking quietly of the events since leaving England. The vehicle returned in just over an hour and they slowly drove back to the camp.

There was pandemonium as they drove into the camp, the staff was running around, fetching and carrying and some just in confused agitation. The surgeon ran up to the vehicle as it stopped, his clothes were covered in blood.

"There has been a terrible hunting accident, the wounded buffalo killed two and the remaining one is barely hanging on, please Bernie, help me. The tracker came and fetched me and I tried under terrible conditions to save the two clients but one died. The professional was dead, mutilated terribly, I have brought both the bodies back, they are covered and lying behind the office tent. The survivor is in the office tent, he has lost a lot of blood and is in a bad way." said Douglas, wearily.

"Go and have a rest in your tent Douglas, I'll see to him with David's help," said Bernie.

"Can I help?" asked Katinka.

"No, Miss Jones, go and clean up and make yourself beautiful for your man, we will be having supper soon," said Doctari firmly.

David and Bernie stood over the badly injured man,

"That fucking tracker was armed. We would have got away after Charlie was gored to death but the tracker shot into the herd and the wounded buffalo attacked us, and killed my partner," said the injured man. Dickson had walked into the tent and smiled at David and Bernie smiled back.

"You planned this, didn't you, you fucking Jew?" whispered the man with hatred

"In answer to your first question, yes, as only an experienced hit man would deduce, and in answer to your second question, when your ancestors were living in trees, mine were forging checks and executing evil men," said Bernie with pride, "I know that wasn't original but it was appropriate. This poor man will suffer from life threatening gangrene if I don't loosen that tourniquet around his thigh," Bernie told David. With that, he loosened the tourniquet and the arterial blood squirted and pulsed out and as the pressure slowly fell away, the man died.Bernie said,

"I wonder if the Safari Company will require a death certificate."

"I had better get onto the radio and inform the company and ask them to cancel the rest of our trip and return us to the hotel in Ndola where we can await His Lordships instructions,"

David went over to the tent that housed the radio and contacted the Safari Company. After relating the tragic events of the day, he warned them of the necessity of bringing a team of hunters to go after the wounded buffalo before other hunters and tribesmen were ambushed by those vicious, vindictive beasts who when wounded actively sought out any human beings who may be about. It was agreed that Lord Montdrago's party would be evacuated out the following day at about midday and bookings would be made with the hotel at Ndola where the group would await instructions from His Lordship.

David strolled back to the area around the campfire where the others were gathered and informed them of the arrangements that he had made. They agreed and instructions were given to the staff that supper would begin within an hour after each one of them had a chance to clean up and change. The staff heaped up wood on the fire and the taxidermist who had completed the skinning of the lion skulls returned to the skinning shed where with various chemical concoctions and lots of salt he practiced his arcane craft and prepared the trophies for packing the following day.

The subdued group sat quietly around the fire, sipping their drinks and listening to the majesty of Africa; the roar in the distance, the yelps of other predators and the sounds of hyenas and other scavengers. With the flickering golden orange light of the campfire reflecting back off the trees and their canopies, with the sounds and the stars in a brilliant heaven, they all sat enthralled and only occasionally passed a comment or two. The same acceptance which the wild animals of Africa displayed towards life and death became part of them in the magic of the moment and there was no regret or morbid thoughts of the day's events; they had just happened, that was all.

The staff served supper with the usual smiles and courtesy of the recently domesticated tribesman who only knew happiness in their day to day lives and did not worry about future events which may or may not happen; they fully understood, although illiterate, the Nazarene's directive, "Sufficient unto the day is the evil thereof."

While eating, talk slowly returned to normal and Bernie was telling of his plans to return to Israel when he retired,

"I am going to build me a nice little house on a smallholding. We build in concrete, you know, it's quick, permanent and cool and do you believe it's expensive. In a country consisting of rock and sand, the price of suitable stone for making concrete is exorbitant. Those bloody Jews are profiteers especially in Israel,"

"Why don't you increase your fees and screw your patients as they do in the rich western states," asked David.

"Well I do part time work for a certain group attached to the Israeli Government but they pay just enough to avoid United Nations sanctions for dealing in slaves. I applied for an increase in my salary and one of the conditions stipulated to qualify is ridiculous, only one man has ever met them as far as is known,"

"What is that condition, Bernie?" asked Katinka,

"Well, they take you to the Sea of Galilee and you have to walk out a few hundred yards without getting your ass wet," replied Bernie.

The evening was joyful and happy and the goring and deaths were not mentioned or thought about, Africa healed the minds of men with her magnificence.

Katinka said that she was going to retire and Bernie stood up and said,

"Let me escort you and check the beasties,"

David left soon afterwards.

Chapter Eleven

The jet's pilots were still living at the hotel and except for a run out to the airport every morning to check the aircraft, they whiled away their time walking around the old Copperbelt town. They had disgraced themselves one night in the hotel bar. On that auspicious night, the hotel had provided an exotic dancer whose specialty was tassel tossing. Except for a G-String her only other apparel were a pair of tassels, one hanging from each nipple protruding from a flabby, flexible support, a tit, in fact. She could swirl each one of them around in a circle independently of one another. The two pilots sitting at the bar loudly started to commentate, one pilot, Jim by name, enthusing to his companion, said in a loud penetrating voice,

"Look, she's feathering the starboard propeller. Wait a bit, yes, now she's feathering the other,"

Just then, the barmaid who sported a pair of huge, magnificent up tilted boobs, walked past Jim's drunken companion, with her lovelies just above the level of the bar counter, causing the drunken one to cry out in admiration,

"I say Jim, how do you feather a jet engine?" They were escorted out the bar.

The instructions came through to the pilot that as soon as Jock and the other two body guards arrived at the hotel, the whole of His

Lordships party must return to Britain. Arrangements had been made to take all their baggage including firearms straight out of the small airport where the jet was usually kept without passing through customs or immigration. The power of money the chief pilot thought admiringly.

The flight was long and boring but Katinka was happy, she was with her man. After a couple of hours, she retired to the luxury cabin to sleep and this gave David and Bernie the opportunity to talk,

"We can expect His Lordship to arrange something very cunning and nasty for us, it must be very seldom that his plans are frustrated and in the process to lose four men so inexplicably and not have the vaguest idea as to how their deaths were accomplished. Any less astute man would put it down to accidents, pure and simple, but he knows better. I hope we survive. We could of course pre-empt him and kill him first, but that may not help, he may have already put his plan into action. I think it better to await events and be very aware," said Bernie.

"I agree. Let's go over and talk to Jock, he hasn't had an opportunity to really talk since we left the hotel, Douglas and the taxidermist have always been around, they are now sleeping, their seats are well laid back and they look to be peacefully deep in slumber land," said David and moving forward to where Jock was sitting reading, Bernie following.

"Jock, could we have a quiet wee word?" asked David as Bernie and he sat down across in front of the huge Scot.

"Sure, Boss,"

"You say His Lordship Flew off with two other men from The Copperbelt in a South African government jet destined for a military base near Pretoria, were those men bodyguards supplied by the SA government?" asked David,

"No, they were foreigners and were referred to as doctor when their names were used and His Lordship treated them with great respect," answered Jock.

"Oh Jesus," exclaimed Bernie, "the physicists,"

"Bernie, ask the pilots if you can use the in flight telephone or what ever the Banker uses or, even the jets radio to notify who you must notify, do you have a contact?"

"Yes," answered Bernie as he got up and made his way urgently to the jet's cockpit.

"What's this all about then?" asked Jock,

"For your ears only, Jock, I am telling you only because we may need your help soon. The evil Lord Montdrago is selling nuclear scientists and probably equipment to certain Arab states we think. Dr Cohen is a Mossad agent and those events on the hunting trip which resulted in those four deaths were caused by Dr Cohen and myself. All four of those men were sent to kill Dr Cohen and myself by His Lordship who suspects Bernie of being Mossad. The first of the assassins to die got the drop on us out in the bush. He was the professional hunter guiding us. We knew each other well from my professional hunting days and while he was holding us at gunpoint, he told me that if I co-operated with him, His Lordship would reward me with a substantial bonus but if not, his instructions were to kill me. I distracted him and drew a concealed silenced 45 and shot him. We threw his body into the river where the crocs attacked it while we watched and staged evidence of a croc attack near the rivers edge having removed the corpse's shoes and socks which were left as proof that the P.H. was paddling.

The other two were sent as "hunting clients" to finish the job and get us.

Fortunately the African who recognized me from the old days overheard radio instructions to the other P.H to help the new clients "fix us" so we were able to frustrate that effort in a deadly sort of way. I am apprehensive of the evil lord's next move. I built a silencer for the 45 and started carrying it some time ago when I realized the terrible truth of His Lordships great power and wealth. I overheard the plan to murder the Congolese president and the arrangements to finance the recent coup," said David "I trust and rely on you completely, Jock, but don't tell your companions. His Lordship knows about our former relationship in the SAS the P.H. told me before I shot him, so be careful and strong, he may offer you or your men a million or two to get Bernie and I," said David with a chuckle.

"It is a simple problem to solve, one of us just kills him and ducks," said Jock seriously.

"No, there are larger pieces to this puzzle, an international conspiracy which he heads; time is needed to clear it up. MI5 cannot be told at this point because nothing can be proved and his fellow conspirators are high officials of banks, government agencies and even a cabinet minister, it is mind boggling," explained David.

"I pledge my full support, Boss, and I will liaise with you constantly," said Jock fervently.

After about five minutes Bernie came back and said,

"I have received instructions; give me time to think and I'll fill you in later. I must go back to my seat and have a rest, are you coming David?"

"Yes, talk to you later Jock," said David as he followed Bernie back to his seat.

Resuming his seat next to Bernie, David asked,

"If your instructions suggest that you may need help in carrying them out, you know that you can count on me?"

"Thank you David, My superiors don't want me to act precipitously, as they want to discover the entire chain of the nuclear command and not only who is involved but where the Uranium enrichment plant is coming from and who all the supply and installation engineering companies may be and where their head offices are located. Therefore we must wait and see what His Lordship's next move is,"

"High on His Lordships list of priorities will be the elimination of you and me.

Can you secure another handgun as he may ask for that one back and if I can't produce it, he may think I'm keeping it to protect myself but if I hand it over, he will think I'm unarmed and not take the precautions he should in dealing with me, giving me an edge?"

"Yes, I have a couple at my home, so I will give to you when we get back to the estate," with that, Bernie tilted his seat into the recline position and started to doze; David copied him and the jet flew on.

There were three vehicles awaiting them at the airport when they arrived in England and they were soon back on the estate where Margaret was waiting to greet them and show Jock and his companion bodyguards to the suite that had been allocated to them, it was on the third floor, directly behind the security control center, down at the end of the passage that passed by Dr. Cohen's rooms.

Margaret was overjoyed to see them and said,

"I have prepared a real Scottish supper for the three of us tonight. I want to hear all about your African trip. His Lordship phoned earlier and instructed me where to settle in Jock and his two assistants and also to prepare the luxury guest suite for two gentlemen who would be arriving tomorrow evening. He told me that the jet had to fly to Germany tomorrow after lunch where he and the two guests would be arriving from the Republic of South Africa. He will be staying on in Germany for a further week before returning home. His instructions are to spare no expense in ensuring that the guests have everything that they want. Their names are Dr. Horst and Dr. Smith and it seems they are renowned academics who are doing some work for His Lordship. I must hurry off now and see Jock to his apartment, so until this evening then,"

"Before you go, I want to go to Dr. Cohen's house and see him, the car he traveled in took him straight home and I didn't get a chance to clear up one or two things that needed clearing up. Where is his house located?"

"Just continue on beyond the nursery, you can't miss it, but be prepared for some harassment by the security guards," said Margaret with a worried look.

"I will be," said David in a steely voice and an angry frown.

David went up to his quarters and once in and with the door closed behind him, he surreptitiously checked the hairs on the bedroom door before entering. He did the same with the secret door and was relieved that neither had been breached; so security hadn't been in his room to fit another surveillance camera while he was away. He unpacked and stowed his clothes and toiletries, then had a hot shower, shaved and dressed in preparation not only for his visit to Bernie's home but also for the dinner with Katinka and Margaret afterwards.

David strolled up past the nursery and was impressed with Bernie's home and the surrounding gardens; your retirement home in Israel will be different to this Bernie, David thought.

David knocked at Bernie's door and was surprised at the beauty of the woman who opened it; after all, Bernie was no oil painting.

"Good afternoon, please come in, you fit Bernie's description of the gunsmith," she said in a deep cultured voice, a voice with a slight French accent, "my name is Rachel, unusual for a Jewish doctors wife. Bernie will be with us shortly,"

"My name is David McAlpine, David being unusual for a Scot whose ancestors painted their bottoms blue," David said with a grin and they both laughed.

As David sat down, Bernie strolled in smiling with pleasure,

"What do we owe the pleasure for this visit," said Bernie going all Jewish and mangling the English language with relish. His wife was laughing gently as she said

"I'll leave you two together while I prepare the tea or would you prefer a whisky, David?"

"I'd prefer tea, thank you Rachel, what Bernie and I have to discuss requires a clear head," David's tone forewarned Bernie that the bantering was over and that there was something serious afoot.

"Margaret told me, after I had arrived back at the house, that His Lordship had phoned earlier and had instructed her to prepare the Guest suite for two men, Doctors Horst and Smith, academics he said, for a stay of at least a week when he will return to join them. They flew into Germany from South Africa and the jet that flew us back has to pick up the guests tomorrow after lunch.

I made a stupid mistake in confiding in Jock on the trip back when he asked me about the accidents that occurred on our hunt. I told him of the attempts on our lives and that the Banker suspected you of being involved with Mossad which I said you were. You must remember that Jock and I served together in the SAS where in fact I was his commanding officer for a few years. It now occurs to me that perhaps he was hired to protect the two scientists who were coming to stay at the estate for at least a week and if what you suspect is the reason for the scientists association with His Lordship is correct, it puzzles me that a former friend and comrade didn't come clean with me if there is an ulterior motive for their presence at the house. Maybe, Jock has been in the service of His Lordship for some considerable time? Could Mossad find out?"

Bernie was quiet and thoughtful for a while.

"Money, big, big money can accomplish the impossible. Beautiful, cultured, highly educated young women can be induced to marry ugly, fat, bespectacled old men, Rachel and me are a good example A young Scottish soldier with an uncertain future could be induced to forego loyalty and comradeship for a great deal of money. But all this is pure speculation nevertheless it must be checked out. When I contacted my superiors during our flight, they insisted that no harm should come to either His Lordship or the two scientists as they are the key to identifying the others involved, including the ultimate destination of the nuclear equipment.

Our organization has the latest undetectable chips which emit a signal that only our monitors can detect, the difficult task is how to plant them. They can be placed in the targets personal possessions, such as a wristwatch, or best of all inserted just below the skin in a position that is invulnerable, like at the back of the neck beneath the skull. Obviously the target must be unconscious when the implant is placed. But how?" Bernie asked.

"Do you have the chips yet? Would you entrust me with a couple in case I get the opportunity and, could you show me how its done and also supply the means to render the target unconscious so that when consciousness returns the target is completely unaware of what has happened?"

"The chips will be delivered first thing in the morning when the technician who comes to the house to sweep for listening devices arrives. He is one of our men and placing him in the company that is contracted to do the sweeping of the rooms in the house was done over a year ago, with great difficulty," said Bernie, "as regards the physical means of implanting the chip, an hour in my surgery is all you would need to be shown how,"

"The other problem we face is the fact that our intelligent employer would almost certainly be aware that the accidents in Africa were somehow contrived and with his deep, financer's cunning, how is he going to respond? Poison, gunshots, the assassin's knife across the throat or what? We will have to be very aware and liaise constantly and not be reactive but proactive; this requires close co-operation. How can we communicate, can cell phone signals be intercepted and monitored?" David asked.

"The cell phones Rachel and I have are special Mossad issue, modified to achieve complete inviolability, I'll have another delivered with the technician tomorrow for your use," Bernie answered.

Rachel brought the tea and sat down with them

"Rachel too is a doctor so if ever circumstances dictate, my lady can help. We have all the equipment we need here in the house," Bernie volunteered "furthermore, Rachel can contact Mossad if I should be incapacitated," Bernie said.

In her lovely low cultured voice, Rachel asked

"May I have one of the lion trophies, David?"

"One of them was for Bernie but you can have both if you want to. From what Bernie has told me, you both intend to retire to a small holding in Israel and it would be appropriate to adorn your walls with the trophies as, historically, out of the lion, came forth sweetness," said David smiling as one does when given the opportunity to please a friend, "now that I have finished my tea, I must depart. Margaret is preparing supper for Katinka and I and I would like to get back. Bernie, I will contact you at the surgery tomorrow and perhaps by then you will have some information on Jock and his friends?"

"Yes, that is what our special cell phones are for. My organization has an unbelievable database and with access to other "Hostile" data bases so, I am sure we will know for sure all about Jock tomorrow," answered Bernie.

David got up and excused himself and they saw him to the door where they said their farewells.

David had barely left Bernie's home and was walking back, when still within site of the home, a security guard approached him and asked truculently.

"What are you doing wandering about the estate; you know it is not allowed?"

"Fuck off," said David in a cold dangerous, steely voice and stepped up to the guard and with his face inches away from the surly uniformed oaf, put his hands on his hips and said

"Take a care, laddie, take a care,"

The guard was startled and backed off muttering about a report as he walked away.

Supper was a joyous affair, Katinka bubbling over with the happenings on their trip, was flushed and beautiful and happy. Margaret couldn't take her eyes off the lovely girl, hanging on to her every word and when Katinka described the two lion charges Margaret turned to David, eyes wide and asked,

"Is that how you made a living when you were a professional hunter?"

"Normally the hunting was quite straight forward and even when a client wounded an animal the follow up was routine and uneventful. But those two lions were man-eaters and had lost their fear of man and were thus very dangerous and had to be destroyed. There are men who are far more dangerous, not only because they are cunning, which a wounded buffalo is too, but because they are wicked which wild animals never are," David said ominously and he could see that Margaret knew exactly who he was referring to.

There was laughter and there was gaiety and when it was time to depart back to their rooms David could see that Margaret wished that they didn't have to. David noticed that since Katinka had started to visit Margaret, the lovely middle aged Scot was always smiling, as if she knew something that pleased her mightily.

Chapter Twelve

David lay on his bed thinking. It had been a lovely dinner and usually after a meal such as that, he would fall into a deep dreamless sleep but he couldn't sleep. If it turned out that Jock was on the other side, he would have relayed David's revelations which he had learned of on the jet. How would the banker respond? How would they kill Bernie and him? He had said to Bernie that they must be proactive but Bernie's instructions were not to kill any of His Lordships immediate colleagues or the scientists. Did that mean that Jock couldn't be dealt with if necessary?

David got out of bed and dressed in his black clothes that he reserved for the chamber and its galleries. He was very aware of his nakedness; the 45 had yet to be unpacked from the firearm crate.

David slid through the secret door and cautiously made his way to the observation slits looking into Jock's quarters. As he opened the slits he heard Jock say,

"Well, what are we to do then? His Lordship says that we must bide our time and when he gives the word, David must be taken out together with the Doctor,"

"Och aye, it's a terrible decision we must make, he was always good to us in the SAS and we all saw action together,"

"I know, Scottie, but we've been with Lord Montdrago for over two years and we are paid handsomely, also we've seen His Lordship deal with those who gain say him. Horrible, horrible retribution and he has men in his employ that will kill us without a second thought if ordered to, regretfully David will have to go. We have taken out several of His Lordships enemies and after the first, it became easier. After all that's what the SAS trained us for and that is why His Lordship hired us in the first place. When he asked us about David long before he sent the Scottish lady to recruit him, he said he needed David for a task that probably only David could accomplish, what that task is I dinna know or whether he still has David in mind," said Jock "furthermore we have to guard the scientists until the Arab gentlemen come to fetch them. I must say that when I told His Lordship that David had asked me to protect his woman, the Jones lass, he said excellent, excellent. I think that he is going to use that poor lassie as bait to force David to do the task he speaks of. He is a cunning man who we should never cross if we wish to live and continue earning the fortune that he pays us. I nearly have enough to buy that grand house I want. It is in Edinburgh's best suburb among the nobs," Jock's face was sporting an avaricious grin.

David knew that he would have to kill Jock at an appropriate time and the others too. Jocks revelations sent chills of fear through him and he wondered what the evil lord had in mind for him and the woman he loved. To hell with Mossad, he would take them all out if his darling was threatened.

Jock said goodnight to the others and retired to his bedroom, the others followed suite.

David went back to his bedroom, undressed and got into bed. His mind was reeling. The banker had sought him out and then sent Margaret to recruit him, knowing full well his background with the SAS and already having Jock and the boys in his employ; perhaps he had sought them out as well as part of his plan. What was his plan? It was obvious that throwing Katinka together with him on safari was initiated by Jock relaying that bit about him saying that she was his woman. What did he hope to achieve by arranging the perfect setting for them to become lovers? Would his love for Katinka give His Lordship some sort of leverage in his proposed plan for David? Was the banker evil enough to use his own daughter to further his plans?

David tried to think like the banker; first what did he, David do in the SAS that made him necessary for the banker's schemes? The revenge attack which had so angered the British Government that they had him dishonorably discharged from the army, was in itself, very unusual; why was there no court martial?

It all came back to David. That terrorist stronghold he had attacked sheltered, he had heard afterwards, two of the tribal villagers who were closely related to the ruling clan who ruled from the capital, a modern city on the periphery of the oilfields. These relatives allocated the oil concessions and drilling rights. He had also heard that those primitive people had placed a price upon his head because he had killed the two blood brothers.

A court martial would have proved that the British government's forces were involved and this placed at risk great commercial ventures; better to quietly remove the perpetrator and not admit liability or any connection to the incident. Had Lord Montdrago offered David up to the ruling house of the nation that he was selling nuclear equipment to as a sweetener to cement the deal; was he to facilitate the means to satisfy a blood debt? Yes, that was it, David thought. The hiring of Jock and then, many months later when the time was opportune and the nuclear deal was negotiated, the banker could use his trump card to satisfy the blood debt and so Margaret was sent to hire David.

Did Montdrago hold all the cards? No, David held all the aces. He would, he decided, remove all His Lordships diamonds and other assets and hide them in the secret labyrinth so when the clever Lord revealed himself as he surely must, sooner or later, especially after the deaths of his agents in the hunting field, David would show him the canniness of the Scot when his back was against the wall.

It was a certainty that the gunroom had been fitted with surveillance cameras and listening devices whilst David was in Africa. These would have to be neutralized before the treasure could be relocated and who better to do that than Bernie's technician, due in the morning. Bernie would still not need to know of either the treasure or the secret chambers and their secret labyrinths which riddled the beautiful old house. David would suggest that Katrinka and themselves also be fitted with locator chips so that Mossad could rescue any of them if necessary.

The technician had other things to do for Bernie so would probably only be able to "cleanse" the gunroom after lunch, which would give

David time to check out the treasure trove's alarm system; the shooting tunnel would definitely not be under surveillance.

The gun crate would have been unloaded from the vehicles shortly after arriving from the airport and placed in the gunroom's ante room so that David could take it into the gunroom and unpack it, taking the pistols and holster into the shooting tunnel where he could strap on the holster with the silenced 45 unobserved. The relief at being fully dressed again with the 45 and no longer naked was looked forward to with joy.

The first priority in the morning was to go to Bernie's rooms and arrange for the technician; also he must decide just how much he should tell Bernie. David drifted into sleep with the many burdens easier to bear now that there was a plan and the floundering around had ceased.

Bernie was usually in his rooms before eight am and when David arrived early, the Doctor was there to welcome him.

"I had been expecting you. The technician is already here in the security nerve center and because of my discussions with my people after you had left yesterday, he has brought an assistant. The house's security staff has dealt with him before and he is allowed to switch off all monitors and surveillance equipment while attending to the maintenance of the electronics; this has become routine on his frequent maintenance checks. If there is anything that you need doing, now is the time when all the surveillance is inactive. The bad news is that my people have confirmed that your former SAS comrades have been in the employ of His Lordship for a considerable time, long before you were engaged," said Bernie grimly.

"Yes, I suspected as much. I had a long time to think last night and I came to the conclusion that the events in that terrorist settlement all those years ago were the beginning. Mossad is aware of the numbers that I destroyed but was it aware that two of the dead were clansmen of the countries ruling family and that a blood debt was incurred and a price was put on my head? The SAS did not court martial me which would have implied the army's complicity so they shipped me back to the U.K. quietly and dishonorably discharged me. Told me to fuck off and disappear. The evil Lord, it seems has planned an elegant scheme to deliver me to the rulers of that oil rich state as a sweetener for his deals which include the Uranium enrichment plant and all the associated machinery needed for a nuclear device. I also suspect that while we were away in Africa, the gunroom was fitted with cameras and listening bugs. Could your man deactivate them?" David asked.

"Yes, I'll send for them and you can take them down. They have a service van that's equipped to do anything that Mossad may need to be done; in other words, the latest in electronic wizardry. Six locating chips have been delivered and as soon as you have time, I will show you how to place them under the skin. Do you still think you can fit them to the physicists when they get here?" enquired Bernie anxiously.

"Yes if you can prepare a sleeping draft that Margaret can slip into their tea or coffee when she serves them. She has been ordered to attend to all their needs, personally, and she could arrange for me to get into the luxury guest suite, which is without surveillance, after the drugs have taken effect," David replied.

"Here is the cell phone that I promised you yesterday and here are three numbers, one to contact me, one to contact Rachel and one to raise the controller of our operation if you get into bad trouble, use it sparingly. Your number is printed on the casing of the phone. It is state of the art and should, say, Margaret call you, it prevents security from listening, despite the fact that the call was made from a tapped line; in fact security won't even know a call has been made. I'll summon the technician; he is next door in the surveillance center," Bernie said decisively, no longer the wisecracking jester, but a no nonsense agent.

The Mossad technician arrived within minutes and Bernie introduced him to David, his name was Moshe. After Bernie explained what had to be done, Moshe nodded and said to David tersely,

"Let's go,"

They both left hurriedly and David led the way down to the Gunroom; Moshe's assistant who was waiting outside the doctor's room, followed them with two cases of tools and instruments which looked like hand held suitcases.

They entered the gunroom and the two men immediately went over the large room with their instruments and soon discovered two cameras, one at each end of the gunroom and several listening devices strategically fixed in the office and on several of the work benches. The shooting tunnel was clean.

David showed Moshe the entrance door's smart card and asked,

"Could you modify this? His Lordship's card, like this one, can open the door from the ante room, but, unlike my card, can also lock the door from inside, denying me access if His Lordship has locked from the inside. I must be able to lock from the inside preventing him with his card from entering and overriding his card in any situation,"

"Yes, we carry many different cards and other electronic devices in our service van and the instruments to program them," said Moshe with pride and gave David's card to the other man and in a strange language instructed him on what was required. The assistant rushed out and Moshe, again with pride told David what he was going to do to the surveillance cameras,

"I am going to place my special digital camera in front of each camera in turn and take an electronic picture of what each camera would normally survey and then I am going to program the cameras with those pictures so that when you press a button on the remote that I am going to give you, the monitor in the surveillance room will only see that view of the gunroom regardless of what is happening in the room. I want you first sit at your desk in your office and I will take a picture and then stand at a work bench holding a gun and inspecting it and I will take another picture. We will take several of you in different locations and then I will program both the remote and the cameras. Last, but not least, I will see that you are thoroughly familiar with the system and can use the remote like an expert," Moshe finished with a proud smile.

While Moshe was doing his work, his assistant returned with the new smart card and gave it to David. David instinctively knew that there would certainly have been duplicates made, one for Bernie and one for Mossad. David decided that he would fit a stout door bolt on the inside, carefully concealed. It would never do for Bernie or his colleague's to slip in while he had the old oak cabinet out, away from the wall or, worse still, while he was counting the bankers diamonds which would shortly go missing.

Eventually, Moshe was finished and rubbing his hands said,

"Voila, it is done. Is there anything else you want done while the surveillance is disabled?"

David considered the secret chamber and the secret room entrance doors from the myriad of passages.No, he thought, leave well alone; to let Mossad do anything to the secret chamber or galleries would be a mistake, and, remove his power.

"Could you do something about the tapping of my phones, both in my bedroom and the gunroom office phone?" asked David.

"We already have programmed a very sophisticated integrated circuit chip to be installed in the systems control computer. This chip will reintroduce past recorded conversations into the tapped line in such a way that it will take a long time for the security staff to realize that there is a fault and even longer to trace it; if we are called in to repair the fault, we can play them along for months. The IC chip will be in operation within ten minutes of our returning to the security center where we are going now," said Moshe as he closed up his tool bags "see you later in Bernie's rooms."

Soon after they had left, David went up to Margaret's suite and after greeting her warmly, said

"A good Scottish breakfast is what we both need, Oatmeal, followed by kippers and toast, topped off with a steaming cup of coffee. While that is being prepared, why don't we take a short walk up to the nursery to work up an appetite? I want to see if there are any Tung nuts on the tree as I would like to extract some oil to touch up one of my rifle's stocks, it collected a few scratches out there in Africa in that altercation with that beastie with the long mane," David's expression conveyed the urgency of the need to talk.

"Excellent idea just let me tell the cook to prepare your Scottish breakfast and we can take our walk." said Margaret as she picked up the phone to speak to the cook.

As they walked up to the nursery, David began to tell her about the attempts on his and Bernie's lives in Africa and his disposing of the four men whom Lord Montdrago had sent to kill them. He told her of Bernie's true identity and the reason that Mossad were watching His Lordship. He carefully explained why his Lordship had her recruit him and how he was being set up. He concluded by telling her that the three new bodyguards, were in fact not new at all and who too had been recruited because of their association with David in the SAS and to confirm David's role in the terrorist attack and the killing of the two members of the ruling house of the country to whom His Lordship was preparing to supply nuclear technology and that the two honored guests who were about to arrive at the house were physicists deeply involved in the nuclear transaction. Margaret was stunned and asked,

"Is Katinka involved and is she in any danger?"

"She is completely unaware of what her father is doing, and is in danger in that she is being used by His Lordship as leverage to ensnare me when the time is ripe.

Bernie and I are going to implant a small locater chip beneath her skin, painless and benign and not detectable so that Mossad will know at any instant her exact location and she is therefore under constant protection by probably the world's best secret service. Mossad does not want me to react yet as they want to trace all the players and industrial organizations involved in the nuclear chain so that they can be completely eradicated. If that were not so, I would have killed the evil lord already.

We need your assistance Margaret. While you are attending to the two scientists personally, at a time of our choosing, we want you to put something, which we will provide, in their evening tea or coffee or whatever they drink before retiring, so as to render them unconscious. After they have fallen asleep, I must then sneak into their sleeping quarters and fit the locator chips beneath their skin so that Mossad can follow their movements and know where they are at all times. Will you do it?"

Margaret had stopped and had brought both her hands to her mouth; David could see that she was shocked by what she was hearing.

"What if they catch you in the guest suite?" she asked in alarm.

"They won't and should those treacherous three former comrades of mine be lucky enough to stumble into me in the good doctors' suite, they are dead men. I once told you not to ask how. Do not ask now but I assure you that I can get in and out of the suite unobserved; do not repeat this fact to anyone. Will you help me?"

"Of course, of course, I'll always help you. Just provide the potion and say when." Margaret was looking into David's eyes and there was more than just care shining out but the pure love of a concerned friend.

"The good news is that those technicians doing maintenance on security's equipment are Mossad's men and have now disabled all the wire tapping on the phone service in a way that will not alert the security staff, so you can speak to me or Katinka safely and securely; remembering that your bedroom's listening bugs are still operative. I don't think it's a good idea to tell our beautiful young lady anything at this stage she is too young and innocent to understand the evil that men do." David said fervently and Margaret understood.

They turned around after inspecting the Tung nut tree and walked back to the house. Their breakfast was ready for them and David wished that Katinka was sharing it with them. After he had drunk his coffee he took his leave of the lovely lady and returned to the gunroom.

First he phoned Mr. Evans the handyman and asked him if he couldn't fit a dead bolt on the inside of the gunroom door?

"It's not necessary, I fitted that electronic lock originally and it has a manual override on the inside which when engaged, completely nullifies the electronic mechanism. You will see that the lock fitting on the inside of the door is a square box which protrudes about three quarter of an inch. Feel around the rebate and at the bottom you will detect a small cover like the one that flaps closed over the gas filling point of a car. Well, flip it open with your fingernail and you'll find a small sliding latch. Slide it forward and it clicks the manual lock in; the door is now manually locked and can only be opened when the latch is slid back and clicks into the unlocked position." explained Mr. Evans. David thanked him and hung up and then strolled over to the door and located the latch and locked the door manually. I hope the Mossad men have successfully cleared the taps, thought David but he knew they had as Mossad did these exercises routinely all over the world and couldn't afford to make mistakes.

Now the diamonds and bearer bonds, thought David. First, he pointed the remote controller at the cameras and isolated them, and then he walked into the shooting tunnel right up the backstop and started to examine every square inch around the sandbags and the surrounding walls. He gave up after a solid hour of searching; there was no switch or lever; there was nothing.

He walked out of the tunnel, despondent. The ammunition boxes and His Lordship's gun cases were still stacked on the bench where he had put them after they were unloaded from the vehicle that had brought them from the airport on their return from Africa. He decided to pack them away and using the remote, returned surveillance so that his work was recorded.

He lovingly oiled the fine guns before placing them in back in their cabinets. The empty gun cases were put back into their designated cupboards. Just the ammunition to go back into the cabinet inside the tunnel and then he would have another go at trying to locate the treasures key or opening switch

He went into the tunnel and opened the ammunition cabinet in the wall of the tunnel. There was a great deal of ammunition stacked neatly on wide, strong shelves. Leaving the cabinet door open he brought the boxes of cartridges into the tunnel and stacked them onto the shelves in the cabinet.

While he was packing away the boxes, he noticed a stout old fashioned wooden box of the type that Victorian sportsmen used to store their ammunition in. He opened the lid and was surprised to see antique shotgun shells of two inch and two and a half inch length, sizes long since superseded by two and three quarter and even three inch shells used in modern weapons. David closed the lid and decided to move the old box to the bottom shelf. He tugged and pulled but couldn't move it; it seemed to be attached to the shelf. He carefully felt all around the box poking his fingers into every nook and cranny to see if maybe there was a bolt or screw holding the box down. His finger touched a metal button right at the back against the wall, he pressed it in and the old box swung easily out revealing a small hinged cover plate flush with the wall behind where the box had been fixed. He opened it and there was the alarm switch clearly labeled ON and OFF and next to it another switch labeled OPEN and CLOSE. David placed the alarm in the OFF position and switched the other onto open and was rewarded by a humming noise at the end of the tunnel.

He looked down at the backstop and was amazed to see the sandbags slowly swinging around on a central pivot and disappearing into the wall while the steel back plate swung out to reveal several wide shelves with the aluminum cases stacked on them. As was his lifelong habit when confronted with a dangerous or difficult decision, he stood stock still and considered all aspects of the situation intently. First, he knew he must go into the gunroom and with the remote, isolate the cameras and then he must decide where to hide the treasure. He walked into the gunroom and isolated the cameras from his office chair and then pressed the remote button which would continually show him sitting at his desk, writing. He sat there for a long while thinking.

He decided to bring the "Cough boxes" from the observation points of his own room and Margaret's room, giving him a total of four boxes. He would strip out the thick sound absorbing felt from the bottoms of the boxes, hide the documents and diamonds beneath the thick felt and return the cough boxes back to their positions.

By the sweat of thy brow, the bible said somewhere, David recalled, after a strenuous two hours relocating Lord Montdrago's massive nest egg. The cough boxes, with their precious contents, were placed back in position in the secret chamber. Everything in the tunnel was returned back to normal and he closed the tunnel doors and locked them.

He phoned Bernie in his surgery and told him the phones were now secure, a fact that the doctor was already aware of, then asked when he should come for the chip fitting demonstration. He said that he thought that Katinka should have one fitted and so should he and Bernie, to anticipate any rough play by the opposition; did Mossad supply enough locator chips?

"Yes, be at my surgery before eight tomorrow morning," with that, Bernie rang off.

David was late again for lunch, he apologized and Margaret said,

"Don't worry; I've had plenty to keep me busy while waiting for you. The two VIP guests are arriving this evening and although the staff has been preparing the Guest suite for a day or two, I'm only just preparing the menus for the week. I have had no instructions for any special food items but both men must have a cup of cocoa before retiring which, according to my written instructions must be exactly at ten pm. It seems our guests lead disciplined lives as the instructions call for early morning coffee at seven am with breakfast following at half past eight."

"I have to see Dr. Cohen in the morning, as must Miss Jones. Something about a routine check up to see that we did not pick up any parasites while in Africa," said David, "this afternoon I am going to rest, I have just been unpacking all the guns and ammunition that we took with us and restacking everything in the correct cabinets; it was very tiring." David hoped that security's eaves dropping would note what he had just said as he needed an uninterrupted few hours in his apartment. I wonder, he thought what Margaret would say if she knew that there were many millions of pounds worth of diamonds sitting in a box just behind her?

After they had finished eating, David excused himself and retired to his rooms. He planned to spend some time observing Jock and his companions from the secret lookout. If he spent an hour or so observing them, he must be able to glean some information which would be of some use. Margaret had mentioned that His Lordship's body guards always had their meals sent up to their room and never ate in the staff dining room so David would take up his listening station after seven pm when they were eating.

David phoned Margaret and advised her that he would not be in for supper as he had some work to do. She said it was just as well, as the two Doctors had just arrived and she was on her way to attend to them and would see him in the morning.

After a shower, David dressed in his black clothes and strapped on the silenced 45 and lay down on his bed to think. Matters were coming to a head and a confrontation with His Lordship was inevitable when he returned to the house. If they were alone, should David kill him? He was worried that a move would be made against Katinka soon and hoped that Bernie would fit the locator chip as arranged and that Mossad would cooperate in keeping track of her. The evil, devious mind of her father could not be fathomed and he undoubtedly had a plan that would tie all the factors together; David, the blood debt and the entire convoluted plot of his conspiracy's main objective, that of the nuclear deal. He dozed off into an uneasy sleep.

He awoke at six pm, refreshed and after a quick wash to bring himself to the state alertness needed for the evening's surveillance, he slid through the secret door and made his way up to Jock's observation position. Immediately he opened the slit he could hear the broad Scots accents of the three men discussing their various interests and other mundane things.

It's going to be a long boring evening, David mused, and why was it that the men's accents were so much broader when they were not in the company of Englishmen? Jock swung their conversation around to their new affluence and how well His Lordship was rewarding them. His voice could not hide the enthusiasm that he felt towards the new house he was planning.

"It's a small wee pub that I yearn for," said Scottie, "and do you believe I'm nearly there. I have saved more since we've been with the Laird than my entire service with the forces, much, much, more. Another few years and I will have my pub in the village where I was born."

All three discussed their dreams and hopes and all three agreed that they were within reach. The conversation dragged on and on and David was considering calling it a night and returning to his bed when Scottie asked Jock,

"Did ye not say that His Lordship had spoken to you on the phone yesterday?"

"Yes" replied Jock "I was going to discuss it with you tomorrow after I had time to think. It is an unpleasant business that is why we are to receive a huge bonus when it is over. Up to one hundred thousand pounds each if we complete the task he wants done, but I repeat, it is unpleasant but, will we ever earn one hundred thousand pounds for a days work ever again?"

"Well, out with it." Scottie could barely contain himself.

"Fifty thousand for Dr.Cohen, and, fifty thousand for our former commanding officer, David." Jock said quietly.

There was a dead silence.

"I am going ahead, with you or without you. A little thought will indicate the options that are open to those who don't join in, after all, would you let a man loose with the knowledge of what I will have done and risk not only the loss of one hundred thousand pounds but a life behind bars?" asked Jock reasonably.

"Who will do the killing?" asked Scottie.

"I will," replied Jock, "You two will only be for backup."

"Ah, that's different then, I'm in."

"And me too,"

"The plan is to lure the two into His Lordship's conference room. I have the key. His Lordship will supply written instructions to the targets to sign some very important documents which will be on his desk in the conference room and that we, His Lordships bodyguards will accompany them. As you know, there is a detector arch at the entrance to the room which will detect any concealed weapons so that the men will enter disarmed into the conference room." concluded Jock.

The air of greed and anticipation of great wealth was so thick; it could be cut with a knife David noticed.

"Tomorrow, we have to accompany the two scientist guests on a tour of the estate with a picnic lunch on the edge of the lake beneath the trees that border the forest. We will implement the plan, the day after tomorrow and His Lordship has arranged for some of his men to remove the bodies during the night.

The surveillance will be disabled all of that day so that there is no record of any activity in the passages outside the conference room or the main house entrances including the access roads to the estate. His Lordship has planned the whole exercise meticulously and every thing will proceed smoothly. The staff, including Margaret and Miss Jones will be diverted on a fool's errand. I will only act after those two have signed the documents, which will be arranged to explain the two deceased's absence, copies of which will be shown to Mrs. Cohen and Margaret when they enquire about their men." Jock explained.

A thoughtful David withdrew back to his room to think out a strategy. The time for a confrontation with the banker was imminent.

David thought long and hard. Should he go back and enter into Jock's bedroom and shoot him? No, that would cause alarm and the scientists may up and leave preventing the tagging of them with the locator chips and the banker would be forewarned and be prepared for anything. He would have to leave a weapon in the conference room, hidden where he could access it soon after entering the room and be able to neutralize any threat swiftly. He would do that tomorrow night using the secret door to gain entry into the conference room, after he had planted the locators on the scientists because he may well need the silenced 45 while still in the guest suite.

David spent a restless night and showed it when he walked into Bernie's rooms the next morning.

"My God, you look rough, is the stress of this game getting to you?" Bernie asked."

"Yes, I am sleeping badly. Have you prepared the Mickey Finns for our nuclear friends, I must do the job tonight; Margaret is ready and I don't want her to get anxious with prolonged waiting?" David asked urgently.

"Yes, everything's ready but you must learn how to plant them first. Mossad has agreed to watch over Katinka and intervene if necessary. They also think it essential for you and I to have locators fitted too." Bernie replied.

David had time during the previous nights thinking session to reconsider his being fitted with a locator. Mossad could easily then plot out the secret chambers.

"No Bernie, I have changed my mind and do not want a locator fitted to me.My instincts tell me that it would be risky in my dealings with the banker. He is now ultra sensitive to me and my actions and he may arrange a sudden assassination if it is detected."

"OK, I am expecting Katinka in a few minutes and then you can see how it is done." Said Bernie but he was puzzled and David knew that his excuse was feeble and Bernie knew that he knew but said nothing.

"Some thought must be given to the best position to implant the chip," Bernie continued, "Experience has shown that certain positions on the human body which would seem ideal, in fact, are not. For example, if implanted in the skin at the base of the skull, an enthusiastic barber with an aggressive pair of hair clippers could damage the chip during a haircut.

In the lobe of the ear might seem a perfect position but the recipient may be the type who habitually pulls on the lobe of his ear when concentrating on a problem. We have found that with males, the small depression below the larynx just above that point where the collar bones meet to be optimum and the skin is nice and loose there. The chip is slightly smaller and flatter than a grain of rice and the inserter syringe has a tip which after breaking through the skin expands the hole gently without tearing the skin, and then when the plunger is gently pressed, the chip is inserted and when the plunger is withdrawn, the hole in the skin closes and soon heals. The trick is absolute cleanliness. You will have a small bottle of surgical spirits and some cotton swabs with the insertion kit and the skin must be thoroughly scrubbed with the spirit before the chip is inserted or an infection is certain and the red mark will be noticed.

With a woman, the nape of the neck just below the hairline is the best position. The chip comes already loaded in the applicator and Mossad has sent me six. Each chip operates on its own unique frequency so to avoid confusion each applicator has the recipients name printed on it and the trackers refer to that name when they pick up that frequency. The chip has a maximum range of twenty miles and the frequency's they use are impervious to the usual urban electrical clutter."

Bernie's nursing assistant knocked at the surgery door and showed Katinka in who only had eyes for David although she greeted Bernie enthusiastically.

"Katinka, I asked you to come in this morning because both David and I think that you may come into some danger at some time. Those men who were killed on safari, were in fact assassins who had been sent to remove both David and I," said Bernie, "and you too have had one attempt to kidnap you. So, we want to insert a locator chip just under your skin which will enable friends of ours to follow you and pinpoint your exact location if you should again be taken against your will to places you do not want to go to. Are you agreeable to having the chip planted in you?" asked Bernie.

"My father must have been behind those men on the safari trip. He is a terrible, terrible man and keeps me here like a prisoner; he says that his enemies would use me against him if he did not keep me protected. Yes, I want that locator and am grateful to you for arranging it." Katinka showed some distress as she answered Bernie.

David took her in his arms and comforted her.

"Soon this will all be over, just be patient, we have some important work to do and when it's complete, you and I will be together and free of any control by Lord Montdrago." David said.

"Your work, does it concern those two men now staying in the guest room?" she asked.

"Yes, but why do you ask?" queried David.

"Margaret and I have been tasked with attending to their needs, Margaret sees to their food and any other requirement that affects their comfort and I have to show them over the estate and through the libraries and even keep them company if they so desire. The little that I have had to do with them so far has been pleasant and they talk quite openly with me; they know that I am His Lordships daughter, a fact that has been kept hidden from the staff and security although Margaret now knows since David told her; we have become the closest of friends which makes my life here much more bearable. My father would be angry if he knew that Margaret knows who I am. Dr. Horst and Dr. Smith are nuclear physicists and are quite unaware of their purpose in my father's schemes, they think he is arranging for them to teach and lecture at a university in the Middle East. As to His Lordships real interest in the two men, I don't know but I am sure that it has nothing to do with higher education, he is too keen to smother them with hospitality and too many of my father's associates have been phoning him and becoming involved in this educational philanthropy. I wish someone would warn those two naïve scientists that they may soon be out of their depth." Katinka said, with concern in her voice.

"Nobody must warn them," said Bernie hurriedly, "we need them to continue colluding with His Lordship. We will look after them and ensure their safety. Now, let me fit the chip, and David will explain many things to you soon."

Bernie led her to a chair and after she was seated he tilted her head forward and draped her hair over her head revealing a beautiful neck as white and unblemished as the purest alabaster. After a careful and thorough cleaning with spirit, he carefully and gently inserted the chip.

"Notice, I insert the applicator with one hand against the pressure of the thumb of the other hand to ensure that the applicator is under control and doesn't go in too deep."

"We do the same when engraving a fine gun, the two thumbs pressing against one another to prevent the cutting edge of the graver from slipping or wandering and stops it precisely where it has to stop." David commented.

"Is there anything that a gunsmith can't do?" asked Bernie with a smile.

"Yes, we have the same problem as Jews living in Israel, we can't make any money," replied David with an even wider smile.

The implant was accomplished and with a long gentle embrace, Katinka said to David

"Please be careful, I love you." and she turned and left the surgery.

"David, I repeat what the beautiful one just said, be careful. Here are the capsules for the two men's tea or whatever, they dissolve almost immediately. Good luck and thank Margaret for assisting."

David pocketed the capsules and the chips and applicators and left the surgery.

He had decided not to tell Bernie of the bodyguard's lethal plans for them, His Lordship's two targets.He would make his own plans and implement them as Bernie would undoubtedly call in Mossad if he knew what David knew and that didn't suit David.

Although too late for breakfast, David called in at Margaret's suite and he was pleasantly surprised to find her in and waiting for him with a late breakfast,

"Miss Jones, or should I say Brenda, phoned in earlier this morning and said both you and her had been summoned to the surgery where Dr. Cohen intended to do some blood tests to see that you hadn't picked up any tropical parasites, such as malaria, on your African trip, so I thought that you would be late for breakfast; I'll give cook a ring so she can start preparing the food." Margaret was smiling broadly, something she had been doing a lot of David noticed.

"Here are the sugar replacement sweeteners you asked for to put in your nightly cocoa, only one per cup. If you put in two, it will be so sweet, it will set your teeth on edge a most unpleasant experience." said David with a knowing look.

"Yes, I understand. I accompanied the dinner wagon with our two guest's breakfasts earlier. What pleasant gentlemen they are. I am going on a picnic with them today, Brenda and His Lordship's three new guards are accompanying us. It is a beautiful day and I am looking forward to the outing."

"Enjoy your excursion. Thanks for the breakfast, I'll see you later, I must go now, bye." with that, David got up and left the suite.

Chapter Thirteen

David spent the rest of the day in the gunroom, he did not cut out the surveillance cameras but ignored them and removed very gently some of the historical fire arms from the old oak cabinet .and laid them out on a work bench, having first laid a large thick blanket on top of the bench. The blanket was kept on a shelf beneath the worktop for use when delicate, easily marred stocks of great historical importance that could not suffer refinishing without a loss of authenticity.

A most beautiful weapon that had once belonged to a French King, a "Louis" who had been responsible for the patronage which resulted in the crafting of many magnificent pieces of furniture and utilitarian works of art which had never been equaled in the centuries that followed. The gun's inlays of precious metals and ivory, accentuated the patina of the marvelously figured walnut which had been selected from the French forests by the stock maker himself. Those same French forests still produced the most expensive stock blanks in the world to this day, David knew. It was rumored that for generations, the foresters who grew the walnut trees knew how to wrap chains around the trunks to distress and encourage the trees growth to produce wood with the most striking figure. The mineral rich soil of those regions enhanced with subtle, rich colors the wood that was fit for the glories of the French Royal guns at the court of the "Sun King"

Running his fingers over the sublime combination of delicately engraved steel and the hand finished ornate hammer spurs and perfectly crafted French walnut was all but a religious experience for David and the soothing feel of the masterpiece affected the flow of thought, inducing a calm consideration of all the factors which he had to deal with.

He had been sought out by Lord Montdrago to ensure that a most lucrative arms deal, a nuclear arms deal, arranged by His Lordship's organization would be given priority regardless of cost. To deliver him to the ruling family of that oil rich, cash flush small Middle Eastern nation to exact revenge for his killing of two members of that family, would place the conspiracy of which His Lordship was the leader, in an unassailable position as the sole supplier of all the small nations wants and needs; but now, the English lord had decided to deliver a corpse instead of a live person. With Mossad now known to be involved, the sooner David was killed and the conspiracy had something sure to trade with, the better. To try and deliver a live David would be impossible with Mossad being involved; they surely had an inkling of His Lordship's plan for David. Those Middle Eastern royal families's multitude of princes and their jealousies and ambitions would be taken full advantage of by Mossad and their intelligence would be superb.

David's execution was scheduled for tomorrow together with that of Bernie's,and, in all probability, his body would be shipped out with the two live scientists; an executive jet would make a fitting hearse for a gunsmith David thought.

The royal masterpiece was carefully replaced in the old oak cabinet and David rang through for a tray of tea and sandwiches, a frugal snack indeed, for someone who now controlled millions in a very liquid form. He wrestled with the temptation to tell Bernie of tomorrow's intended actions but knew that if he did and he relied on Mossad to save him, Mossad may allow his killing to take place in order to have another traceable delivery and to ensure that the scientists could be used to fulfill their plans. No, he would save himself and tonight, after implanting the chips in the two scientists, he would secrete the silenced 45 in the conference room. He daren't switch on the conference rooms lights at night, so he thought it would be better to go up to the Room's secret observation slits and do a thorough survey and decide where to hide the 45, while there was still daylight.

The ante room's intercom informed him of his teas arrival and he collected the tray.When he had finished his tea, he used the remote to neutralize the surveillance cameras and then entered the chamber behind the oak cabinet and crept up to survey the conference room.

Looking through the observation slits and carefully noting all the contents of the room, he became aware of many things that he had not noticed before on his brief visits to that hallowed room. There were tastefully sited green decorative plants growing in richly figured and highly polished wooden containers, one in particular that seemed to David to be in a perfect position for the concealment of his 45. Standing next to it, he could slip his hand beneath the over hanging foliage and retrieve the gun instantly. Its container, a square richly carved bin, was waist high and it would be easy to reach the weapon unobserved with no body movement to give his intentions away. All the other likely places to hide the 45 were poorly positioned and would require a short dash to reach them, which would be fatal.

As always, David stood dead still as he thought; yes, he decided it would be the plant stand, situated perfectly, just to the side of The banker's main desk. David crept back to the gun room, observing the pre-entry ritual, and then carefully closing up after walking into the room and, when seated at his office desk, re-activating the cameras. David took the tray out to the ante room notifying the kitchen and after locking up, went back to his apartment to rest and then get ready for a very busy night.

Margaret phoned just after he had emerged from the shower; it was just before seven pm.

"We've had such a lovely day, those two men are the nicest guests the estate has ever had; they're childlike, not childish, but childlike. Full of wonder and enthusiasm, shouting with joy at every butterfly in the woods and awed by the birdlife. Are all scientists like this?" Margaret asked.

"Only if they are unmarried, there after they become tame and domesticated and can only dream of woods, butterflies and birds," David said lightheartedly "Will you be taking their supper to them soon?"

"Yes, that is why I phoned, do you mind having dinner on your own?"

"Am I to be jealous, then? And as I know you'll be taking them their cocoa at nine, I suppose with your new found admiration for the guests, you'll be making them an especially special cup of cocoa?" David asked anxiously. There was an ominous pause and then she replied,

"Yes, it will be a special cup of cocoa to help them sleep after such a strenuous day."

"I will see you tomorrow, both you and my lovely woman." With that David rang off. Should he go and conceal the 45 immediately now that it was dark, no, he would do it after he had attended to the scientists, he decided.

Promptly at nine pm, he slipped into the darkness of the chamber and made his way cautiously to the observation points serving the guest suite. On opening the slits, he observed Margaret with the dinner wagon making the mugs of steaming hot cocoa; they were all talking of the picnic and the wonderful day that they had enjoyed. They spoke a great deal about the loveliness of Katinka and how she and Margaret seemed to have a perfect bond and how pleasant it was to observe. The two men were sipping their cocoa and remarked on how good it was. David fervently hoped that Mossad hadn't changed their minds and that that was to be the last cup of cocoa that they would ever enjoy. Margaret said goodnight to the men and left the guest suite.

The drug took effect rapidly and shortly after Margaret had left them, they both decided to retire. Dr. Smith switched off his light once he was in his bedroom and promptly went to sleep. David moved quickly and had soon implanted the locator exactly as Bernie had shown him, he then went back up to the observation slit and was astonished as he opened the slit to Dr. Horst's bedroom to see Lord Montdrago bidding the doctor good night and then leaving the suite. The doctor switched off his bedroom light and almost immediately fell into a deep sleep. David entered his room and rapidly completed the implantation and withdrew back into the chamber and then made his way down to the conference room.

He entered and swiftly concealed the 45 in the chosen plant bin, briefly adjusting its position whilst practicing a fast draw from a few different positions that he may be forced to stand in the next day. When satisfied, he withdrew and had barely closed the secret door behind him when he heard the key being turned in the conferences entrance door and shortly after, the lights were switched on. He took up his position at the observation slits and listened in astonishment as the banker called to some other men who were standing in the doorway to enter and to close the door behind them.

"Be seated, gentlemen and let us discuss our next moves. It has now been confirmed that Dr. Cohen is a Mossad agent and we suspect that his beautiful wife is too. The gunsmith, our most valuable pawn in the nuclear deal is thought to have struck up a relationship with Mossad for no other reason other than they have probably approached him with a good financial inducement to betray me. He and Dr. Cohen will be shot in this very room tomorrow morning. All surveillance will be disabled for the entire day and you will bring in your body bags after lunch and remove their bodies and take them to the jet which will fly out shortly thereafter. All security staff will be prohibited from the ground floor of this mansion tomorrow and they have been tasked with preventing anybody else from entering the forbidden area either."

"Why take the doctor's body to the jet, couldn't he be disposed of locally?" asked one of the men.

"We are dealing with Mossad, need I say more? If the body was discovered by them, and let me remind you that they have agents every where, they will go on high alert and they will retaliate. Most Jews in this country, although not Mossad agents know how to contact them and the discovery of the doctor's body would certainly be known by them almost immediately." said His Lordship, "Gentlemen, return to your rooms and await orders, thank you and goodnight." Lord Montdrago ushered them to the door and they all left, the lights being turned off and the door locked behind them.

David thought deeply and as usual when thinking on matters of life or death, he stood stock still. . He would now resume carrying the Browning which Bernie had returned when they arrived back from Africa, while the 45 was hidden in the plant foliage. The gloves were off and the confrontation would take place soon after he had attended to Jock and his men. A silenced weapon would no longer be necessary, the gloves were off; even after Jock and the other body guards had been killed tomorrow, he would leave the 45 under the foliage of the luxuriant pot plant in preparation for the final showdown with the banker which he was certain would follow.

The banker would be unlikely to be carrying a concealed weapon but there would be others at hand during the final confrontation. David went up to his bedroom and after closing the concealed door behind him, climbed into bed and calmed himself secure in the knowledge that he would survive tomorrows meeting with Jock in the conference room.

The new morning's breakfast was a Scottish delight and Margaret was showing relief that all apparently went well. As they were finishing their coffee, there was a knock at the door; Margaret rose from the table and went and opened the door, Jock and his men and Bernie were standing at the door entrance,

"Sorry to bother you madam but I have an urgent note for Mr. McAlpine from His Lordship which arrived by courier early this morning could I see him?" asked Jock pleasantly.

"Of course, David," she called, "Jock to see you," David came quickly to the door,

"Morning Jock, morning Bernie, what's all this about then?" he asked with a broad smile.

"Morning David," Bernie said quietly, "His Lordship wants us to sign some documents urgently down in the conference room so that the courier can take them back to his lawyers in London as soon as possible,"

"I hope that it concerns a huge bonus and a pay rise," quipped David with a chuckle, "Let's go then."

They all walked down to the conference room and as they walked along, Bernie asked David,

"Did you manage to get that spring made for His Lordship's double rifle alright?"

"Yes, it went off perfectly, I had to locate the swivel in precisely the right spot, near the throat of the chamber, yes, it went in very smoothly and I am sure that it will function correctly. By the way, there wasn't one, but two that were fitted."

They had come down the stairs and as they reached the conference door, Jock produced a key and opened the door. Bernie walked through the metal detector and a shrill alarm went off.

"Could you give me your keys or what ever triggered the alarm and I'll stow it in the drawer next to the detector where we always keep things until the business in the room is over," Jock asked pleasantly.

Sheepishly Bernie removed a small automatic from his pocket and gave it to the huge Scotsman.

"That's a prostitute's weapon," laughed Jock "what do you use it for, Doctor?"

"Prostitutes, sometimes they won't give me my change or they overcharge me?"

Everyone laughed and they trooped in.

"The documents are on the desk," said Jock.

"You sign first Bernie," said David extending his arm towards the desk and as Bernie moved to the desk and sat down, the gunsmith positioned himself behind the pot plant, adjacent to the desk.

"Do you remember that old Scottish saying I used on you when we were in the SAS together, well it is appropriate to use it again."

Jock tilted his head and looked at David in a puzzled way.

"Long may your lum reek," said David as he whipped out the 45 and shot Jock dead and then his companion standing next to him.

"Sir, Sir I didnee want to be part of it," Scottie wailed, terror stricken.

"I know. You said that you didn't want to be part of it and when Jock told you that he would attend to the killing, you said, that will be alright then."

David shot him and as soon as he had fallen, he asked Bernie to help and pick up the empty cartridge casings.

"I am a member of the chosen race and have a medical degree and am held in high esteem by my colleagues but you," said Bernie indignantly "treat me like a skivvies and expect me to run after you picking up your ejected brass whenever you feel like killing someone. I won't stand for it, I tell you, I won't stand for it," and he stamped his foot. David burst out laughing as Bernie's tantrum took away the horror and the tension they both felt. Bernie then asked seriously,

"How did you know, David, and how did you manage to secrete a gun in here?"

"Margaret. For over forty years the lady has been walking around this house minding her own business but missing nothing, becoming part of the furniture when necessary and lingering in concealed positions behind a drape or a piece of furniture and nobody takes any notice of her. She has certain keys which allow her to go where she is not supposed to. She also told me that all surveillance has been disabled and no staff or security would be allowed on this floor today, it is out of bounds.

So, you leave first; pick up your highly perfumed whore's gun and go back to your rooms. I want to lock after you leave and then I want to search the bodies and several other places where Margaret says that I ought to. Incidentally the chips were planted successfully. One last thing, there are some strange men in the house who are waiting to hear from Jock so that they could remove our bodies to the jet to be flown out."

David went through Jock's pockets swiftly, found the door key and ushered Bernie out and closed and locked the door.

There was a lot of blood around the corpses so after searching them thoroughly, David pulled one of His Lordship's priceless Persian carpets off the wall, where it was hung to enhance the other oil paintings, and lay it next to Jocks huge frame. He rolled the body onto the carpet and dragged it over to the secret door which he opened and lifted the body into the chamber. The carpet had successfully prevented any blood stains from making a trail to the entrance to the chamber. He soon had the other bodies in the secret chamber and then he closed the chamber door and had one last look around the conference room to satisfy himself that there would be no give away trail to the secret door; he had left the Persian carpet with the bodies in the chamber. He went out the conference room door and locked it, leaving the key in the lock.

He made his way to the gunroom and after locking himself in, using the lock's manual override, in case the banker should come in, he brought all the bodies into the gunroom. Using the Persian carpet, he dragged them to the end of the shooting tunnel. He switched off the alarm and swung open the former treasure compartment and struggled for some time to load the bodies onto the shelves, especially Jocks. Jock's legs had to be bent and crushed into the space available.

Sweating profusely he completed the task and closed the compartment, rolling up the carpet and secreting it back in the secret chamber. Painstakingly he checked the floors to see if there may be a spot of blood or a smear but there was not drop or mark to show that three bodies had been dragged across the floor.

David went back to his bedroom to clean up, using the main passageway and the stairs quite openly as if he had just come back from the gunroom. There was nobody around on the ground floor. As he reached the top of the stairs, he saw some security guards walking back and forth but they ignored him. Once in his room, he phoned Bernie and told him he was back in his bedroom where he intended to stay until supper time when, as usual he would dine with Margaret. Bernie said he was just waiting to hear from him and now that he had, he was going home. He said he was going to contact mutual friends and bring them up to date with events at the mansion. If there was no cargo for the jet, would the two guests still depart on the jet? David said that they would just have to await developments.

David strapped on the shoulder holster with the Browning and put on his hunting jacket to conceal the weapon and then lay down to wait for supper time.

Supper was served a little earlier than usual and David asked Margaret why?

"Our guests are leaving in an hour's time and I must see them off and check that they haven't left any of their possessions behind. Our lovely young lass went into London just after lunch with those friends of His Lordships who arrived yesterday. Lord Montdrago instructed them to accompany Katinka around London and then take her to the airport to say farewell to those two lovely men whom we shared that delightful picnic with yesterday and after the jet has departed to bring her back to the house."

David jumped up and dashed to the phone.

"What is the matter, why are you so alarmed?" asked Margaret.

"I must contact Bernie immediately, thank God the phone taps were disabled," he said as he frantically dialed Bernie's home number.

"Glad you phoned," said Bernie as he answered the call, "our men responded to the movement of Katinka's locator move to London and noted that one of her companions is known to Mossad and is under suspicion of being part of a Middle Eastern group potentially dangerous to us. Furthermore, we have been monitoring all flight plans and passenger manifestos connected to the Montdrago corporate jet. The jet is flying out in a few hours time and apart from the scientists, a Miss Brenda Jones is listed as a passenger. Did she inform either you or Margaret that she was flying out tonight?"

"No, she thinks she is being taken to the airport to say goodbye to those two men whom she enjoyed the picnic with yesterday, please Bernie, your men must prevent this blatant abduction," David begged,

"A rescue plan is already in hand, we have several very competent men hanging around the airport waiting for the beautiful one; I shall inform our controller that she is unaware of her being flown off and would be most reluctant to board the jet. Don't worry, situations like these are Mossad's specialty so don't worry." Bernie concluded and then hung up.

"What is happening?" Margaret asked, thoroughly alarmed and scared, "Nothing must happen to that young woman; I have grown to love her very much,"

"Fortunately, all the surveillance equipment was disconnected this morning by order of His Lordship, so I think that I must bring you up to date with all the events that threaten us. The reason that the bottom floor was placed out of bounds and the surveillance switched off was to facilitate the murder of both Bernie and myself in the conference room this morning and to make sure that those men, now in London with Katinka, could remove our two bodies unobserved. The body bags were to be flown out on the jet where my body would be used to close a very, very lucrative contract for His Lordship," David then proceeded to tell Margaret everything, right from the beginning; everything except the secret chamber and the observation and the entry of most of the rooms in the mansion. That must remain his secret until all was settled and Lord Montdrago was dead and Katinka was his wife.

As the tale unfolded, Margaret's face took on an unusual expression, and she kept muttering, the time has come, the time has come. David did not ask what she meant; she was obviously deeply shaken and stunned by what she had heard.

They both sat silently for a while before Margaret said,

"That Jock and his men, both Scots and former comrades of yours could comply with the evil lord's instructions to murder you, indicates to me that Montdrago can and will corrupt anyone without compunction if it suits his needs. The time has come." Margaret said with finality.

"Now don't be putting yourself in any danger, leave it to me and Bernie and Mossad." David said emphatically.

The phone rang and Margaret took the call and told the caller that she would be down presently.

"The guests are leaving, I will return as soon as they have left, please wait here for me."

David sat quietly at the dinner table thinking calmly whilst he waited for Margaret to return. After Mossad had secured Katinka's safety, he would just wait and let events unfold, he could do no more until clarity dictated the actions that he must take.

They sat for many hours after Margaret returned to her suite. They spoke of many things not only of recent events but of other times in other parts. Margaret spoke of her lost lover, the soldier Jock and of her early childhood. She still owned the small cottage that she grew up in and would like Katinka to have it one day, not that she would ever need a refuge after her father was no longer living.

"What makes you think he is going to die? His power and wealth protect him and as I am going to marry Katinka as soon as possible, I can hardly become involved in his demise. Bernie, a worldly wise Jew, warned me not to kill the banker as he said that in the years to come and Katinka has children of her own, her memories would blur and as blood is always thicker than water, she would resent me if I had killed her father. Even Mossad would think twice of eliminating a man of such unlimited wealth and influence. Perhaps the Israeli government may one day need his wealth and influence.Pragmatism has always been the norm in International politics. Today's terrorist is tomorrow's freedom fighter or Nobel laureate. So hopefully, one of His Lordships associates will do the necessary."

The phone rang and Margaret answered it,

"Bernie would like to speak to you," and she handed the phone to David.

"David, I have just had word that our team arranged for another of our people who works in customs to take Katinka into custody. He had slipped some cannabis into her handbag to convince her companions that it was a genuine arrest, everything is alright."

"Where is she being held?" David asked anxiously

"At one of Her Majesty's correctional facilities my house actually. There will be no record of her detention which will puzzle His Lordship and his lackey, the Chief Constable. Mossad has provided me with several gardeners who although they don't know one end of a rake or spade from the other are very familiar with a Uzi machine pistol, so the daffodils should make a magnificent display this year." Bernie concluded and hung up. Margaret wanted to dash up to Bernie's house after David had related Bernie's conversation but David stopped her,

"His Lordship is on the premises and if you are seen going to Bernie's house, as you are sure to be, Katinka's safety will be compromised. Just wait, now with Mossad involved, Katinka is perfectly safe. He was only using her as leverage to force me to do his will. Now that the assassination has failed, I suspect that a direct confrontation is imminent."

"Will you be harmed?" She asked tearfully,

"No, I will be offered bribes beyond belief for a deal that will satisfy both of us. I must go to my apartment and sleep. It is certain that the surveillance will be kept inoperable for another day and that the ground floor will still be out of bounds until the banker and myself have concluded a deal. Goodnight and don't worry, all will be well."

"It is time," she mumbled quietly to herself as she showed him out.

Chapter Fourteen

David slept well and got up early to shower and shave. He dressed carefully and strapped on the Browning then putting on a sports coat made of Scottish tweed, still smelling faintly of peat smoke which all good quality tweed sports jackets smelt of. It was nearly time to have breakfast when his phone rang,

"Good Morning David, Montdrago here, after you have had your breakfast with Margaret, say about nine, please come down to the conference room, we need to speak. You will be met by my new bodyguards who have been in my employ for a number of years but not stationed here, please humor them and obey their directives. So, nine o'clock then." The Banker hung up.

At breakfast, David was quiet and thoughtful, Margaret was too.

"I have been summoned to meet the banker in his conference room at nine am. His tone indicated that both of us must now confront the issues which we both are familiar with. He has some new bodyguards who will escort me into his presence."

"Do be careful and remember he is at his cruelest when he is at his most polite and displaying reasonableness inconsistent with his usual behavior. Be canny and ruthless."

There was a knock at the door which David answered. There were three men at the door and one of them said,

"Good morning, Sir, His Lordship asked us to escort you down to the conference room where he is waiting to see you."

"Thank you," replied David, noting the thick bodies and the hard looks of the professional killers masquerading as gentlemen's "minders"

. They walked down to the conference security barrier in silence and when David triggered the metal detector, one of the men behind David stuck the muzzle of a gun in his back as the other said.

"Remove your weapon and no tricks." They all had now drawn their handguns and looked very dangerous. The door was opened and he was ushered into the room.

Lord Montdrago was seated at his desk and said with a broad smile as David walked in,

"My dear David, so nice of you to come, please sit down," the banker gestured towards a chair next to the pot plant.

"I would prefer to stand, thank you Sir," he said as he positioned himself next to the pot plant, his right hand hanging loosely next to the concealed 45.

"As you wish. Now let us see, you have something I want and I have something you want. In discussions between statesmen and business men of our caliber, only the bare facts are considered. Time is not wasted with trivialities or inanities; there is neither ego, nor pride, just plain talk. I want my stolen money back and you want to live. That was a nice touch leaving the bodies of my former bodyguards in the treasure strong room, I've no doubt that an empty treasure chest is as offensive to you as it is to me so that was indeed a nice touch leaving something in it for me to find. I want to know two things, one, why haven't you tried to kill me, and, two, where is the treasure?" His Lordship smiled broadly his cruelty shining through.

"Well, Sir, in answer to your first question, I cannot kill you because I am in love with your daughter and shall be marrying her soon. Two, I don't know where the treasure is, you should be addressing that question to Mossad,"

The banker was very quiet. David surveyed the bodyguards, they had put away their guns and he noticed that they were wearing body armor; it would have to be head shots. He psyched himself up to fire carefully aimed head shots but to do it very quickly, these were professionals he was dealing with.

"You are not the sort of Scottish scum that would be permitted to marry Katinka, in any case I have been informed that she was arrested by customs at the airport for being in possession of the drug, cannabis; is that what you have taught her to indulge in?"

"No, Sir that was a piece of subterfuge to prevent her boarding your jet. She was not arrested and is not under detention, you may check with your friend the Chief Constable."

His Lordship picked up the phone and dialed a familiar number,

"Montdrago, I am informed that an employee on my staff was arrested and detained last night by customs as she was about to board my Corporate jet, it seems that she had in her possession a banned substance, Could you please confirm that and find out where she is being held, please expedite the enquiry as I must know immediately." and he put the phone down

"If you are right, you will then have two questions to answer, one, where is my money and, two, where is Miss Jones. Those three gentlemen over there have worked for me for some years and they specialize in encouraging people to reveal their deepest secrets. The tall one with the anticipatory smile, once cut off a child's fingers, one by one, in front of the child's intransigent father who thereafter, couldn't stop talking," said the banker with an amused smile.

"Well, that moves him to the top of the queue," said David as he whipped up the 45 and fired, hitting the target in the head and a second shot hit the man at his side before the first body had hit the ground. The final man was moving fast as he brought his handgun up and David's shot hit him in his upper arm and he dropped his weapon.

David walked swiftly up to him and placed the silencer an inch from his head and fired, he then walked back and stood in front of the banker's desk,

"Even Scottish scum floats to the top and I promise you that your grandchildren will have the best of everything that my money can buy," said David with a grin.

The phone rang and His Lordship answered it, listened and then replaced the receiver,

"There is no record of my daughters detention, where is she?"

"With friends; I am sure you will manage to clear up the debris," David picked up all the weapons from the corpses including the confiscated Browning and walked out of the conference room, closing the door behind him. He then ran down to the gunroom and after manually locking the entrance door's over ride from the inside, he crept into the chamber and silently and swiftly slid along to the conference room's spy slits.

Lord Montdrago was just sitting at his desk, hands resting outstretched in front of him. The bodies now surrounded with blood stains seemed unreal and an atmosphere of tragedy pervaded the room. David watched in silence and wondered what the evil man would do. His vengeance would be terrible and cruel and cunningly convoluted, backed by all the skills that a lifetime of international finance had imbued him with. A wise man would kill him at once before retribution was set in motion.

The metal detector alarm shrilled as the door opened and in stalked Margaret, dressed in an old fashioned ankle length waterproof cloak which Scottish women of her generation wore with their brogues when walking in the rain through the heather covered countryside. She looked at the bodies and said to lord Montdrago,

"David has been here I see. It is time; I have something to say to you Thomas."

"How dare you, get out, you old bitch, immediately."

"No, I won't, Thomas. When you were a baby, I loved you and when you became a little boy I loved you more. Then your father took control of you and trained you to become the wicked, wicked man that you have become and now the time has come." With that, Margaret dropped off her cloak as she brought up a light, short barreled ladies shot gun and leveled it at the sitting banker's head.

"The lady your father married was ridden with cancer before he married her. He only married her to consolidate the two families banking interests. I am your mother and I have come to destroy you before you destroy my grand daughter." said Margaret calmly.

"So that's why my father settled you with the lifelong monthly salary and the cottage. As a banker I find this an intriguing situation. I have had many years of experience dealing with supplicants who have displayed great cunning and ingenuity in trying to convince me to either lend them money or back their schemes; I have never made a mistake, my training has been too thorough and my experience too extensive. You, as my mother, can be considered as an emotional supplicant. You are trying to get me, not to lend, but to give you my daughter. I would say that deep down in the maternal recesses of your mind, you crave my love and that your grand daughter is a pawn you hope will somehow bring us all together as a loving family unit. My banker's instinct tells me that you will not kill me because you love me and that as a woman, and a mother, you haven't got the guts."

David was fascinated as he watched the unfolding drama below his spy slit. Lord Montdrago placed his hands behind his head and leaned back in his sumptuous reclining chair. Looking from above, the pleasant smile of the banker was transformed, from an insincere mask of joy to a triumphant smirk of superiority, by the angle of truth presented to David

Margaret's face was racked with emotion. David watched fascinated as her expressions revealed the tug of war between her mother's instincts and her love for her grand daughter. Her love for Katinka won

"It is time." sighed Margaret.

Margaret fired and the full charge of shot from both barrels all but decapitated His Lordship; just a sitting corpse with a shredded bloody neck with a few pieces of skull and hair attached, remained. David dashed out the secret door,

"Margaret, Margaret, put the gun down and come in here now, hurry, hurry, the noise of the gun's report will bring the staff,"

He caught hold of her and pulled and pushed her into the chamber, she was in deep shock.

"Stay here and keep quiet, I'll be with you in a minute."

He rushed to the shotgun and using Margaret's cloak wiped it thoroughly and placed it in the headless corpse's hands, left hand on the muzzle, right hand holding the grip with the thumb through the trigger guard. He bent the arms so that the muzzle was right beneath where the jaw had been and the butt away from the body and resting on the desk. He rushed over to the other bodies and after wiping their pistols, he put them back in their hands and finally, he put the browning on the desk next to the Banker and quickly slipped back into the chamber and closing the door behind him.

"Keep very quiet and if you want to cough, put your face over the cough box," he pointed out the box and placed his face onto it to demonstrate what to do.

"Who are you?" she asked, clearly bewildered and in a state of shock,

"I am the phantom of the opera skulking in the secret tunnels observing this grand opera of high finance and evil doings" and placing his mouth close to her ear he said,

"I sing Scottish love songs such as, - "Stop your tickling Jock, stop your tickling Jock, stop your tickling, tickerlickerlickerling, stop your tickling Jock. There you are Sir Harry Lauder couldne do it better."

Margaret looked at him lovingly and said,

"Thank you, I feel better now," and smiled

There was a hammering at the door and some of the staff ran in; all showed horror and expressed it. Behind them, Bernie appeared and took charge.

"I will phone the Chief Constable so no one else must touch or do anything, nor leave the estate, neither must anyone phone out. Security, will see that those orders are strictly complied with until the Chief Constable gets here and takes control," said Bernie to the chief of security and his men

"Except for security, will everybody leave the room immediately," said the chief.

"What the hell went on here do you think, Doctor?" asked the chief of security,

"Well he obviously committed suicide but it will have to be kept very quiet. In fact, the news of his death will have to be suppressed for a long time otherwise there may be a collapse of several large finance houses and the government would never permit that. Even we employees would suffer financially if his death were to become public knowledge, so please impress upon the entire staff the need to be discrete. Let me phone the Chief Constable." Bernie concluded as he reached for the phone. He found the policeman's number and was soon speaking to him, and gave him the same summing up that he had just given to the Chief of security, after a minute, he put the phone down,

"The Chief Constable will be here soon, please see that everyone is under your control, you know what your own financial consequences will be if you do not control the staff," Bernie said "Now please leave me alone. No one must enter whilst I carry out my Medical examination, put one of your men at the door and if someone must enter, knock long and loudly as it will give me time to cover His Lordships private parts; we do not want any disrespectful gossip from the staff."

When Bernie was alone he said out loudly to himself

"David, you careless sod, don't you know how to arrange a decent staged suicide?" with that Bernie rearranged the bankers arm position and after another critical examination from a few different angles, slid the body into a slightly different angle.

David touched a fascinated Margaret on the shoulder and indicated that she must follow him. He led her back to her own room and let her in and whispered, "Never repeat what happened today, you have saved Katinka's life and future and also the future of your great grand children too. I will be back for supper tonight with Katinka" and kissed her cheek.

David dashed back to the gunroom and made sure that everything was normal. He checked the backstop and was not surprised to see that when the shelves pivoted around, they were empty but there were a few bloodspots which he quickly wiped clean and closed up. Before closing the secret chamber he quickly went up to the cough box behind his bed room and withdrew a small bag of diamonds and returned to the gunroom and closed everything up and, unlocking the manual override, left the gunroom and strolled up to his bedroom. He phoned Bernie on the cell phone he had been given by Mossad and when Bernie answered, he asked

"When will you be home, and can I invite myself for a sundowner?"

"Go up now and make yourself at home, I'm waiting for the Chief Constable and clearing up for some clumsy bastard that shouldn't be allowed to arrange his own funeral, let alone a faked suicide, but thankfully I don't have to grovel around on my hands and knees looking for spent cartridges." Bernie hung up.

The road up to Bernie's house was beautiful as it curved around the lake, and looking back, David could see that some official police cars were parked outside the front entrance to the mansion. Luckily, David thought, I used the side entrance, would they detain Bernie long?

The Chief Constable would certainly take the finger prints of the three dead body guards and search through their clothes and the rooms that they had stayed in, David thought, and he wondered what the police would uncover? That the banker had some unsavory employees and that there were some unsavory documents in his conference room that would soon be uncovered. The mansion would be crawling with police for many days and everyone would be questioned including David and Margaret. She would need support and advice; it would be imperative that both she and Katinka reveal their relationship with Lord Montdrago immediately, so that their claim on his assets could be established and proved with DNA evidence before clever, avaricious associates of the deceased banker could purloin what was rightfully Margaret's and her grand daughters. The lawyers and accountants of the various companies that the late Lord Montdrago controlled must be vigorously monitered. Mossad's advice must be sought on how to immediately cancel the nuclear deal and any other arms transactions that were illegal or immoral.

The conspiracy that the English Lord headed would be impossible to cast off and confound without Mossad, but on the other hand it would be unwise to give Mossad a free hand as they might embroil the deceased's estate in some equally dangerous venture of opportunity to suit their country's interests. He would have to trust Bernie to advise on that one. Where Israel's interests were at stake could Bernie be trusted? Would Mossad use their knowledge of David's recent actions to force him to comply with their wishes?

David knew he must gather all the evidence of everything concerning the two women and himself before it gets lost or is compromised. He must compile an accurate diary of everything pertaining to the two women which might influence their claims on the estate, to lodge with their lawyers. Copies of all documents must be secured in their bank's security boxes with each one of them having a key.

The conspiracy worried him as there were some very powerful men involved who might do anything once the death of Lord Montdrago became known; who these men were, was anybody's guess.

As David approached Bernie's house's front door, he was challenged by two very tough looking men and asked to state his business. David explained that he was Bernie's associate who was helping to foil the nuclear threat and that it was his young lady that they were guarding. One smiled and said "The Gunsmith" and let him pass.

Rachel opened the door when he knocked and with a warm smile said

"Welcome, Bernie had just phoned and said he was on his way. Katinka is sleeping, poor woman, she has had a frightening experience and I don't want to wake her yet. Would you like a drink?" she asked as she led David into the spacious and beautifully decorated living room.

"No, I'll wait for your overworked husband to join me and then we can all toast the passing of the evil Lord. The relief that event has brought is tremendous for all on the estate especially Bernie and the two ladies. I must admit to feeling safer and more relaxed than I've been for months."

"Yes, Bernie told me over the phone that he was dead, I wonder how Katinka will take the news." Rachel asked.

"With relief, I expect."

Bernie arrived within ten minutes and walked towards David with both arms extended and gave him a bear hug.

"We are alive, we are alive," he said joyfully

The beautiful Rachel walked up close to the pair of them and standing on tip toe, kissed David on the forehead, "Thank you for keeping my man alive," she said with feeling.

They were all seated around a small table with a thick exquisitely woven covering, there was no conversation, they all were thinking of the dangers they had survived when David said,

"Remember confiding in me your dream of owning a small holding in Israel? Your complaint of the high cost of building materials, especially the crushed stone for the concrete, really touched me, so I have been picking up stone all around the estate when I've had the opportunity. Well, here's what I have managed to find and it is good English stone and will make the walls of your home strong."

Bernie and his wife looked puzzled and Bernie started to ask David how a small bag of stones could build what they wanted to build, when David drew out a small bag and opened the drawstring and poured out a cascade of sparkling white fiery stones which glistened and sparkled with many colors as only superbly cut and polished diamonds could.

There was a long silence. Eventually David said,

"Lord Montdrago tried twice to kill you so I sued him on your behalf for damages citing mental anguish and he settled."

There was still silence

"You didn't steal them did you," whispered Bernie.

"No, I've just told you they are for payment for the two attempts at trying to kill you. In any case his assets now belong to his family and I can guarantee that not only would they approve, they would insist."

"What about you? He tried many times to kill you," asked Bernie.

"Oh my reward is the beautiful one who is sleeping in one of your bedrooms," David said

Every one was smiling and David said.

"You had better put your treasure back in its bag and put the bag in your safe before we wake up Katinka. Furthermore, write down this old Scottish recipe for making quality concrete which is rigid with great compressive strength and put it in the bag too, it is priceless."

Bernie took a pen out of his pocket and asked David,

"Shoot, give me the formula and rest assured that I shall keep it secret like the secret of Heather Ale."

"Three stone, two sand and one cement, identical to the constituents of your injection for erectile dysfunction," said David with glee.

Bernie blew David a raspberry.

"Before the lovely lass awakes, some questions. Why did you decide to eliminate the late banker today? With your wedding pending, I thought you would have taken a wise Jew's advice and leave it to someone else." Bernie asked

"I didn't shoot His Lordship, his mother did."

"Don't be ridiculous, his mother died when he was a baby, Mossad's research is very reliable and that is from the mother's family documents, a family of European Bankers." Bernie stated emphatically.

"The putative mother was ridden with cancer before the banker's father married her; it was a marriage of convenience to consolidate two banking houses. It was the sickly woman's companion come nurse, Margaret, that was His Lordship's mother and she shot him to protect her newly acquired grand daughter whom she has grown to love so dearly. I did try to stage the suicide and get Margaret to safety as she was in a shocked state after she had shot him." David declared.

"Did he know that Margaret was his mother?" Rachel asked,

"Yes, she told him about a minute before she shot him. I think that both Katinka and Margaret's relationship must be declared openly immediately to secure his estate and I think you should guide them and organize the DNA tests. Please seek Mossad's advice on what the ladies should do to stop all illegal arms deals and crush the nuclear deal. We must see that a large firm of "clean" lawyers moves in to protect the bankers assets, bearing in mind that he was the head of an international conspiracy who will try to conceal all financial activities as soon as his death is made known; the lawyers and auditors will have to act quickly. Could you contact Mossad immediately, Bernie?"

"Right, excuse me; I'll phone from my bedroom." Bernie rushed out the room with his bag of building material.

Rachel walked out of the room saying,

"Katinka should be woken and told that you are here."

She came back and on resuming her seat, she said,

"She is dressing and won't be long; will you be staying for supper?"

"No, Margaret is expecting us. I wonder what her reaction is going to be when she learns of her father's death and that Margaret is her grand mother? Will she still want to go home to Russia?"

"She will soon have control of the executive jet and the means to go where ever she wishes and a husband to accompany her too." Rachel laughed.

Katinka walked into the room, a vision of loveliness and upon seeing David gave a cry and rushed over and as he stood up, flung her arms around his neck whimpering like a puppy.

"It's all right, the nightmare is over, and your father is dead."

She stood dead still and moved her head back and looking into his eyes, asked,

"Is he really dead? Am I truly free?"

"Yes, he is dead and you are free. Margaret is waiting with supper for you, so as soon as I have spoken to Bernie, we will stroll over to the mansion and join her, so collect your travel case and we will leave soon after I have spoken to our favorite Doctor."

Katinka rushed out to fetch her baggage just as a beaming Bernie strode into the room,

"Good afternoon, my lovely," said Bernie "the wheels have been set in motion, David, one of the most prestigious law firms in London has been engaged, a firm with many partners, each one a specialist in his own particular area of expertise, such as finance, business, wills and estates and forensic experts who investigate large corporations whose books, and records and intertwining companies, would normally be difficult to unwind. The estates security must be instructed to immediately stop anything from leaving the premises and to spread out and prevent anyone from prying into any records or documents.

The chief constable is still in the house with his staff and the bodies have not yet been removed to the mortuary. I will accompany you both down to the house and Margaret and Katinka must call a staff meeting immediately and assure them all of their job security and of their employment and ask for their help during the next few, difficult weeks."

When they arrived at the house, Bernie suggested that Katinka go to Margaret on her own whilst he and David confronted the Chief Constable and his staff whom they found still in the conference room. The Chief Constable waived them in and Bernie introduced David to him,

"Before anything further is said or done, I would like to inform you, Sir, of the following indisputable facts. Fact number one, Margaret Hamilton is Lord Montdrago's mother. Fact number two the young lady known as Miss Debra Jones is His late Lordship's daughter. DNA tests, which I shall organize with the laboratories who specialize in these tests, will prove conclusively the relationships between the deceased and the two aforementioned ladies." said Bernie, "Furthermore, the prestigious firm of Isaacs, Brown, Cowper, Worthington and associates of London have been engaged on behalf of the two ladies. They have advised that the estates security personnel immediately ensure that nothing, absolutely nothing except the bodies of the deceased leaves the estate. A private security firm is manning all exits from the estate and only official vehicles will be permitted to leave the estate until the lawyers give their permission, they will arrive in the morning." and turning to the chief of the houses security staff, he said, "Will you advise all staff of what I have just said and assure them that their jobs are secure for as long as they want to continue serving the family. A staff meeting will be called soon, probably tomorrow and that handsome bonuses will be paid to the staff for helping the family through the next few difficult months. Please attend to that instruction as a matter of urgency." The head of security rushed off bursting to tell of the new, fantastic developments.

"I say, you can't do this. On whose Authority do you issue those orders?" bellowed the Chief Constable.

"On the authority given me by the deceased Lord Montdrago's two heirs and confirmed by their legal advisors who are treating this commission as urgent and of high priority; they are approaching the courts first thing in the morning to confirm their status in these matters. Excuse me, I must make an urgent call," with that, Bernie using his cell phone spoke urgently to someone in a strange tongue for a while and then after ending the call, said to the Chief Constable,

"That was the private security firm's officer in charge of the group that is presently manning all the exit gates and he assures me that he will obey his instructions to the letter."

"Well you get hold of that firm's general manager and inform him that I give the orders as to what can or cannot be done on this estate," the clearly agitated Chief Constable barked out.

"I am unable to contact the head office of the security as it is an international company based in Israel and does do a lot of work for the various departments and arms of the British Government. Here is the number of the lady's legal representative and they are always telephonically available at all hours, their staff will wake up a senior partner if necessary and the Montdrago estate is their highest priority."

Bernie could understand the chief Constable's anxiety; would his kick back payments be traceable once the forensic lawyers started nosing around?

"Would you be kind enough to notify me when and which mortuary Lord Montdrago's body is to be taken to so that the DNA procedures can be initiated. The family's new legal representatives insist on an early DNA report for submission of papers to the master of the Supreme Court?Me and Mr. McAlpine are having supper with the two bereaved ladies and hopefully we can be of some comfort to them, good day, Sir." David and Bernie made their way up to Margaret's suite.

There was no bereavement or sadness at the supper table, only happiness and joy. Bernie had located the Chief of security as soon as he entered the suite and had phoned him and instructed him to immediately disable all security devices except the burglar alarms and lock the security control room door and post a guard outside to see that no tapes or documents pertaining to security surveillance be removed. He also advised him of the Israeli based security company and the six men on the gates and that this relieved his men of that duty allowing him, the chief, to concentrate his men on preventing any breach of His Lordships documents especially by the police authorities who must be kept under open, obvious surveillance at all times, day and night. Should the police hamper them in the execution of their duties, they must contact Dr. Cohen immediately, no matter what the hour.

In the middle of the magnificent dinner David asked Margaret,

"Have you told Katinka yet who you are?"

"No, I am afraid."

"Well all the staff has been told and it would not be nice for my darling to hear it from them." Katinka looked puzzled.

Margaret hesitated, looking apprehensive and a little frightened, and then she said,

"I am Lord Montdrago's real mother and your real grandmother."

There was a moments silence and then Katinka got up and flung her arms around her grandmother's neck kissing her again and again and then they were both crying.

Bernie, moist eyed said that he'd had enough to eat and after thanking Margaret profusely, he left to go home to the beautiful Rachel.

"I am so happy" said Katinka wiping her eyes.

"Now listen carefully, you both know of the secret chambers and passages, you must never, I stress, never tell any body about them and never even try to use them. The only reason that I was never caught out was because I developed and used a ritualistic, cautious system that I adhered to at all times. Better to forget that they exist, for if others find out about them, they can be used with devastating effect against us."

The supper continued joyously late into the night and when they left, Margaret asked,

" In which suite shall I contact either of you should I need you urgently?"

"Stop fishing, you inquisitive future Great Grandmother." David replied.

Margaret was smiling happily as she showed them out.

Chapter Fifteen

The next morning Bernie phoned David,

"The bodies have been taken to the police mortuary and so have all the hand guns found on the scene, including the Browning and shoulder holster. I have ordered another Browning and another silenced 45, both with spare magazines, and a young Mossad recruit, who is not showing much promise, to walk behind you picking up empty cartridge cases; they will be delivered tomorrow. Be very wary of any policemen, many, even the highest were being bribed by the banker and are now trying desperately to cover their tracks. Fortunately the legal teams will be on the estate just after ten am. They will surround all the available documents with a bulletproof system. They have also sent a team to the late banker's bank and one to a large finance house in London. Were there any documents in the concrete constituents?"

"Yes"

"Keep them in a bullet proof condition too and do not even reveal that you have them, not even to the two lovely ladies, ever."

"Thank you Oh wise and learned Jew and I mean that sincerely." David said.

The forensic lawyers and accountants arrived precisely at ten am and proceeded immediately to pull out every piece of paper and every book and every document in the conference room but told Margaret later that they had a particularly rich haul from the deceased banker's bedroom safe, which was, in fact a strong room. The forensic financial scientists had brought with them a highly qualified locksmith as a matter of routine so the strong room was quickly opened.

The legal team, admitted to Margaret and to Bernie that the strong room had yielded secrets of international holdings and massive deals all around the world that amazed even their worldly wise legal colleagues, Lord Montdrago had died as one of the richest men in the world but many of his assets were teetering on the ragged edge of illegality.

The new Ladies of the manor were informed, as was Bernie, that several high court interdicts had been obtained to prevent many of the very wealthy vultures, who had been associated with His Lordship, from chancing their collective arms, as Bankers and financiers were wont to do.

In the days that followed, the two women were inseparable and roamed around the estate enjoying the forest and the woods; wildlife abounded, to the intense interest of Katinka. Margaret insisted that she be called Margaret and not Grandmother. Katinka asked her if they ought not to ban the hunting and shooting of wildlife on the estate?

"No, my dear, wildlife should be managed and shooting is a useful game management tool. Speak to the estates game keepers and foresters and ask them to advise you. Those men are university trained and have many charts and records and instruments to help them manage the wildlife and are right up to date with the latest research. His Lordship never interfered or questioned their judgment."

That evening at supper, David felt that it was time to discuss the banker's death as Katinka had grown stronger daily and seemed to be fit enough to learn of the Banker's "suicide" This would prevent her asking questions when perhaps Margaret was not as strong. It would never do for Margaret to tell her the truth in a misplaced bid to clear her own conscience as she aged and became frail.

"Bernie tells me that the lawyers and forensic accountants are uncovering some terrible facts about His Lordships business and say that he may have been near breaking point and that his conscience almost certainly led to his suicide," David said.

"Did he commit suicide? I thought that he perhaps had a heart attack," asked Katinka in a muted voice,

"Yes he did, he shot himself. I thought you should know because sooner or later the servants would let slip, and still might, and it is better to prepare yourself. In any case all that is over and you and Margaret must not let anything spoil your happiness and when you have your own children, you can prepare them for any thing that might spoil their happiness and ensure that they have a perfect childhood; they must grow up strong and without any hang-ups." David said and stretched across the table and kissed her lovingly.

"You're right, I am so happy and I am not going to let anything, even my own thoughts, spoil my happiness and my life. Since I have got to know Margaret, I have lost all desire to go back to Russia except to visit my people there, sometimes with Margaret. Is it true that when everything is settled, I can use the Jet?"

"Yes, I am sure that you can. There is a big wide world out there waiting for all of us." David lent across again and kissed her again.

A few days after the supper when Katinka learned that Margaret was her grandmother, she phoned Bernie and asked if she could come to his rooms, as she was not feeling well? He told her to come to the surgery immediately. After examining her he phoned David and asked him to arrange a meeting with both Margaret and himself present and he would come immediately, bringing Katinka with him.

Bernie ushered the lovely girl into Margaret's apartment shortly after he had spoken to David.

"What is this all about then?" asked David,

"Katinka asked for an appointment with me this morning as she hadn't been feeling very well recently. After all the tests, I diagnosed a condition that she had picked up in Africa," Bernie said gravely.

"Oh my God, what is it?" Margaret asked anxiously,

"Morning sickness, I'll send my account for my difficult diagnosis through the post, Remember I only accept guineas, that is, not pounds, but a pound plus a shilling, Good night." And he turned and walked away from the astonished family.

They sat around the dining room table after Bernie had left, their happiness was intense.

"It was barely a couple of months ago when every day was a grey, dreary, hopeless day and I remember one day kneeling in my room and praying to God to deliver me from my adversity," Margaret told the two star struck lovers, "so, if you will excuse me, I am going back to my room to kneel in gratitude and thank my God for having delivered me and blessed us all." Margaret got to her feet and walked out of the dining room, leaving the two young lovers to sit in a haze of joy in the presence of Margaret's God.

The following morning, David received a call from Bernie, who suggested they meet in his rooms,

"Are you going to give me a pregnancy test too?" David asked "I will be there in a few minutes."

They sat in the surgery and Bernie said,

"I shall be leaving soon, my work is done here but we will keep in touch. Would you lend a helping hand if you are needed? Now that you are financially independent, you are a very attractive proposition to Mossad, they won't have to pay you.

The two scientists have been persuaded to work in Israel where their knowledge will complement those of our own physicists. The people that they were supposed to join, in that bogus nuclear educational scam, have all been attended to but the secretive conspiracy, of which the evil Lord was head of, is as elusive as ever. The preliminary report from the forensic investigators of the late banker's financial affairs reveals a world wide complex; a convoluted web of interlinking industrial multinationals and media empires which boggles the mind. Both of Britain's intelligence services are involved in their own investigations and have been for some time it seems; they were and are very worried about the banker and his fellow conspirators.

We of Mossad have infiltrated some of our men into both your lawyers and the investigating team and, we suspect, so has MI5. Incidentally, the pilot Jim, he of the handle bar mustache and the loud guffaw and the expert on the tassle tosser's tits, is MI6 and has been flying the bankers executive jet for three years; this has only been known to us in the last week. We have been told that the investigations will continue for at least two years and you and your family will be under close scrutiny, not because you are in any way wrongdoers but because with the bankers far flung empire, many will try to use you. There will be documents to be signed from time to time and I implore you, not to allow Katinka to sign anything until her lawyers have examined the document. Not even a donation to a local charity. In your new world there will be many pitfalls so remember what I am telling you," concluded Bernie.

"Phew, as the Scottish Laird's engraving on his shotgun warned, "What a lot of fucking Indians". Certainly, Bernie, I will help as long as anything I do does not clash or is detrimental to the United Kingdom's interests and of course my duty to Her Majesty, to whom I once attested to when I joined the SAS and will always be bound by for the rest of my life," said David.

The listening devices which had been placed in the doctor's surgery by a suspicious MI5 team as soon as the news of the international bankers death had reached them was manned by two operatives who listened and recorded the conversation. They turned and smiled at one another and one gave the thumbs up sign.

"I hope David that we never have an enemy who is a gunsmith. The way you got rid of those four in Africa who were assigned to kill both of us and made it appear as accidents was nothing short of brilliant. And Jock and your other two comrades from the SAS, how did you hide that silenced 45 in the pot plant in the conference room before they lured us there and tried to kill us. Did you not feel awful when you shot them?" asked Bernie,

"They had accepted huge amounts of money to kill us and we were close to being assassinated and don't forget they were trained SAS men, they had to be dealt with the instant the opportunity presented itself; thank God I left the 45 back in the leaves of the pot plant because those other three who confronted me were professionals and very dangerous. The banker sat at his desk with a smile of anticipation as he waited for those hit men to shoot me. I told the evil lord to clean up the mess and get rid of the three bodies and walked out. Imagine my surprise when as I turned to go down to the gunroom out of the corner of my eye, I saw Margaret go into the conference room.

I heard her say to His Lordship, I see David has been here as she walked past the three bodies and when she told him that she was his mother and pulled that shot gun from under her cloak and blew his head off, I rushed in and shoved her out of the room, wiped her prints off the gun and quickly arranged the gun to indicate a suicide."

"And, what a fucking mess you made of that, if I hadn't re-arranged the gun and the body that corrupt, dumb Chief Constable would have twigged. What did Margaret say to you when you got her back to her room?" asked Bernie,

"She was in shock but after she knew that Katinka was his daughter and therefore her grand daughter she had to destroy him as quickly as possible before he destroyed her new found grand daughter. She knew he was holding her at the estate against her will and that he was using her to lure me to the middle east where those tribal rulers had a price on my head for the killing their two brothers. Strangely enough, handing me over to them would have assured him the nuclear deal, even if he was vastly more expensive than other suppliers; honor and blood debts and Tribal etiquette" David said with a grim chuckle.

"Well alls well that ends well," a grinning Bernie.

"I need some help too. You remember on that African trip, we were helped by my old tracker's son, Dickson who warned us that he had overheard that those two new clients were being sent out to get us. Those two professional Killers sent by His Lordship who got killed on the buffalo hunt were helped into eternity by Dickson leading them into a dangerous position and then, while they were all pre-occupied with one wounded buffalo, Dickson deliberately wounded a few more. Well, I need to send him a gift. Do you have a Mossad man in Lusaka who could help? Dickson is a tribal man and every member of the tribe is regarded as either a brother or a sister or a father or mother so the money that I want to send to him must be put into a trust or he would have distributed it to the tribal people within a few months. After helping him buy his immediate needs, the rest must be paid as a monthly draw that must last him for the rest of his life. Could Mossad arrange that?"

"Yes. I meant to tell you that the rifle of the professional hunter, who led that fatal buffalo hunt, was inspected by an expert and he found that someone had broken off the tip of the firing pin deliberately before the hunt. You must have left a file mark or something. While they were taking the rifle for a more thorough inspection, the bolt with the damaged firing pin got lost. Dickson was in charge of the baggage porters." Bernie laughed with delight.

"My God, what a tale," whispered one of the listeners to the other.

"Bernie, could you see that your technicians continue to sweep for bugs regularly especially as there are so many other interested parties floating about. There have been all the Chief Constables men in the house, could it be swept immediately?"

"Definitely?" replied Bernie.

David made a mental note to engage a completely independent company to sweep again after Mossad was through. David's experiences of the last month or two, had shown that the second sweep was essential.

After a few more playful remarks, David left the surgery and went to look for Katinka.

Chapter Sixteen

Within a week the DNA tests had confirmed the relationship of the two women to the deceased Lord Montdrago and the following week, David and Katinka were married in a small church in Scotland, a stones throw from Margaret's cottage where she had spent her childhood. The wedding was attended by some of the lawyers, who made sure that all the documents and licenses were in order, and Bernie and Rachel, and by the staff of David's gunmaking firm.

The bride was radiant and like Margaret was dressed simply but elegantly. The ceremony was conducted by and old Presbyterian minister with a broad Scot's accent which neither Bernie nor Rachel could make out. The reception was held in a small country hotel and was quiet and subdued. The food and drink were of the finest, but again, simple and varied. Bernie gave a speech without humor but with much sage advice on the family and of family love. David and Katinka and Margaret were surprised when the senior partner of their legal firm rose up and gave a speech. He too stressed family love and said that blood was always thicker than water and to prove that, he declared, he would like to announce that Lord Montdrago's last will and testament had been found in the bank's vault. He had left everything to Katinka and the will had been accepted by the Master of the Supreme Court. Bernie stood up and started clapping and all the others followed suit.

The three of them as a family, left for Russia the following day in the executive jet. Jim the chief pilot congratulated them as they boarded and David said by way of a reply that it was comforting to know that a member of Her Majesty's secret services was just an arms length away as they flew over the former Soviet Union. Jim was taken aback and quickly retired to the cockpit.

It was becoming increasingly obvious to David that the vast financial empire that Katinka had inherited would always have the agents of certain governments trying to gather information about the financial affairs of that vast empire. Bernie had revealed that his technician had uncovered numerous bugs and removed them. The independent electronic experts that David had hired to sweep the very day after Mossad had concluded their sweep, had uncovered bugs of Israeli origin in every room in the house and had destroyed them.

As money was no object, David had decided to carefully select those security guards that were part of the mansions staff, and he had told them, at a private meeting he had called, that their salaries would be doubled immediately but that the second salary would go into a trust account and would be paid out yearly only if they were not caught being disloyal and treating with outsiders such as government agents or any other officials, such as police or hired investigators. He stressed that they too would be constantly under surveillance He then said that they must never leave any visitors to the estate that may plant a bug or two or other information gathering devices alone and by themselves.

David reminded them that the family, as the owner's of several banks and finance houses, with vast intelligence gathering networks, had instructed that their bank accounts be under constant scrutiny and any financial instruments they transacted would be known of and that bribes would be instantly discovered. However, he said, there would be performance bonuses and if any one of them needed help for any reason, the house of Montdrago would always be available to provide it.

David pondered long and hard as whether to ask Bernie to remove the locator chip from Katinka's neck and eventually thought that he must wait a while before making a decision. He still intended to hang on to the cell phone that Mossad had given him. He also decided to ensure that no one ever discovered the secret chambers and that only his family would know of them.

He realized that the intense interest of the government agencies was solely due to Lord Montgrago and his associates' worldwide deals which were not only against international law but against the vital interests of both Britain and Israel. The constant surveillance by the various Governments would cease when the conspiracy was destroyed.

Katinka's mother was a slim beautiful woman in her late thirties or early forties with a sad, mournful demeanor. She lived in a smart well furnished house on the outskirts of Moscow. The forensic accountants had informed David that the house was owned by the Lord Montdrago's estate and that the Russian lady received a handsome monthly stipend from the estate. Mother and daughter were excited to be together and Margaret insisted that Nadia return to the mansion in England with them, to await the birth of her grand child.

David decided to go for a walk through a nearby park and let the women folk talk about womanly things. It was summer and it would not get dark for a few hours. The park was lovely and had a small artificial lake with water birds swimming about. He sat down on a bench and reviewed the past few months; he had hardly started his review when a familiar figure strolled into view. It was the SAS's former commanding officer, Colonel Dempster, the man who had informed him of his dishonorable discharge and told him to disappear back to Scotland. As he approached the bench, he smiled warmly and said,

"Good lord, if it isn't David, my, my this is a coincidence, fancy meeting you here,"

"Yes, it is a coincidence meeting my old commanding officer in a small suburban Russian park. Are you on a recruiting drive for the SAS then?" asked David sarcastically.

"I have not been an officer with the armed forces for many years, I have, in fact, been the director of a combined service organization that oversees both the internal intelligence group, MI5, and the intelligence group which looks after Her Majesty's interests outside of the British Isles, MI6. Before my unit came into being, there was so much rivalry and deliberate non cooperation between the two arms of our intelligence services that many of the nation's enemies were not brought to account.

And, yes, I am on a recruiting mission, not a drive, just a mission to recruit one man, you." replied the Colonel.

"No, I do not need to do any work for anybody and I am sick and tired of being manipulated by people who seem to be above the law and who always have ulterior motives and do not hesitate to sacrifice their own loyal agents if it suits them. Please go away and leave me and my family alone and never forget that my family has control of a large proportion of the media,"

"My, we are irritated and tetchy this evening, even, if I may say so, petulant. But please just listen to two important pieces of intelligence that directly affect your family before I leave. One, those three assassins that you killed in the mansions conference room while Lord Montdrago looked on, were members of the Russian Mafia. We recovered their bodies after the good Bankers staff dumped them. The Russians were supplying the conspiracy which Lord Montdrago was head of, with stolen Soviet arms of a most advanced and sophisticated design; many of those arms are, note are, still being supplied to our nations enemies and will kill many of our soldiers and airmen one day.

The second piece of intelligence is more personal. Your new, beautiful, mother in law has been virtually held hostage by the same Mafia and your lovely wife has been terrorized ever since she went to stay with her father. The Mafia threatened to kill her mother if she did not keep them informed of her fathers business at the mansion, matters such as the number and names of his visitors and certain other items.

We managed with great difficulty to place several listening devices in your mother in law's home, and we gather that your wife and her grandmother wish to take the lovely Nadia back to England with them. Nadia has a personal staff of two, a maid and a man servant, who were foisted on her by the mafia and who keep her terrified at all times. They will accompany her to England. Please be kind to them especially with their meals, give them the best because when they land in England, customs will discover packets of heroin in their personal luggage placed there by your pilot, Jim, and they will spend the next ten or fifteen years in a prison where the food, although nourishing and adequate, is very bland, not to say awful.

If you do decide to join us, please try and imbue Jim with a little of your Scots canniness, he has grown very fond of your dear wife and when he was told of her mothers treatment by the two servants, he wanted to kill them during the flight, assuring us that no one would know and he could throw the bodies out over the sea without depressurizing the aircraft. Please impress upon him that there are more ways of killing a cat than shoving its head up its ass. So what do you say, old man?"

David was angry, very angry as he heard how Katinka had been terrorized by the Russian Mafia and he knew that the only way he could protect her was to join the British intelligence services.

"Yes, I will join, but I must tell you that I assisted Mossad over the last few weeks although I am not in any way connected to them," David said.

"Yes we know. However although your cooperation with them seems to be at an end, with Dr. Cohen leaving the estate to go and live in Israel, Mossad must never know that you have joined us although they will find out in time and may attempt to use you." replied the Colonel.

"Mossad swept the house at my request and removed all your bugs and then" said David with a laugh, "replaced them with their own bugs which I had removed the following day when I called in an independent sweeping company."

"Very prudent, you were born for the Great Game as Kipling would say. Be very aware of everything around you and I shall contact you in due course. Thank you David, we knew we could count on you," The Colonel stood up, nodded at David and walked away.

When David returned from his walk in the park, Katinka said that her mother would be taking her servants with her to England and didn't David think that was unnecessary?

"No, I think that's a jolly good idea as they speak the language and they are used to your mothers ways. No, I think it's great,"

After supper, all the women were occupied packing Nadia's things. David said that Nadia shouldn't take too much as he was sure that Katinka had many shopping expeditions planned in London over the next few weeks.

They all boarded the jet the next morning and David asked the chief pilot

"Did you attend to the stowing of the luggage, Jim?"

"Yes, Sir, I put Madam's mother's servant's baggage in the forward hold as the other hold was fully utilized," replied Jim,

"Thank you."

The flight was smooth and Nadia was excited as she had never flown before.

The jet landed eventually at the small airport where it was normally kept between flights, and they all disembarked.

There were only two scheduled flights per day for those who wished to avoid the hustle and bustle of the larger London airports, so when David and his family passed through customs and immigration, it was an unhurried, casual procedure. The family passed through first and after some delay the two Russian servants entered the custom zone. They placed their hand luggage on the counter and as the customs officer opened their bags and started checking through the contents, he called out to his assistant loudly,

"Come and have a look at this,"

David and the ladies looked around in time to see the officers take out some packets from each suitcase

"What have you got in these packets?" asked an officer.

The Russians started shouting in their own language and Katinka walked over to the custom officer and translated,

"They say that they have never seen those packets before and want to see a member of the Russian embassy."

"Yes, they all say that madam," as he slit a corner off the one package and with his finger, tasted a small quantity of the white powder that the packet contained.

"This is heroin, a prohibited drug and I am placing them both under arrest, sorry Madam, they are going to be held in detention until the police arrive,"

"Surely there has been some mistake?" Katinka asked,

"Yes Madam their mistake was in trying to smuggle heroin into Britain," and with that they were both marched off through a door behind the counter shouting loudly.

Katinka rushed back to David,

"Can't you do something?"

"Afraid not, they have committed a very serious offence," replied David.

As they all walked out of the building and over to their transport, Margaret sidled over to David and asked quietly out of the side of her mouth,

"What was that all about then?"

"Russian Mafia, Nadia's jailers," replied David,

"What does that mean?" she asked,

"Nadia is now free," David answered

Nadia was overwhelmed at her daughter's estate and, since the arrest of her "minders", had lost her mournful look and was smiling and happy.

Margaret was alone with David briefly while Katinka was showing her mother the magnificent works of art which filled the various rooms so tastefully without ostentation.

"That succinct but elegant reply to my question concerning the arrest of the two Russian servants did not make me any the wiser," said Margaret,

"The Russian Mafia with whom the late Lord Montdrago did business had forced Katinka to spy on the Bankers visitors and any thing else that might be of interest to them and warned her that they would kill her mother if she betrayed them to His Lordship. Those two servants were Nadia's jailors and are extremely lucky that they were not eliminated. Katinka is unaware that I know, and she mustn't know; the poor darling has gone through enough. I will discuss it with her when I judge the time to be ripe," replied David.

"Bernie phoned, as he is leaving soon to go to live in Israel, he would like to see you as soon as possible to discuss certain matters."

David phoned him immediately and made an appointment to see him in the surgery at eight the following morning.

Sitting in the surgery next morning, both men knew that it was the end of a very interesting association but also knew that their friendship would last solidly.

"I have some confidential news to give you. The search for the uranium enrichment plant was fruitless and not successful as I was initially led to believe. An entire nuclear facility for the assembly of a nuclear device has completely disappeared. The evil lord bought a stolen plant from the Russian mafia with a huge down payment and it was dissembled and loaded onto a large cargo ship at a port on the Black Sea. The final payment was to be made shortly after the unhappy suicide of the banker which prevented the transfer of the funds. The

Russians want either the money or their plant back, Mossad wants the plant so that they can destroy it and the British intelligence, helped by the CIA, also wants to locate the plant. So, you see Davie boy, you are up to your ass in the Luangwa river with all those crocodiles circling round you,"

David then told Bernie of Katinka's mother being used as leverage to find out more about the bankers visitors

"It all makes sense now. The Russians were trying to identify the banker's associates in the conspiracy but unbeknown to the Mafia, was the fact that the deal was being done for His Lordships own account only. I have since learned that those three that I shot while His Lordship looked on were Mafia hit men." David told Bernie.

"How did you know?" asked the Doctor, "Did Margaret tell you?" Bernie grinned.

"I was accused by a certain Colonel who works for the British Government. He was on a fishing expedition; I denied knowing anything about it, only that the mansion staff and the resident Doctor found the deceased Banker with three dead men beside him and that I was only told afterwards by the aforementioned doctor of the tragedy. The Colonel was my former commanding officer in the SAS, the one who kicked me out. He showed no remorse, the son of a bitch,"

"Well, you have been a naughty boy and an ungrateful one too. After our technicians swept your home and removed all the MI5's bugs and replaced them with their own, you called in an independent sweeping firm the next day and removed all Mossad's bugs."

"Well Bernie, I had just moved in with my betrothed and I had to maintain a degree of decorum." They both laughed.

"Bernie, in this dangerous situation, can I count on Mossad if I phone them on the cell phone to initiate an immediate search if Katinka is kidnapped?"

"That, you can stake your life on, we owe you David and one of the reasons for Mossad's success is that they always pay their debts. They save those they owe, and kill those who owe them."

"There are a few other things you can help me with. Could you steer me to an investment bank that will hold my personal assets without informing any of those who might cause me trouble, such as any of the Montdrago institutions, the forensic auditors, the Russian mafia, the

Montdrago conspiracy, British Intelligence or any other Government institution and especially not Mossad. Also a dealer who will convert some diamonds into negotiable instruments, such as bearer bonds; the dealer must be a person of integrity and beyond reproach. You see, my Scottish canniness indicates that all of Lord Montdrago estate may be frozen to assist any of the aforementioned bodies to lodge a claim or to initiate a legal action; British intelligence, aided and abetted by the internal revenue service, might prove troublesome at precisely the time when I and my family are at our most vulnerable.?"

"David, we shall be leaving for Israel in two weeks time and there will be a small get together for both our families a few days before we leave. I shall have all the information for you which I will give you at that small party." Bernie said,

"Remember, Bernie, anything and any time you need help, contact me, even if you need a heart transfer, I will somehow get you the organ, a special kosher one, taken from the bosom of one of those profiteering Jews in Israel who you complained of, the ones who are going to rip you off with the building materials."

"Bad choice, David, you won't find a heart in any of them,"

David left the doctor and sought Katinka out. He found her sitting on her bed, looking nervous and frightened,

"What is the matter, my darling?" He asked gently,

"I know that I should have told you before, but I was so scared, my mother was under threat from those Russian criminals who had forced me to report to them on the people who visited my father even though he was doing business with those very self same criminals. Now that my mother is here and safe I have been trying to pluck up the courage to tell you. I thought that you may suspect that I was betraying you too and I love you so much and don't want to lose you." Katinka started to weep quietly. David took her in his arms and held her tight,

"Nothing could ever alter my love for you. I had learned of your mother's plight and why the mafia was holding her; she was the means of controlling you. That is why I arranged for the drugs to be planted in the baggage of those two dreadful people who were her jailers. Hush, it is all over now." crooned David.

"But it is not," wailed Katinka, "When my father was taking me away from my home to bring me to England, he met with those Russian mafia in my mother's house. I was standing upstairs on the balcony behind a drape and I watched them as they were talking, they did not see me. The leader of the mafia was a tall man who spoke English very well. I have just seen him downstairs talking to our lawyers in the conference room. David, I am so frightened."

David as was his wont, stood up and was very quiet and still for a few moments and then he said,

"You are my wife and my beloved; no harm will ever come to you. Remember what happened to those men who tried to kidnap you?"

Katinka covered her face with her hands and said,

"No more killing, David, please no more killing."

"My darling, as your father told you, he had many enemies and always with great wealth comes problems that must be attended to promptly. Just carry on with your daily meetings with your mother and Margaret, go down to London for the day if you wish. Be happy and know that I will attend to all our temporary problems and they will soon be over and when our baby is born our lives will be perfect and free of any care. If you bump into that man in the mansion, just behave normally and as the very wealthy woman that you are. Security chief Brown and his men are always walking about the house and the estate and are aware of everything that is going on. I am going down now and will meet this man in a friendly way and find out why he is here. Let us meet at Margaret's for lunch." With that, David kissed her and left the bedroom and strolled down to the conference room.

David did not knock, but walked into the conference room purposely as the owner of the mansion was entitled to, and with a broad smile walked up to the tall man who was talking to the senior partner of their legal advisor's firm, Mr. Isaacs, and said,

"Good morning, I am David McAlpine."

The tall man was taken aback but quickly resumed his air of superiority. He was tall with a long handsome face, a prominent nose and high cheekbones. His hair was black and streaked with grey and long and carefully groomed. He wore a beautifully cut suit that had obviously been made for him by a master tailor. He was a man of substance.

"I am Sir Horace Blakely an associate of the late Lord Montdrago. I am in steel mainly and several of my companies supplied His Lordship with his engineering needs." Sir Horace did not offer his hand but smiled imperiously at the Scottish upstart, "I am having a confidential talk with Mr. Isaacs concerning certain records of various transactions that took place between my companies and His Lordship."

"I have my wife's power of attorney and she depends on me to assist her with the affairs of her father's estate, so there is no confidence that does not concern me. Mr. Isaacs will tell you that we hired his firm to audit the estates affairs and to advise us of any steps that have to be taken. You are probably aware that Lord Montdrago took his own life and this has made it a necessity to have a forensic audit," said David in the most insolent tone he could muster.

"Suicide was it. Have the police considered foul play, many stood to profit by his death?" the English knight asked with even greater insolence.

"Mysteriously, there were three other bodies found with his corpse and the authorities have determined that they were men of the Russian criminal syndicates. These men are often led by foreign trash from countries other than Russia, this of course made the forensic investigation imperative," said David haughtily.

"You will be kept informed of all details of the investigation, Mr. McAlpine" interjected Mr. Isaacs in a conciliatory tone.

"Excellent. Good day Gentlemen." David turned and strode out the room. secure in the knowledge that Mr. Isaacs would relay the conversation to Mossad.

.Lunch was a delightful affair; the three women were becoming more joyful by the day. After lunch, David made arrangements for the chief pilot of the jet to be brought to the estate that afternoon.

When Jim the chief pilot arrived, David met him in the main entrance foyer.

"Pleased to see you, Jim, have you been to the estate before?"

"No, Sir." answered Jim.

"Cut the sir crap, call me Mr. Gunsmith if you wish to be formal but otherwise it is David and my wife's name is Katinka," David replied with a smile. "Let me show you around, come and see the gunroom first, the most important room in the mansion."

When they were safely in David's office in the gunroom, David asked Jim,

"Can you arrange for a meeting with Colonel Dempster in the jet, I do not want to be seen with him?"

"Yes, David, would tomorrow morning do?"

"Perfect. Have you been officially told that I have joined your group?" asked David,

"Yes, welcome, we and the rest of the department are so pleased because this business with Lord Montdrago's estate has ramifications that affect Britain's vital interests and so far you have played a significant role in the recent affairs of His Lordship. Tell me David, were the accidents on the hunting safari really accidents?" asked Jim,

"Well, all those men that died had been instructed to kill both the Israeli doctor and myself and in trying to fulfill their tasks, they were either eaten by crocodiles or killed by wounded buffalo, so how on earth could it not have been a series of unfortunate accidents. That the victim of the croc attack had a bullet wound in the head and that the hunter who was gored by the buffalo had his rifles firing pin shatter and that the two assassins that were with him were attacked by buffalo who had been wounded by the son of my old tracker is neither here nor there, accidents will happen," said David sagely.

"Nicely put, Mr. Gunsmith, oh breaker of firing pins and friend of the tracker who randomly fired into a buffalo herd at the appropriate time," laughed Jim "and as for shooting the other hunter in the head before feeding him to the crocs, well, accidental firearm discharges are very common."

Jim was driven back to the airport after he had eaten scrumptious scones and strawberry jam, covered in thick clotted cream with some Earl Grey tea on the side.

David met the Colonel in the jet at the airport. The aircraft was parked a long way from the airport building so it was unlikely that he would have been seen entering. Jim sat beneath the wing reading and keeping watch.

"Well now David, do you have something to report or are you eager to meet me so as to establish our contact details? I was going to meet you soon to give you the details as to our arrangements for contacting the various controllers at headquarters,"

"A new development in the saga of His Lordships interaction with the Russian mafia has come up," said David and told the colonel of

Katinka's identification of Sir Horace Blakely and the run in he had with him and Mr. Isaacs's involvement.

"So, another member of the unholy conspiracy has revealed himself. I will detail a team to investigate every aspect of the man's life; where he comes from and what he is doing, although I do recall his name in connection with some British trade delegation visiting Russia some years ago.

I will pass on to you all the details and emergency phone numbers of those people in our organization with whom you will be dealing and the routine procedures which are used by agents in the field. If you need any specialized equipment for your work, do let us know in good time. We have an advanced weapons department who also deal with sophisticated signals and communications such as locator chips and homing devices. You leave first and I will leave later, I must have a word with Jim before I go." David got up, shook hands and left.

Bernie's going away party took place the night before he and Rachel were to depart. Apart from the three ladies and David, there was only Bernie and Rachel and a man that David had not met before; he was introduced as Saul Abrahams a friend and colleague of Bernie's. David's assumption that he was a member of Mossad proved correct as the evening wore on.

There was much laughter and gaiety and the food was outstanding. The Israeli wine was superb and the piece de resistance was an impersonation of an intoxicated Turkish belly dancer energetically danced by a shirtless Dr. Cohen. Katinka laughed as she hadn't laughed before and both her mother and grand mother couldn't take their eyes off her.

In due course after the eating and the Turkish diva had put her shirt back on, the party followed the pattern of most small family and friend get togethers', the men sat out side on the verandah and the women remained inside talking of babies and recipes and clothing fashions and other subjects of high intellectual interest.

"Here are the names and locations of those dealers you wished to consult," said Bernie handing a sealed envelope to David "and Saul here has a list of all the various holdings and companies that the forensic investigation has so far revealed and that Mossad has managed to acquire. As you can see by the bulk of the documents His Lordships interests were vast and worldwide. Saul, give David a quick run through of what has been uncovered." Bernie asked.

"There are many nominees that have been uncovered but they all have been traced to the deceased banker. Mining consortiums and companies, media holdings which include many influential newspapers and opinion makers, varied industrial holdings and, of course, powerful banks and financial houses. Strangely there are some companies where His Lordship was less than astute. He bought a fishing company that has two large factory ships that were operating off Angola and another that had fishing boats on the Black Sea catching the small sardine called Kilka using unusual methods. These boats fished at night with underwater lights dangling at the end of a cable and the mouth of a large suction pipe near the light which was attached to a fish pump. The English Lord had a theory that those boats could be used along the South West African coast to catch sardine and anchovies. The theory never had a chance to be proved as he could not get the necessary licenses nor could he acquire the fishing quotas, so the boats and the factory ships are mothballed at Boma, a port up the Congo river about one hundred miles from the mouth , I think; I am not sure of the exact distance.

There are some other very small companies that the banker owned which can only be put down to sheer self indulgence. He owns a small saw mill in Russia on the eastern coast of the Black sea which converts the much sought after Circassian walnut into rifle and shot gun stock blanks and they have quite a high inventory of the wood; it is not traded but was kept purely for his own use. The extraction of the trees is done by a separate company which has the concession. That company is owned by Sir Horace Blakely, an English entrepreneur who has a number of companies in Russia and holdings in steel and engineering in the West.

The other strange asset is a small company with just a few employees based in London. This company has a workshop which hand crafts custom designed furniture and restores antiques, including furniture, clocks and other valuable artifacts, and would you believe, His Lordship used to go to that work shop regularly and personally work with hand tools on the restoration and crafting of furniture. The men there say he was highly skilled and were unaware of either his title or his vast wealth.

It was his stress relieving hobby about which he was quite passionate. He even restocked a rifle to a fairly high standard." Saul concluded and handed a heavy parcel of bound up files and documents.

Bernie and David were flabbergasted.

"My God, the man had a soul" said David.

"However," continued Saul "not a single clue as to where the cargo ship with the enriched uranium plant machinery on board sailed to after it left the Black Sea via the Dardanelles. Nothing."

"Anything else," asked a bemused Bernie,

"Yes, that hunting outfitter in Zambia whose reputation for solid hunting expertise you two fucked up also belonged to the banker. His Lordship's aircraft company owns three executive jets and three helicopters. One of the jets is based in England, one in the USA and one in Rep. South Africa at Johannesburg, as are two of the helicopters. Now here is another anomaly, the third helicopter is based at Kinshasa in the Democratic Republic of the Congo. All aircraft have a full compliment of pilots and ground staff and in South Africa a full team of maintenance technicians. The aircraft are never hired out but are lent to various heads of state in Africa and their ministers.

There was an exception recently in the Congo, the aircraft were not made available for the late president to escape although it is on record that he requested the aircraft to evacuate him repeatedly; this leaves no doubt as to who instigated the coup that toppled him and killed him."

"A most resourceful and diligent banker," Bernie sighed.

"The Sir Horace Blakely you mentioned who has the timber concessions has an interesting association with the Russian mafia," said David and proceeded to tell them of Katinka's story and his own clash with the man,

"Could Mossad perhaps look into him?" asked David,

"We will tell you where and exactly when his mother went into labor and precisely when his bowels work and when he farts within the next three weeks," answered Saul.

"When did you learn about this?" asked Bernie.

"Shortly after I had left you, the other day; that's the day he was having a meeting with Mr. Isaacs," said David.

"Isaacs did not mention this and he is supposed to be a Mossad informant. I had better pass this information on. Money can turn all men but perhaps he didn't think it important; but it must be checked." said Saul.

Rachel came out onto the verandah and said,

"We ladies feel neglected; I am now serving coffee or tea if you wish."

The men got up and went inside

After coffee, David and the ladies said their farewell and David said to Bernie,

"Please give me your address and contact number in Israel?"

"The information is in the envelope I gave you" he replied.

They left the house and made their way back to the mansion.

Chapter Seventeen

The telephones were vulnerable, David knew, even if they were not tapped. The American security administration, it was rumored, had a super computer that monitored every telephone conversation in the world and was programmed to react whenever key words were spoken, such as money. David wanted to make arrangements with the Swiss bank that Bernie had recommended, to open an account for himself that would involve millions of dollars, possibly more than a billion; it would have to be a one on one meeting.

The flight to Switzerland was quick and pleasant and David soon found the Swiss bank he was looking for. It was tucked away unobtrusively in a side street in a quiet backstreet in Berne.

After outlining his requirements to the Swiss manager, who spoke impeccable English, David asked the inevitable question about secrecy.

"We, Sir, have a long history of complete integrity and secrecy regarding our client's affairs. It is true that the pressure applied to our government has resulted in our paying lip service to their instructions. We have people world wide who advise us whether a client is abusing our facilities. If a client is reported to us as having any links to any criminal elements or crime of any sort, we report the matter of his deposits to the government concerned but if the client is a bona fide business man such as you are, your secrets are safe with us.

Let us commence and open your account which only has a number and which only you know, apart from three of our highest executives who are all family members and are the owners of this house. We suggest that when you transfer funds to us, it is not done electronically, a system we do not favor for some transactions but which are adequate for others. We will advise on the instruments to use for the large sums you will be depositing," the manager explained.

The flight back to England was pleasant and David sat up with Jim in the cockpit until the descent commenced when the co-pilot resumed his seat.

The next day, David visited the diamond dealer and apprised him of the quantities of diamonds he intended to bring to him after a satisfactory arrangement for the transaction had been concluded. The dealer said that small manageable bite sized chunks should be dealt with at the rate of one bite per week and the financial instrument that would be tendered as payment would satisfy whichever bank he dealt with.

In preparation for the money transactions, David spent an entire day in the shooting tunnel in the gunroom practicing with the silenced gun that Bernie and Mossad had supplied. The holster needed a small alteration and an equally small adjustment. He would use Jim to bypass Swiss airport checks, an inconvenience that pilots could easy circumvent. His first deposit would be all the bearer bonds and any share certificates that were kept in the same files would placed in the Swiss bank's safety deposit system.

The deposit went off smoothly and David's account was credited with six hundred and thirty million dollars. He flew back to England a happy man.

On his second visit to the diamond dealer, anticipating that he may be watched, he strapped one packet of diamonds, carefully flattened, to his stomach and chose a suit that had a loose fitting jacket that aided in the concealment of the slight bulge. The deal went of smoothly and David received negotiable instruments to the value of just over a hundred million dollars, seemingly His Lordship's idea of a bite sized chunk and he was sure that the remaining seven packets would be the same.

David deposited the money the next day and as he flew back home he decided to cool it for a few weeks as he was certain that Jim would have reported the flights to MI6.

The next few days, David spent with the ladies exploring the estate and meeting the foresters and the horticulturists and the game keepers. Being shown around by the experts was enlightening. The late banker had spared no expense in ensuring that everything that those experts did was done correctly and that they had all the equipment they needed. The picnics were delightful and Margaret said to David while Katinka and her mother were frolicking about,

"I hope all the estates affairs are settled by the time our baby is born."

"Yes, they will be, both Mossad and British intelligence are involved and as soon as one particular transaction that His Lordship was conducting, and, thank God, was prevented by his death from being completed, has been unraveled, we will be able to concentrate all our energies on our family and their happiness.

Towards the end of the week, David had his driver take him out to Romford, a suburb in the east side of London where, in a pleasant side street His Lordship's antique restoration and furniture making workshop was located. He entered the premises and in the reception area asked the pleasant young woman seated at a desk if he could see the manager. The girl phoned through and after ringing off said that the manager would be coming through from the workshop presently.

Displayed on the walls of the reception area were large photographs of various pieces of furniture which seemed to David to be of exquisite design and manufacture.

The manger arrived, an elderly man in a white dustcoat and smelling of exotic woods, a fragrance very much to David's liking. After introducing themselves to each other, the old man ushered David into his own office.

"How can I help you?" The manager asked.

"I represent the owner of this establishment and there are some important matters that I must discuss with you," David began

"Ah you mean Mr. Jones, how is he, we haven't seen him for some time?"

"I think there is some mistake, Mr. Jones you say is the owner. Could you describe him for me?" David asked.

"Good lord that is an unusual request," exclaimed the old man but nevertheless gave David a detailed description of the banker which was very accurate.

"Your Mr. Jones, in fact, was Lord Montdrago, the international banker and financier, and I am the deceased Lord Montdrago's son in law. I am married to his only daughter, Katinka"

"But Mr. Jones told us his daughter's name was Debra, a beautiful blond lady whom I glimpsed in his car one day when he was visiting the workshop. Can you show proof of what you say?" the old man was thoroughly alarmed.

"Yes, I shall give you the name of the large London legal firm which is handling all the estate's business. However, the reason that I am here is to assure you and your staff that your jobs are secure and that everything will continue as they always have, in fact we may have to bring a lot more work to you and invest more money if necessary. Please tell me more about His Lordship; from what we can establish he used this workshop as a sort of therapeutic antidote to the high pressure world of high finance. Was he really skilled, or did he just assist the men, or did he build pieces on his own?" asked David.

"Occasionally he would assist the men if there was a particularly difficult assembly but usually he worked on his own. He had his own private workshop cum office attached to the main workshop and he would while away the hours there. He never allowed anyone into that private retreat and it was kept locked when he was not here, the keys are in the safe in my office. I will get them and accompany you to the private workshop." the manager explained.

His Lordship's private workshop was an eye opener. The hand tools in their glass fronted cabinets told it all to David; they spoke of a craftsman who was more than just competent; the tools were well chosen and although well worn were razor sharp and well maintained.

"Could you leave me here for a while and if, after you have explained to the men the current situation, there are any queries, I shall be glad to answer them," David said.

The manager withdrew and left David to browse around and investigate. There were a few half finished pieces of wood on the work bench and on the shelf behind and above the bench, which was attached to the wall, were some miniature Seaman's Chests, made of highly figured quarter sawn oak with brass straps and hinges.

He wandered into the paneled office that was richly furnished, as befitted an office in an establishment that crafted the beautiful pieces, and which smelt of perfectly seasoned wood.

David went through all the drawers in the desk and found only very well drawn sketches, to scale, of period pieces and the sketches had the familiar signature at the bottom. There was a bookcase, well made and of unusual design, which housed many specially bound books covering most aspects of wood identification and various classics by Sheridan, Applewhite and the "Gentleman's directory" by Chippendale. The great French designers were represented too. David was impressed.

Before going back into the main workshop, David paused at the bench and took down one of the oak model chests. He lifted the brass locking devise and lifted the lid. Inside was a rolled up old fashioned naval chart covering most of the Atlantic and the Mediterranean and the Black sea. It was about a yard square when rolled out and it was a reproduction by a well known art house in London. His Lordship had drawn on it and there were many scribblings and figures in the familiar hand. David rolled it up and decided to take it with him.

The staff were all lined up and waiting for him.

"The men and the office lady want to know if they are to be given written confirmation that their jobs are secure and any new conditions that may have to comply with?" asked the manager,

"Of course, I will send them down in a few days signed by His Lordships heir, my wife, and counter signed by the senior partner of the law firm handling the estate. I would have you know that when it becomes known that Lord Montdrago spent time here, many newsmen and nosy parkers will come and worry you, so I shall send two of the estates security staff to stay here in your front office to steer away the unwelcome. You will also receive a written commission to design and build a baby's cradle, a replica of those built in the days of Chippendale and Sheridan, to be crafted from the finest walnut and finished with a modern finish which is non toxic and durable; my wife is expecting our first child. I shall call in from time to time. Incidentally I am a time served Gunsmith who still has a share in my family's gun makers shop outside Edinburgh, so you can rest assured that I understand your worth as craftsmen and shall see that you are always treated with the respect that a craftsman deserves." David bid the men farewell and left.

As soon as he had returned to the estate, David summoned the chief of security and gave him his instructions as to the posting of security at the furniture factory and also to contact the contractors who did the electronic work and to have them install a VCR, attached to surveillance cameras that monitored all visitors to the small furniture workshop. Strangers had to sign in and produce some sort of identification. David explained that as soon as word got out of His Lordships strange hobby and his anonymous behavior, there would be all sorts of dubious people calling on the workshop. It occurred to David that the manager and his foreman should be brought to the estate to discuss the matter of the babies cradle with the womenfolk and he instructed the chief to arrange it for about ten am the following day.

That evening during supper, David told the ladies of his visit to the furniture makers workshop and what he had learned of the late bankers eccentric behavior; they were astounded and comments flew back and forth. He then said that the manager and the foreman were coming the following day to discuss the building of a cradle. The conversation became animated as to whether it should be a cradle or a traditional Russian crib or a rocking cradle or a cot. David suggested all three be made and excused himself, saying he was going up to his study.

The study was a large one and attached to the late bankers bedroom. David and Katinka had moved into the banker's personal suite of rooms as soon as they were married. The study was the nerve center of His Lordships Empire. It was lavishly equipped and furnished. There was a large leather topped desk and a separate table against the one wall with the tools of the banker's trade. A computer, a printer and a scanner; nearby was an elaborate telecommunication center with a phone and a specialized computer that not only had a scrambler but a monitor with a speed dialing feature connected to other phones around the world which also had scrambling devises. On the wall were fixed half a dozen clocks all reflecting the time at different locations around the world where His Lordships business interests lay. An ingenious electronic devise connected to a separate monitor with a printer attached continually spewed out information that bankers need such as stock market data, political events, coups, riots, and any other event that could affect the strategy of a big player in the world of finance.

David had smelt it the first time that he had entered the study; this was where the brilliant mind of Lord Montdrago schemed, strategized, manipulated and gave orders that started coups and even liquidated those that frustrated his schemes.

Incongruously, in the far corner of the study stood a cabinet that concealed a water faucet, a kettle, a coffee peculator, a miniature refrigerator, a teapot and cups and saucers. On the shelves were expensive tidbits, dried fruit, biscuits and various custom blends of coffee and teas. The banker was well equipped to work around the clock if proved necessary.

The large bundle of documents that Saul had given him which detailed the many interests that the banker had investments in, was on the desk and spread out alongside was the pseudo ancient map that had been rolled up in the small wooden chest.

David considered the map. There was a line drawn from Odessa on the northern coast of the Black Sea down to a small port, Sochi, on the south east coast of the Black Sea. The small Russian saw mill, listed in the Banker's portfolio, which specialized in producing Walnut stock blanks, was located within a reasonable distance of the port. The country was wild and mountainous and the walnut trees were not from a formal planted orchard but were wild and sparsely located and difficult to harvest. Walnut trees that struggled to grow in inhospitable soil produced magnificent wood as connoisseurs knew.

The documents showed that only about three or four trees were felled per month; hardly a commercial proposition, more like another of His Lordship's self indulgences. But what was the significance of the line on the map? Both Mossad and MI6 had known that the cargo ship that transported the stolen nuclear machinery had been loaded at Odessa before it disappeared. And what did the letters and words mean that were scribbled next to the line; rich. fac. k. b. trans.?

David pondered for a long time and he realized that he would have to visit the saw mill as soon as possible. Where was the nearest airport and would an executive jet alert the Russian Mafia? David was sitting at the desk of the late master of the art of innovative, manipulative and cunning implementation of successful action, surely, he thought, he should derive inspiration from this study where many earth shaking events had originated?

He phoned Margaret's rooms and told her to tell his wife that he would be shut up in the study for a few hours, so she must not hurry back on his account, but must just be happy with her kinsfolk and avoid gossiping about his bad habits.

He made some coffee using a special blend that he had not tried before. He was staring at the large bay window at the far end of the study which overlooked the lake and at the pair of expensive Leica Binoculars, mounted on a tri pod which had been used to watch the water fowl, many of which migrated from the cold Russian winters to this very lake. Some species molted while in Britain, and regrew their feathers before returning to the swamps and marshes in Mother Russia; a kind of transference of plumage from one lake to another. An ignorant but enthusiastic bird watcher would assume if he found the foreign feathers that there were exotic waterfowl in Britain that no one knew of.

What had initiated those strange and irrelevant thoughts, David wondered. He returned to the map and the strange thoughts did not leave him; what if some of those birds originated near Sochi and transferred a little bit of that border region between Georgia and the Ukraine to Britain. Suddenly it hit him, his subconscious mind was stressing transference and maybe the nuclear machinery had been transferred to another ship at Sochi? The word rich on the map referred to uranium enrichment plant. Could the word fac refer to the large factory ships now fishing or waiting to fish off the Angolan coast? The letters k and b could refer to Kilka fishing boats and the word trans was obviously transfer. Yes, that was it, he thought, excitement overwhelming him that was it.

He and a team of his security staff could locate the factory ships and the fishing boats and search them. If he did find the missing plant, then what? If he told Mossad, they would take the plant back to Israel and would then be less amenable to any restraint that the USA might wish to place on them, although it was rumored that the Americans had supplied them with small tactical nuclear weapons; but with the Russian plant the sky would be the limit and they could produce weapons of any size they wanted. If he told MI6, what devious game would they play in the murky world of national gamesmanship? The Romans had referred to Britain as Perfidious Albion and nothing had changed. Ideally, David thought, the agency that promised to sink all the ships that carried the deadly cargo would be a perfect recipient of the intelligence. Perhaps the Americans would be the best bet; yes they would certainly sink the boats with their horrible cargo. How to tell the Americans without the other agencies finding out? Jim, his pilot had been with MI6 a long time and he would almost certainly know several of his CIA counterparts, he would be the best person to ask; very subtlely and with great care.

It is imperative to visit the Russian Sawmill thought David, and as a gunsmith, with an interest in the gun making firm in Edinburgh which still operated under his name, it would be natural to buy some gunstock blanks whilst visiting his wife's newly acquired property. David could visualize Mr. Isaacs face when he approached him and told him what he was going to do and asking him and his colleagues to establish a price for the blanks, as David could not, without being thought to be biased. This piece of subterfuge would certainly give the impression of Scottish self interest and allay any suspicions that he had an ulterior motive for visiting the sawmill. He would phone Mr. Isaacs in the morning and also notify Jim of the impending flight. He would like to liquidate another packet of diamonds and deposit the money if he could stop off in Switzerland without arousing suspicion.

The next day after speaking to Mr. Isaacs who would notify him later in the day as to the gunstock prices, David drove out to the airport and caught Jim just before he was about to leave for London.

"I want to fly to Russia tomorrow to visit a sawmill that the Banker owned, it is near the port of Sochi on the East coast of the Black Sea and on the way, I want to stop off at Berne, you remember that I went there before to see if they would let me look into a safe deposit box which the banker kept there. Margaret seems to think that there may be some shares there. The bank wouldn't let me last time, but I have since faxed them all the documents to establish my bona fides so perhaps I will have better luck this time. Can you file a flight plan and arrange for the flight?" asked David.

"Sure thing, I will get on to it right away." Jim replied.

David who had raided the secret cache of diamonds early in the morning, continued on to London after leaving the airport and concluded the deal with another bite sized chunk of the high value merchandise which the dealer obviously relished.

They had taken off early and David had brought his silenced 45 rig which Jim assured him he could get through the customs at the airport in Russia. They landed in Switzerland and David soon concluded his business with the bank and they took off a few hours later.

"We will have to land at Krasnodar and then hire a car and drive down the coast to Sochi. There are some decent hotels near the airport where we can spend the night and leave early tomorrow as it is quite a long drive," said Jim.

The hotel at Krasnodar was not at all bad and after supper, they found themselves a secluded little nook near the bar and had a nightcap.

"Tell me Jim, do we ever liaise with members of the CIA? You know, of course that prior to joining you I had a loose relationship with Mossad through my friend Bernie Cohen, the in house doctor who shared a few tight moments with me. Why I ask, one Mossad member told me that members of the CIA are mostly untrustworthy and liable to let one down."

"That's true, but most agents unless tightly controlled usually know their counterparts on the other side and often all sorts of convoluted antics take place. I've only met one whom I would say could be trusted to play it straight down the line, and that's O'Reilly attached to the American science and technology organization based in London. He is lily white and does every thing according to the book. He has never pulled off any spectacular coups like the naughty boys of the CIA sometimes do."

"Is he a scientist?" asked David,

"Yes, he roamed around all sorts of remote corners mainly in the tropics researching certain species of plants and their possible use in medicine, that's why he was recruited into the CIA, he had a perfect cover for those far off places where a casual traveler would have immediately drawn suspicion on himself, but a man investigating plants was always considered harmless and generally helped by the locals. He is a bit of a bore and simply cannot stop talking about his beloved plants."

The conversation drifted onto the dangers and difficulties of the business they were in, and Jim reminded David to collect the 45 from him in the morning before they left as it would never do to arrive at the sawmill naked..

They arrived at Sochi after a long but not uninteresting drive and soon were directed to the Sawmill which was in the foothills of a rugged mountain range where the wild walnut trees grew. There was a village inn for travelers that occasionally drove through the district, within a few miles of the mill and they booked in.

It was late afternoon when they arrived at the mill and introduced themselves to the manager and David was surprised when he said in broken English that he had been told by telephone in a call from London to expect them. The mill was well equipped with modern machinery and the storeroom was full of correctly cut blanks with the grain taken into account so that it flowed along the length of the stock, where it should, without weakening those vital areas where recoil would split a stock if the grain was not exactly following the lines of the finished stock. The wood was beautiful, the color and figure sublime in the eyes of the gun maker.

"How many of those can we fly out in the jet?" David asked.

"It is more a question of how many we can get into the car," replied the pilot.

"London said that you were a hunter from Africa and that I should arrange for you to hunt a wild boar in the mountains, there are many where we cut the trees and I can provide the rifles." said the sawmill manager

"Come on Jim, why not?" asked David and Jim readily agreed.

"This young boy knows the mountains very well and he knows where to get the boars," with that the manager called over a young boy of about sixteen and instructed him in the local dialect.

"Can he speak English?" David asked,

"Yes I can," replied the boy in an accent that showed that he could and a lot better than the manager.

"Tomorrow morning then, after breakfast?" enquired David and the boy nodded his assent

"It is still light, could we see the rifles we are to use?" asked David,

"Yes, I bring them now," said the manager and went off to fetch them

The young boy went to the back of the building and returned shortly with two steaming hot cups of strong coffee. They were just finishing their coffee when the manager came back with the rifles. They were two old bolt action army rifles from the First World War; Mosin-Nagant model 91's a crude but reliable rifle shooting a seven point six two mm rimmed cartridge.

"Can we try them out and sight them now so that we are prepared for tomorrow?"

The manager looked alarmed and said quickly,

"Wait, I will change them for something better," and took the rifles back and dashed off.

"What does that mean David?" asked Jim.

"That means that we are being set up. I know, having recently sabotaged a professional hunter's rifle in Africa. However, wild boars seldom charge even when wounded, I suspect there is bigger game waiting for us, very dangerous game with two legs and the ability to ambush. We can call off the hunt now but that will only encourage an attempt when we are unarmed and probably distracted while driving.

Better we take them on whilst armed and aware. They probably want the rugged country where very few people go and there is many an impenetrable ravine to hide the bodies," David replied.

The manager hurried back into the building with another two similar rifles which he handed to David. David took them outside into the bright light and inspected them carefully. He noticed that the front sights had been tampered with on both rifles. The front sight blades dovetailed into their basis from right to left across the axis of the barrels and both had witness marks indicating alignment after sighting in. The witness marks were a scribed line which should show precisely when the line was perfectly mated but, someone had tapped the blades to one side and the witness lines failed to mate up by about an eighth of an inch. David estimated that the bullet would strike about a yard or more to the side of the intended mark at about a hundred yards. Fortunately just a tap or two would realign the witness marks.

"That's just fine "David said to the manager with a grin and turned to the boy,

"See you in the morning, we will be at the inn, fetch us there,"

They both clambered into their hired car with the rifles and the boxes of ammunition and drove off to the inn.

Later in the inn's cozy bar after supper, David explained the sabotage of the sights and that he would have them realigned within a few minutes in the morning before breakfast. The beer was exceptionally good but bearing in mind what tomorrow held, they just had two and then retired for the night.

The boy was waiting for them after breakfast and they set off in the hired car,

"Where are you taking us to?" asked David,

"The manager told me to take you to a place where we drag out the trees after we have cut them down. It is thick forest and in some places quite steep with some deep gorges. I don't know why he says we must hunt there, there are no wild boars there, it is too rough and rocky and there is no food for pigs," said the boy with a puzzled frown.

"That's fine, just stop about half a kilometer before we get there and we will go the rest of the way by foot." said David.

They stopped and David asked the boy,

"Where exactly did the manager tell you to we must park the car and then where must we walk to begin the hunt?"

"Half a kilometer ahead, a small logger's track turns to the right into the forest and it goes in about two hundred meters and ends. That is where I was told to stop the car and get out and begin the hunt."

"This is what we will do, Jim. I will get out here and walk into the forest about two hundred yards to the right and then I will stalk forward, parallel to this road which will bring me approximately to where we are supposed to stop and begin hunting. Hopefully I will have located our prey and can engage them from an advantageous position. What you must do is to give me about five minutes and then cruise to the turn off but don't drive in. Stop there and open and close the doors, banging them loudly and calling out loudly as if you are directing me. That should stir up some movement so I can see our hidden ambushers but do not come up into the forest until I shout the all clear.

If after gunshots, I don't shout the all clear, clear out and head for the Inn and wait; if I am not back at the Inn within an hour, call in the local police and tell them that we were shot at while out hunting and notify MI6. After you have banged the car doors and the action starts, get back into the car, and hold the rifle out the window loaded and ready. There is no safety catch on these rifles only a method of twisting the cocking piece to make the loaded gun, safe. Don't touch it, leave the rifle cocked and ready to fire and prepare to pull out fast."

"Roger David, good luck."

David moved into the woods and calling on all his experience from his African hunting days, he silently, with intense concentration and with the excited anticipation of a born hunter, slid through the trees and the undergrowth. The ground was sloping slightly and within five minutes he could just make out the track ahead. He stopped and carefully swung his gaze around, slowly looking in the shadows and at every piece of cover that the ambushers may be using. After a minute, he heard Jim banging the car doors and out of the corner of his eye he caught a slight movement. There was one of them, standing in deep shade at the side of a large tree not fifty yards away. The car door banging continued and the man was concentrating on the track and brought his scoped rifle up and was taking a dead rest against the tree. David slid forward silently to within ten yards of the man and drew out the silenced 45 from its shoulder holster. He quietly placed his rifle on the ground, stood in a steady two handed pistol holding stance, took careful aim and fired. With the almost inaudible plop, the man dropped down with the rifle making a slight clatter as it fell on some rocky ground. At the sound, David caught another movement a hundred yards down to his left; there stood the other man, rifle also held to his shoulder pointing down the track. Another door bang concentrated his attention on the track and David picked up the rifle and put the 45 back into its shoulder holster. He, too, took a dead rest against a tree and drew a bead on the other man's knee. Hoping that the sights were accurate after their tampering, and knowing full well the limitations of plain iron sights, David squeezed off a shot. The loud report shattered the silence of the forest as did the scream of pain the surprised ambusher gave out as he collapsed.

David cupped both hands to his mouth and yelled out as loud as he could,

"All clear, all clear."

Jim and the boy came running up the track and saw David walking towards the spot where the man had fallen, holding the 45 in one hand and the rifle at the trail in the other. They both arrived at the desperate man who was grunting and whining with pain, together. The boy was wide eyed and David said to him,

"They would have shot you too after they had killed us so there were no witnesses,"

"I know, they are bad men," he said in a fearful tone.

"Where is the other one, or was there only one, I heard only one shot?" asked Jim.

"The other is just up there; I used the silenced 45 which you so generously smuggled through. Our friend here is lucky but his luck will run out if he doesn't tell us what we want to know. I will even deny him a tourniquet if he doesn't talk fast and he is bleeding heavily." David said in a steely voice,

"Who sent you?" he asked as he drew out the hand gun and held it to the wounded man's head.

"The Colonel, Colonel Dempster, he is involved with our employer, Sir Horace Blakely. Please help me, please"

There was a stunned silence and then Jim said,

"Only two things are going through my mind at this moment. One, we are in a dangerous pickle and two, that you are very good at this killing business. I have never shot a fire arm in anger in my life."

David could see that Jim was scared.

"Search him while I stand over, then remove his rifle from his reach and then put on a tourniquet while I go up and search the dead man."

At the mention of a dead man, the bleeding thug groaned and turned his head and began to weep.

After searching the body, David dragged it down to where the others were standing. The tourniquet was in place and the bleeding had stopped.

"We have to make some decisions with as much forethought as we can muster," said David, "let me ask the boy a few questions first. What is your name boy and do you live with your parents?"

"My name is Ivan. My father was a soldier and was killed in Afghanistan, my mother died soon after. I live with the managers friends, who live near the sawmill," the boy answered.

"Listen very carefully, Ivan, my name is David McAlpine, I own the sawmill and many other businesses and I am very rich. These men that tried to kill us today work for people who want to steal the things that I own. Now I want you to work for me and you can work in any of my companies, and can be trained to do any type of work that you want to and can live in any country where my businesses operate. Do you accept my offer?"

"Oh yes, oh yes" answered Ivan, his eyes shining.

"Could we fly him out with us without any papers and fix it all when we get back to England, Jim?"

"Piece of old cake, with my MI6 contacts, he will become a British citizen within a month," answered Jim.

"Now, Ivan, tell me all about the sawmill and the work and the strangers that have visited from time to time?" asked David.

"Well, Sir, we don't cut many trees, they are so few and we sometimes do other work. Some months ago we all had to go to the docks to help take many big crates and machines from a very big ship and then to load them into two big factory fishing boats. There were also some small fishing boats which we loaded with small boxes that came to the port by trucks. One of the drivers said they were guns for Africa and that they had been supplied by the gangs of Moscow."

"What happened to the empty cargo ship?"

"The crew said that it would sail to the scrap yards in India as soon as its cargo had been transferred to the fish factory boats," answered Ivan.

"If there are any streams around here, try and get some water for this man Ivan," ordered David.

"There is a flask of coffee in the car, I will go and fetch it,"

"We will go with you and you can bring it back to this man and watch over him as me and my friend want to be alone at the car as we have to talk." Said David and they all walked down to the car.

Sitting in the car after Ivan had taken the coffee up to the wounded man, David said to Jim,

185

"We now know where the missing nuclear plant may be and we know that Colonel Dempster was involved with the attempted assassination of both of us. Your co-pilot is back at the jet, what do you know about him, could he possibly be the Colonel's man?"

"I don't know, he was hired by Lord Montdrago. He is a very tight lipped man and never discusses his family or his past flying work."

"In that case we will assume that he is hostile and will take that into account. I think that as soon as we get back to England, I will hire another co-pilot for you and transfer the present one. I will also make arrangements for our debugging experts to sweep the aircraft for hidden recording devices and if you can recommend a company that is expert at checking aircraft electronics and radio and navigational aids, we will get them in to thoroughly check the Jet and the work must be done quickly. With the new developments, the jet will be needed to be ready at all times.

First, we must neutralize the sawmill manager so he cannot report back to the Colonel or others. Remember the CIA man, O'Reilly you mentioned, we should consider bringing him into the loop as both Mossad and the Colonel will want the location of the nuclear machinery. My personal view is to tell the Americans as they will definitely destroy the machinery whereas both Mossad and the Colonel and his Russian friends will recycle the plant and put it back into production which will frustrate the West's nuclear anti- proliferation efforts.

The Factory ships are stranded up the Congo River at the port of Boma as far as I know, waiting for operating licenses, which is just a subterfuge.. There is an even larger facility further up the river at the port of Matadi, just below the Livingstone falls which is an impassable barrier to any sea going ships; although there are large vessels above the falls which can navigate the rest of that large river. What puzzles me is why His late Lordship took the machinery down to Africa when the buyers were supposed to be in the Middle East. Was he negotiating a deal with the Republic of South Africa?But enough of speculation and planning for events ahead, what do we do now with the wounded man and the Sawmill manager, not forgetting that I do want to take some walnut blanks back with me," said the gunsmith with a laugh, "We will have to take a chance on the immediate course of action. I searched the body and have his passport and you have the wounded ones too, quickly copy all the details down and we will take the passports back and replace them. How much cash do you have on you?"

"About five hundred American dollars and a small amount of local currency," answered Jim,

"I have about five thousand American Dollars and some local currency too. Let's walk back to the wounded thug and negotiate a deal."

As soon as they had joined Ivan and the thug, David said,

"I am a very rich man and have vast resources and a large security force with some very dangerous men amongst them who will hunt you down and kill you if you don't cooperate and do exactly as I say. We are leaving now and Ivan will go and fetch the police. He will tell them that he witnessed the manager shoot you and your companion and then rob you while you were on this hunt which the manager had invited you to attend with him. You can say that he robbed both you and your companion of about three thousand dollars and stick to that story. They will take you to hospital and do not attempt to contact the Colonel or Sir Horace or his staff. I have your passport details and if you betray us, you will be as dead as your friend within days. Do you understand?"

"Yes Sir." the man answered through clenched teeth.

"Just hang on, the police will be here within an hour with a doctor," said David as he motioned the other two to follow him to the car,

"Don't forget the flask and the rifles. We must hurry."

"Ivan, when we get back, go and take the police to that wounded man and tell them that you saw the manager rob them and that he threatened to shoot you too if you told anybody what you had witnessed. Say that you had come straight to them as soon as you had the chance to run away. Get away from the police as quickly as you can and meet us at the Inn and we will leave for the airfield at Krasnodar and fly off to England immediately. Do not bother to bring any clothes, you must be as fast as you can and we must be out of the country before the police become suspicious and want to question us. Be very, very fast. We will drop you off near the police station and then go and see the manager." David instructed the eager boy.

The surprised manager greeted them with caution and David said as he handed back the rifles,

"We had some trouble with two men in the forest and must leave immediately, here is Three thousand dollars for you to keep quiet about the trouble until we have left, in the meantime fill the car boot up with some of the best blanks and also some on the floor beneath the rear seats."

The manager was smirking and gloating and thanking David profusely as he shouted for some men to load the car.

"Hurry, hurry," David urged and they were driving off within ten minutes on their way to the Inn.

David settled the account, with a handsome tip saying they would be leaving right away and driving down to Turkey for the next stage of their tour of the region. They ordered some tea and waited for Ivan. He was late, arriving an hour later. They all got into the car and Jim drove off heading back to the airport.

"There was terrible trouble and the police arrested the manager and when they searched him they found three thousand American dollars, they took him away together with the wounded man and the doctor who said that they must go to the hospital first. They left me at the sawmill and said that I must be prepared to go to the police station tomorrow to give them more evidence, so I borrowed a friends bicycle and rode to the Inn."

At the airport, Jim filed a flight plan and arranged to drive right up to the jet taking Ivan as a servant to help load the luggage and saying that he would send him out of the aircraft parking area as soon as he had done with him and as David had instructed, gave the official a five hundred dollar tip. It was late so they spent the night at the hotel adjacent to the airport

David boarded the Jet early the next morning as soon as he had cleared officialdom, again with a five hundred Dollar tip which expedited his progress. Ivan had sneaked through with Jim via the flight crew entrance to the jet parking area. They took off and soared up into the blue with the power and panache that only an executive jet can muster. Ivan was thrilled and gaping with wonder at the sights which a first ever flight always engenders.

Chapter Eighteen

David advised Jim to get the electronic experts in to attend to the jet immediately and he took Ivan back to the estate with him after phoning to let them know he was coming.

He was met by an agitated Margaret who said that a friend of Bernie's was waiting to see him in the conference room who said he had checked with flight control as to the ETA of the jet at the airfield. He gave his name as Saul and said that David had met him at Bernie's home.

Saul greeted David cautiously and looking nervous said to David

"I will not beat about the bush. Word has come to us that you now know the location of the nuclear plant. It is vital that Israel obtains the plant as soon as possible and our sources say that the Russian mafia are closing in as they too suspect that you know where the plant is. We took the precaution of taking your wife and her mother to a safe place where no one can touch them. We told her that you had asked us to. They are with Bernie in Israel under heavy protection. We advise you that British intelligence has been penetrated as it usually is and if they approach you, to be circumspect in your dealings with them. But to the kernel of the problem, could you help us to take possession of the nuclear plant immediately?"

"When will my family be returned to me?" asked David in a tight voice

"Emigration officials are very difficult in Israel but we could speed things up. We could even eliminate those Russians that pose a threat to your family. This affair of the nuclear plant is such a worry to our government. They would risk a rift in their relations with Russia and sanction a promiscuous strike against the Russian mafia; what is your answer?"

"The world of the spy is a curious one. I have only just been told of the location of the plant, and why did the double agent not tell you himself?" asked David coolly.

"He says that you are a natural born killer and he is frightened of you," answered Saul, "He said that he would be dead within an hour of you finding out of his duplicity and wants us to proceed amicably. He also says that you are both cunning and devious, characteristics that Mossad is well aware of, and that you have probably made irrevocable arrangements that anticipate his status and that he might be killed even if you do not do it personally."

"Jim flatters me. Come back tomorrow and I will tell you all you wish to know. I await your visit at nine am tomorrow." David rose and left the room.

David first sought out Margaret and found her in her room. She gave him Katinka's letter which had been brought to her by that same Saul several days before David's return. It was a cheery note which just informed Margaret that David had instructed his friends to take her and her mother out to Israel to stay with Bernie for a few days until David came back from his trip. They said she was in danger from the same people that had been disposed of in her father's conference room and who had kept her mother in detention in Russia. They had whisked her away so quickly that she had been unable to wait for Margaret to return from London. She ended by saying that she was sure David was right to have her protected by his friends and that she would be home soon.

"I was tricked into going to London that day by a telephone message from Rachel who said to meet her in London at Claridges hotel and not to tell the others. She stressed that it was urgent and that if she was late, to just wait for her. She never arrived so I eventually came home and was given that note by one of the staff. David when will all this end?"

"Soon now, Katinka is in no danger and is probably safer where she is as those bloody Russians tried to ambush me and kill me while

I was at the sawmill in Russia. That business concerning his Lordships deal with the nuclear machinery has reached a climax and I am going to the American secret service that has a vital interest in that deal for help. Excuse me now; I have to go to my study to use the special equipment there to get the ball rolling with the Americans." David said as he took his leave and made his way to the study.

Sitting in the study, he reviewed the events of the past few days. Jim had given him a break by not mentioning the intelligence they had obtained from Ivan as to the transferring of the plant from one ship to the others. This had forced Mossad to deal with him face to face. The CIA man whom Jim had recommended in a roundabout way would obviously belong to Mossad or be a sympathizer. David had made up his mind and picked up the phone. The American Embassy's number was on the bankers speed dial system. A lady with a voice of authority answered the phone.

"Good day, I am David McAlpine, the son in law of the late banker, Lord Montdrago and I wish to speak to the Ambassador or his private secretary on an urgent matter,"

"Certainly Sir, I will put you through to him."

After a lengthy pause, a firm strong voice answered,

"Ambassador Brady, How can I be of assistance?"

David went straight to the point

"I have information and the location of a missing nuclear plant that was stolen in Russia and which my late unlamented father in law, Lord Montdrago was involved with. I am being harassed by both Mossad and the British MI6 and I would like a senior intelligence officer of the CIA, a genuine agent on nobody else's payroll to visit me this evening at the Montdrago estate as the Mossad agent in London will be here tomorrow morning at nine am for information. They say that they have taken my wife to Israel in protective custody and will return her when I give them the information they need. There are other players and only I know the full story. Can I expect your man this evening then?"

"Ah, the gunsmith, we will both leave immediately. Expect us within an hour or so, Thank you," he said as he put down the phone.

The ambassador was as good as his word and he and his senior CIA agent arrived on time. The ambassador was a tall, man with silver hair accentuated by a deep tan, David judged him to be about sixty. His eyes were intelligent and piercing and not without humor. The CIA man was also tall and very muscular, about forty with a pugnacious air and unlike the ambassador spoke in a clipped manner when he was introduced to David, his name was distinctly Russian, Kerensky.

David led them into the conference room and immediately launched into the events since he had been employed as a Gunsmith leaving out only the secret rooms and the bankers treasure, He concluded the monologue with the events at the sawmill.

"Are you sure that Colonel Dempster ordered the hit and that he is colluding with Sir Horace Blakely?" asked Kerensky.

"Yes, the wounded hit man told me that and as he was in fear of his life and in pain, it has to be true. I promised him that he would live and would be given medical attention if he told the truth." David replied,

"Why did you join MI6?"

"I was recruited by Dempster my former commanding officer when I was in the SAS and what with the Russians and Mossad, I was in the middle and needed the help of an interested party who had the expertise and the muscle. Now is all I want is those ships and that bloody machinery at the bottom of the sea and I think the USA is the only power that wants the same and does not want to use the nuclear plant for political purposes."

The ambassador spoke for the first time, quietly and with authority,

"We have been following events concerning that nuclear plant for some time and naturally, since your joining the Montdrago staff, you have interested us immensely. We have applauded the way you have dealt efficiently with the evil men that seemed part of this illustrious mansion, but those first four bodies that included the two security guards, what was that all about?"

"I think that was a piece of opportunistic free enterprise, Sir. I caught two of the strangers in my wife to be's apartment and they were armed and were in cahoots with the guards in a kidnapping attempt,"

"If you could attach a label to all the corpses that you create, it would cut down on the overtime we pay our staff in following up these unhappy events," said the Ambassador, "and now for the sixty four dollar question, where is the plant hidden?"

"It is stowed aboard two fishing factory ships belonging to His Lordships estate and they are tied up at Boma, a port up the Congo River and also in that vicinity is a fleet of former Russian fishing boats loaded with arms for sale to certain African states."

"I suppose the estate will want to be compensated for the boats if we sink them?" asked the ambassador,

"No Sir, we just want those weapons destroyed," said David emphatically, "and the inheritance of the evil lord to be sanitized and cleansed. The Mossad man will be here at nine tomorrow morning, what do I do?"

"Tell him the location of the nuclear plant and leave the rest to us." Kerensky said.

"Now if you will excuse us David we have a lot to do and we have to do it very quickly. Our deepest gratitude to you, you do not realize the full ramifications of the nuclear deal," the ambassador said as the two men rose and left purposely.

The Americans had just left when there was a call from the security guard at the main estate entrance gate saying that there was avionics service van that had arrived from the airfield with a young Russian boy answering to the name of Ivan and twenty five pieces of wood; should they be allowed to enter? David instructed them to come to the mansions main front entrance and to bring in the boy and help him to unload the wood and stash it in the ante room at the gunrooms door. David went down to welcome Ivan. With the stock blanks stacked neatly on the ante rooms table, David thanked the security men and took Ivan up to Margaret's apartment and introduced Ivan to her.

"Could you allocate him decent living quarters and tomorrow have someone to take him into London and buy him some clothes and foot ware and anything else that he needs," asked David with a smile at the boys obvious delight.

"I will take him myself and together with the driver, we will turn him into a Londoner of fashion but as soon as he has seen his room and washed up, we will all have supper together. I can see that he only has the clothes he is standing up in, so I shall ask the chief of security to find someone of his size to give him a change of clothes which we will replace tomorrow," said Margaret and clapped the boy on his shoulder in an affectionate gesture.

David spent a restless night, although he was worried about Katinka, he knew that Bernie would protect and look after her, nevertheless the audacity of Mossad infuriated him and emphasized the vital importance of this operation was to Israel.

As had become an increasingly enjoyable habit, he arose at dawn and padded through to the study and sat at the bay window with the binoculars and watched the waterfowl coming and going in the early morning light. He made a mental note to instruct the horticulturist to plant more wild rice and other natural foods that would satisfy the migrant water birds. He was taking in the beauty of the scene when the telephone rang and the scrambler light was flashing. This caused David to be very alert as that had never happened since he had come to occupy the banker's suite.

"McAlpine," he answered,

The sharp abrupt voice of the CIA London head said,

"Kerensky. We have worked non stop since we left you yesterday, this operation is of the highest priority and importance. We instructed our man in Mossad last night to reveal to Mossad the location of the nuclear machinery whereas we had previously told him to with hold the information to force Mossad to approach you. Our man had already given us that information, before you contacted us but we came immediately you called yesterday to gather up the loose ends and establish a working arrangement with you.

Our other man, Isaacs had discovered the late Lord Montdrago's financing and involvement in the Congo coup and the providing of white mercenaries to lead it. He contacted the new Congo President last night and informed him of the death of his English Financier and reassured him that under your, David McAlpine's leadership, things would continue as normal and that he could rely on your support. Furthermore he told the President that you would be visiting shortly and to expect you. Your identification will be no problem because when Lord Montdrago hired those ex SAS men, he hired ten of them. Three stayed in England with His Lordship as his body guards and the other seven were sent to the Congo to train and lead the men of the successful coup.

The leader of the mercenaries served with you in the SAS. His was known to you as a Captain Billy Steele, now known as Colonel Steele.

The factory ships are heavily guarded by Congolese soldiers commanded by well trained mercenaries. The Israelis have been allowed to learn all this by some very clever work by our double agents and they know that you will have to go with them to organize the release of the boats, so expect their man, at the meeting you are having with him this morning, to insist on your accompanying them. They have already notified our double agent, known to you as Jim, to file a flight plan and be ready to fly to the Congo today. You may ask why the US did not just go and take those boats. Politically it would have been disastrous. Furthermore, the blood bath that would have ensued would have focused the world's attention on matters the US feels should be kept quiet. Incidentally, your friend Bernie is in disgrace as he went right to the very top of the Israeli government to complain about Mossad snatching your wife and threatening to kill any Mossad agent that harms her. However he is guarding her and her mother jealously and we too have agents watching the situation and will make our concern known to the Israeli government if it is necessary, so don't worry, your wife is as heavily protected as our First Lady. Hope to have a drink with you when this is all over. Goodbye and good luck." Kerensky rang off leaving David in deep thought. In the world of high finance and espionage and great power's vital interests, all was smoke and mirrors and constant change.

David left his rooms just before eight to go for breakfast and was surprised to see Ivan standing at attention at his door

"Why are you here?" asked David smiling hugely,

"I am here to serve you Sir," replied the boy in heavily accented English

"Well come along and have breakfast with me and we shall make a plan,"

While breakfasting with Margaret, David said,

"I have to go away for a few days, and until I get back could you take Ivan up to the nurseries and introduce him to the horticulturist and the chief forester and ask them to take Ivan in hand and teach him a thing or two?" David asked Margaret.

"Yes, I think that is a splendid idea. How long will you be away?"

"I don't know, but it shouldn't be more than a few days," he replied.

After breakfast David collected the 45 rig and strapped it on beneath his coat, and went down to conference room and waited. Saul was shown in promptly at nine.

They greeted each other, David without warmth and Saul in a guilty conciliatory way

"There has been certain developments," Saul began "and we will have to insist that you accompany us to the Congo with your executive jet. The boats are heavily guarded and it will need you there to secure their release. Our government urges you to help us, we must have that machinery"

"When must we leave and how many are to fly in the jet?" asked David curtly.

"There will just be four of us on your aircraft. The seaman and other members of the crew will be flown there in two large amphibian aircraft which will land on the Congo river at Boma, they have already left Israel and will be standing by at Kinshasa airport where they have filed a flight plan to refuel before flying on to Angola, to mislead the Congolese. After getting the go ahead to land at Boma, the flight plan will be re-filed as the circumstances dictate." Saul explained, "We would like to leave immediately."

"I will go and pack and will be down within thirty minutes," said David and stood up and walked out of the room.

They arrived at the airfield; David had just a small suitcase and had changed into a lightweight tropical suit, the jacket not revealing his pistol. Jim was standing on top of the boarding stairs.

"Good morning Judas," said David with a grin,

"Not really, welcome aboard, David," replied Jim with a smile,

"Aboard the jet, or the triple spook coach train? How I wish that I could draw four salaries," David muttered quietly as he passed the sheepish pilot.

The flight was a long one and looking out, the vastness and richness of Africa entranced the gunsmith. After the desert with its golden hues and strange beauty, the thick jungles and forests made one realize that the magnificence of it all could not be ascribed to chance.

It was just after sunset when they landed in Kinshasa. Stepping out of the air conditioned executive Jet into the hot humid air gave the body a quick shock which it soon adapted to. There was a delegation of black presidential aides to greet David and a tall tough looking white officer dressed in a ridiculous over embellished uniform whose face David instantly recognized, it was the mercenary, Colonel Steele. They nodded at one another.

After an interesting drive through a boisterous, run down, former colonial city, the convoy arrived at the Presidents palace, a grand building that had been redecorated in the poorest possible taste.

The president was a chirpy little man who greeted David warmly, constantly glancing at the white Colonel as if seeking guidance or approval every time he opened his mouth. No doubt who runs this country, David thought, and who will prove very troublesome as the situation develops.

At a nod from Steele, the president cleared the room leaving only David, the president and Colonel Steele.

"What are your intentions, David?" asked Steele bluntly,

"To sail away the factory boats as was originally planned," replied David.

"That could be difficult. There are heavy dock dues and various taxes and levies to be paid, for starters, before those boats are allowed to be released," said Steele with a grim smile,

"Let us not beat about the bush. My organization will pay all costs as were negotiated by Lord Montdrago plus bonuses for the expeditious releasing of all the boats. I learnt a lot from my father-in-law before he was shot; he did not commit suicide. I have left a letter with our attorneys to immediately notify one Kerensky of the location of the boats and what cargo they are carrying. Kerensky is the chief CIA man in London, furthermore, a large, well led and well equipped force to the north of the Congo which is preparing for certain actions in that part of Africa will be re-directed here to support some of your troublesome opponents, the rebels, who are too weak to increase the trouble you are already experiencing; with the large force that my organization controls up there, you, gentlemen will speedily be overthrown. When your comrades, big Jock, Hamish and Scotty tried a wee bit of coercion, the delayed contracts that had been placed on them when they were recruited, were called up, and as you know, Colonel Steele they were instantly taken out. Lord Montdrago was a prudent man with long experience in dealing with dangerous men so it was his practice to anticipate trouble and therefore he took out delayed contracts on each of the former SAS men that he had engaged. The holders of those contracts are not individuals but organizations of known competence, in your case the Russian mafia who in any case have a vested interest in the cargo of those boats. The cargo was originally bought from them and only half paid for, the balance to be paid when we deliver it. The Russians are growing impatient. The letter will be delivered next week if I do not return to London. Incidentally the cargo was stolen by the mafia from the Russian government and they too are not disinterested. Do I make myself clear, Colonel Steele?"

A look of pure fear shone out of Colonel Steele's eyes as he answered meekly,

"The clearance will be given immediately and the boats can leave as soon as they are ready."

"Thank you Colonel Steele, and your moneys will be paid as soon as you submit your accounts. Your personal bonuses will be paid into your accounts which are held in my bank in London. I hope we can do much more business together in the future and now I must leave, could we be taken to the Hotel, and then first thing in the morning, to the airport where our company helicopter is always stationed both for our use and yours, with permission of course, Mr. President. It has been a pleasure," said David as he took his leave of the fidgety little man who was striving not to shit himself.

The next morning the Mossad men accompanied David to the helicopter with Colonel Steele. The amphibians were told to take off an hour after the helicopter had taken off and to be prepared but not to show aggression nor their weapons which might spark a panic reaction.

The helicopter landed at Boma and David was surprised at the size of the river port, there were concrete wharves and large cranes for loading and off loading ocean going ships. The factory ships were anchored a short distance off shore and Colonel Steele had soon mustered all the soldiers and their officers and told them that the boats would be sailing soon when their replacement sea going crews arrived.

David called the Colonel aside and said,

"Billy, advise your men not to stand down and if I signal you, like this," and David placed both his hands behind his head, "Come in force, that is all of you, and insist that I stay behind with you, don't let me be taken aboard. There will be a fifty thousand dollar bonus paid into your account when I return to London," David said,

"Yes Sir," said the Colonel smartly "we shall be on guard and act decisively."

David nodded and walked towards Saul who was standing nearby.

"The planes have just radioed, they have the port in sight," he said.

The amphibians made an impressive sight as with a trail of spray and a wake of a foaming river and sea water mix they landed and taxied gracefully near to the wharf. A large tender sidled up to each of them in turn as the crews debussed and then they were taken out to each factory boat in turn and the guards who were on the boats taken off.

The tender tied up at the wharf and after the guards had climbed onto the wharf, Saul said to David,

"We will go aboard now and I am afraid you must accompany us David, please, don't cause any unpleasantness."

David put both his hands behind his head with his elbows raised up level with his shoulders and he stretched and said,

"No I'm not."

As he dropped his arms down to their normal position, all the Congolese soldiers rushed up, arms at the ready and formed up behind David in extended line. The Colonel marched up smartly and stamped to attention in front of Saul,

"Sir, Mr. McAlpine stays with us, any attempt to take him will be met with deadly force. Your aircraft are under the sights of three heavy machine guns located in bunkers nearby and will open fire if your aircraft use their weapons, Sir." The last "Sir" shouted in a very loud and menacing tone.

"Nicely done David, You are both ex SAS and we should have anticipated this" said Saul.

"Colonel Steele, please order your machine gunners to sink those aircraft if they leave before two hours have elapsed after my helicopter has taken off, is that clear?"

"Yes, Sir, Wilco" and the Colonel saluted.

"What does Wilco mean Colonel?" asked Saul,

"Will comply with, Sir," replied the gallant Billy Steele.

David strolled over to the helicopter, trying to give the impression of one who has planned for every contingency and Saul was duly impressed.

They slept overnight at the hotel and the Jet took off from Kinshasa the following morning as soon as David had boarded. David was exhausted and slept most of the way back home.

There was a car waiting when they touched down just after four pm. to take David to the estate; traffic was light and they were soon at the estate gates. The guard did not open the gate immediately as the guard usually did when an estate vehicle drove up. A surly looking guard approached the driver and asked for identification and after it was produced, let them through.

"Drive very slowly," David instructed the driver and thinking furiously tried to fathom out what might be wrong. As they car inched round a bend in the driveway, a figure darted out from behind a shrub and waved them down. The car stopped and a clearly frightened Ivan climbed in.

"Master David Sir, there are bad men in the house, Russian men, the same ones who were on the docks back in Russia when we worked to load the boats, I have seen them." Ivan said fearfully.

"How many?" asked David?

"Ten, Sir."

"Driver stop the car, I need to go into my suitcase." David got out the car and opened his case and took out a box of cartridges, drew out the 45 from the holster and checked the magazine. It took eight and David slipped one extra in the chamber and put the box in his pocket.

"Drive on" he said to the driver after closing the boot and settling down next to Ivan,

"Don't be afraid, Ivan, there will be some shooting but just obey me and you will not be hurt."

The car drew up at the entrance to the grand house and David motioned Ivan to follow him. The chief of security stood in front of the conference door with a terrified look on his face and was blinking deliberately and continually trying to warn David.

"There are some gentlemen waiting to see you in the conference room, Sir."

David gave him a broad smile and said cheerily and loudly,

"Just have to drop off something down in the basement and will join them in a jiffy," and he and Ivan breezed past and turned down into the gunroom. David quickly unlocked the door and pulled Ivan inside and locked the door manually behind them.

"I am going to show you something now that you must never tell anybody about, ever, and when we go in, you will see some boxes with big holes in their tops. They are for you to cough into so you do not make a noise. So if you want to cough or sneeze, do it in the box and you will not be heard." David said and Ivan nodded

David slid open the oak chest and they entered the secret room and David closed the entrance behind them. Putting his finger to his lips to emphasize silence, they climbed the stair and when they got to the observation slits, David again placed his finger to his lips as he opened the spy slits. The men were talking and all were facing the door. The diamond dealer that had bought David's diamonds sat in a chair and his face was horribly beaten up and he was terrified,Colonel Dempster and Sir Horace Blakely were talking to one another.

"What if he wont show us where the diamonds are?" asked the Colonel,

"Boris is the best in the business, it has never been known for anyone to be reticent when Boris questioned them, to call a spade a spade he is the most terrible torturer that Russia has produced, his knowledge of torture is immense and his victims never pass out or die on him, he is superb," said Sir Horace with admiration. There were two men flanking Boris and the two Englishmen were standing about six feet behind them leaning with their backsides against the desk.

"Ah, here he comes, I hear someone at the door" said Sir Horace.

They all stood facing the door expectantly with their backs to the secret door when David slipped in and shot Boris and the two beside them with accuracy and speed.

"Ah Sir Horace, so good of you to drop in," said David cheerfully from behind them.

They spun around and the Colonel said frantically,

"You won't get away with this you know,"

"I will" said David as he shot him.

"The CIA have the nuclear plant and as you know of the diamonds regretfully you must follow your expert Boris," and David shot him too. The distraught diamond dealer said,

"I did not tell them anything, I had nothing to tell, they had you under observation and followed you to my shop and over to the bank in Switzerland"

"I know, and you have nothing to fear and I want to do a lot more business after tonight when all these evil men will be no more, Ivan, go over to that cabinet and pour my friend anything he wants and stay with him until I get back."

David strode over to the main entrance door and locked it and then walked back to the secret door. Before entering the hidden chamber he said,

"Don't open the entrance door until you hear my voice when I call you to open it,"

David slipped away into the secret maze, closing the door behind him. First he crept up to the security center to see why the security guards were not around in the main building. They were all huddled together and one was lying on the floor with his face all bashed open and was groaning in pain. There were two strangers with guns in their hands sitting down and looking bored. The chairs as usual had their backs to the chamber door. David slipped in and shot them both from behind in their heads. He asked the astonished security guards.

"Where are the others?"

One of them said,

"One is in madam Margaret's room and one is behind the chief downstairs, covering him to make sure that he didn't warn you when you came in,"

"Look after your comrade, is he badly hurt?"

"No Sir I don't think so just a heavy blow to the head," said the spokesman.

"Wait here while I attend to the others."

"Sir, there are five in the conference room."

"They are all dead." said David grimly, as he slipped back into the chamber and its galleries.

The man in Margaret's room was sitting opposite to her at the dining room table and David had to be quick. He stepped into the room quickly and fired instantly over Margaret's head as the surprised man tried to stand and draw his gun. He slumped back into his chair and Margaret called out softly,

"Is that you David dear?"

"Yes, my sweetie, There is only one left, I shant be a minute and slid past her and left by her main entrance door and made his way to the top of the stairs just above the ground floor. The Russian was standing behind a cabinet in the main walkway keeping watch on the chief security guard who was standing outside the conference room. David fired obliquely down, hitting the man behind the neck. He fell with a crash and the chief spun around terrified. He looked up and saw David, who lifted the 45 and waved it and said,

"Relax, it's all over. Those inside the conference room are all dead."

David walked down the stairs to the conference door and knocked and called out loudly,

"Ivan, open up."

The door opened and an excited Ivan asked

"Is Madam Margaret, she is well?"

"Yes, thanks to you. Chief, this beaten up gentleman is my friend and an honored guest, please escort him up to Miss Margaret's room and see that his wounds are dressed and he has anything he wants. I have to go to my study and phone certain people. This is British intelligence business so impress on our men not to phone out and we will have a meeting when those highly placed officials arrive," said David.

"Are you one of them, I mean Intelligence Sir?"

"In a way, Chief, in a way," responded David as he made his way up to his study.

It was the same lady who answered the phone at the American embassy,

"This is David McAlpine, may I speak to Mr. Karensky, please," He was put through immediately.

"Mr. Karensky, I need your help. When I arrived back at the estate, there were some of those dreadful uncouth Russian mafia people who wanted their nuclear plant back. Well one thing led to another and they are all dead, could you send a large mortuary vehicle around and take them away without any fuss with the British authorities?"

"My name is Bud, David, and did you put labels on them as our Ambassador requested, and how many are there?"

"Well, Bud, if you pop off the guard at the gate, who is one of them and probably will not let you enter, there will be ten and that includes Sir Horace and Colonel Dempster, who said that I wouldn't get away with shooting him."

There was a long silence and then Bud said

"Shit"

"You will then Bud?" asked David anxiously.

"Yes, we will be there soon, are you sure the one at the gate is definitely one of them?"

"Yes, Bud, he was so ugly and badly dressed, I first thought he was a member of the CIA, but he was very polite and I knew that he had to be one of the Russian mafia" said David with a giggle. Bud hung up but immediately and before David could hang up, the Lady with the authoritive voice interjected and said,

"Go and have a bath, Mr. McAlpine and thank you for calling and have a nice day," and she too hung up.

The Mortuary van, preceded by a large American car drew up in front of the mansions impressive entrance and Bud and the Ambassador got out. A struggling trussed up security guard was dragged out the car and thrown into the back of the van

"Good evening David, may we come in?"

"Please do, Sir, you are most welcome and thank you for bringing the sanitizing crew,"

Chapter Nineteen

They were all seated in the conference room, the Ambassador, Bud Kerensky and two other men who had been introduced as officials of the state department. The Americans from the morgue where just completing the removal of the bodies. They had been placed in body bags and a man was attaching labels.

"He is doing your job," said the Ambassador dryly smiling at David

As the last of the sad bags were being taken out, David's chief of security wheeled in a tea trolley laden with delicious tidbits and the tea and coffee pots with sufficient cups and saucers. The chief was clearly in a stunned state of disbelief and a little yellow around the gills; he asked if he should pour and when refused, left the room closing the door behind him.

"Let me commence by thanking you for your help in concluding a matter that has troubled our government for some time and it distresses us to have to come here and warn you or even threaten you to desist from pursuing the course of action which we have been told you are contemplating," the Ambassador said firmly.

David was puzzled and said,

"I don't understand, Sir,"

"I am referring to the large force of men you are financing and directing based to the north of the Congo," answered the Ambassador coldly, with a brittle steely tone in his voice.

David burst out laughing,

"Good lord, news travels fast in Africa. No Sir, there is no third force. I was threatened at the meeting I had with the President and the head of the army that the boats anchored at Boma under guard with a large force on standby would not be released until huge sums of money were paid and that the money would have to be in their possession before any release would be granted. I told them that I had left letters with my lawyers in London to redirect this large fictional force which we controlled onto them if I was not back in London within a week and that there were contracts out on them which would be activated if the boats and myself were not away within the aforementioned week. They became very humble, one could almost say meek, very quickly and the releases were given and their guards at Boma were very co-operative the next day,"

The relief in the room was tangible and Bud Kcrensky said,

"So I can tear up that label we had prepared for you and cancel the body bag?"

"Oh yes, my life has become far too interesting to risk irritating the state department. However, I am worried about the British authorities especially as two of those body bags contain the corpses of Colonel Dempster of MI6 and an English knight, Sir Horace Blakely. I am anticipating great trouble." said David earnestly.

"We can and will clear all those problems up. I assure you that MI6 will be relieved, if somewhat stunned at the course of events; they are still smarting from the effects of Kim Philby and his gang. You will not hear of this matter again, we will squash it at the very highest level of government. Now, to another matter. The Israeli ambassador has requested a meeting with me tomorrow, urgently. I think that he wants to discuss the matter of the boats and of the abducting by the CIA of your wife and her mother and your friend Dr. Cohen and his wife. They will be here tomorrow morning and will be delivered to this house in the morning, as soon as the aircraft bringing them puts down. I want to have that meeting here at ten am, OK?"

David was overjoyed and a great load suddenly had lifted from his shoulders,

"Thank you Sir, thank you. Yes, the meeting is looked forward to." David said happily.

"As soon as we have finished our coffee we will leave. Everything has ended successfully," said the Ambassador.

David got up and walked to the door and called for the Chief of security .who was standing outside the conference door.

"Chief, this is the London Ambassador of the United States of America and officials of the State Department; will you impress upon your men that everything that has occurred in this house today is to remain secret. There will be large bonuses to compensate you and your men for your loyalty in the handling of the difficulties of the day." said David.

"Yes, absolute secrecy," repeated the Ambassador.

"Yes Sir I will tell my men, Thank you Sir, may I go now Mr. McAlpine Sir?"

"Yes Chief." The chief left the room.

The Ambassador and his entourage then bid David farewell, the Ambassador saying,

"Until tomorrow then," and they all departed.

David hurried up to Margaret's apartment as soon as his important guests had left. Margaret was deep in conversation with the battered and bruised Diamond dealer

"The Chief of our security has just told us that The American Ambassador and several other men were here and that they brought a team who has taken all the bodies away. One of them came in here and removed that dreadful man's corpse; it was quite disconcerting having him lying over there while Mr. Solomon and I were trying to enjoy our tea and a chat. What was it all about David?" asked Margaret.

"Those men with the Ambassador were State department officials and one of them was the head of the London arm of the CIA. Our family inherited some secret baggage including a deal with the Russian Mafia concerning a stolen nuclear plant for the enriching of Uranium. Every one wanted it for different reasons; the USA to destroy it, the Israeli's to utilize it and the mafia to redeem some money from it.

I, knowing nothing about it, stumbled upon the location of the ships which were carrying the plant and which had disappeared and hence the Mafia's interest in me and their following me about. I had done some business with Mr. Solomon and they concluded that he was involved, I am so sorry that you were dragged in, Mr. Solomon and any medical expenses we will obviously meet. I hope that you will continue doing business with our family. There will be no more trouble. Once more I apologize."

"I should be so lucky to have been part of this exciting adventure at my age. You must teach me how to use a gun and I will seek employment with the CIA. Of course we shall continue doing business. Good business is good business and shooting crooks is shooting crooks."

David realized there was a great deal of wisdom in what the old man had just said

"Your granddaughter, her mother and Dr. Cohen and his wife will be delivered here by the American officials as soon as their plane arrives tomorrow," David said with a broad smile. Margaret gave a small shriek of joy and clapped her hands to her cheeks.

" I will send you home with a driver Mr. Solomon, please direct him anywhere you wish to go and I hope that you and your wife will come and spend a few days with us in the near future, the estate has many interesting features" said David,

"I have no wife, have never had one, I live with a nephew and his family,"

"I will send for the car now," said David and picked up the phone.

The old man left none the worse for the manhandling he had received and David said he would see him within a week to do some business.

David slept like a log and woke as soon as the pre dawn light seeped into his room and as had become his habit; he walked through to his study and went straight to the binoculars. The water birds were just starting to move about and some were flying out to forage on the surrounding fields. The birds made David feel calm and relaxed but could not dampen the joy he felt knowing that Katinka would be home in a few hours. David knew that the secret chambers were now common knowledge amongst the security staff and that he must remove the last of the diamonds. All the share certificate had been lodged in the Swiss bank as had the bearer bonds and other financial instruments that had formed part of His Lordship's nest egg. There would be death duties and other taxes and levies when the estate was finally wound up but the secret cache that David now had for his family would ensure that all those he loved would always want for nothing.

The Americans were as good as their word and delivered all four of their passengers just before nine. There was much joy at the reunion but Bernie and Rachel stood back in embarrassment and looked both sheepish and ashamed.

As soon as he had hugged and kissed his wife and her mother, he rushed over to Rachel and kissed her too, enthusiastically and then flung his arms around Bernie and gave him a joyous hug and said,

"Thank you both for what you tried to do and also for making such a fuss with Mossad and your government. I have been told that you have blotted your copybook with them and severely jeopardized your career. I hope we will always be your best friends and please don't say another word about your dilemma, I understand." And David gave Rachel another kiss.

"Hey, don't let that become addictive," said Bernie with a grin.

"There is to be a meeting at ten, in about an hour's time. The American Ambassador and the Israeli Ambassador plus the CIA and Mossad will attend. The meeting will take place in the conference room and I would like you to attend with me, Bernie. Will you?"

"Of course, I look forward to it," replied Bernie.

"I am sure the ladies will find a great deal to talk about and maybe even a picnic under the trees at the side of the lake. I think champagne and caviar would be appropriate, Don't you, Margaret?" asked David.

Margaret, bathed in a glow of happiness, could only nod.

The meeting commenced soon after the mansions staff had brought in the four trolleys with their coffee percolators, tea pots, crockery and all the paraphernalia associated with the ritual of tea drinking, David would have preferred a Geisha girl or two to sanctify the ritual. The other trolleys had a wide selection of cakes and savory snacks and there were the inevitable English cucumber sandwiches too.

"Gentlemen, as the Israeli Ambassador asked for this meeting, it is fitting that he opens it," stated the Ambassador representing the USA, nodding at the Israelis.

"Thank you Mr. Ambassador, these three of my fellow countrymen were the last of the Israeli contingent to see the factory ships with their cargo of nuclear machinery sail out of the port of Boma on the Congo river. They flew out of Boma two hours after the ships sailed. Our radio listening posts picked up signals from those ships five hours later when they were out on the Atlantic Ocean in deep water. The signals were of a desperate plea for your navy not to sink the ships until the crews had abandoned the craft. Since then we have heard nothing, absolutely nothing. We would like an explanation, please?" asked the Israeli Ambassador angrily.

"Bud Kerensky here is the senior CIA officer that was in charge of the operation to destroy the nuclear machinery. Could you explain exactly what happened because I too am puzzled as to why you did not hear those distress calls that I have just been told about. Your official report just said that the ships had been sunk together with their cargo and all hands." asked the American Ambassador.

"Gentlemen, my name is Nathaniel Kerensky, my Grandparents were Russian Jews who emigrated to the USA. My father was a first generation American but could speak both Russian and Hebrew fluently. Hebrew was the language which was spoken in his home when he was growing up. I, too, speak the language fluently.

Now in the fog of war communications often suffer and many accidents occur, take my father, for instance, he was the radio and communications officer aboard the USS Liberty in the Mediterranean when it came under friendly fire from the Israeli forces, he was killed in that action as were thirty three others and one hundred and seventy four were wounded. One of the survivors testified that my father told his shipmates around him, while the attacks were taking place, yes gentlemen, there were at least three separate attacks over a space of time, seventy five minutes of being attacked by both aircraft and torpedo boats; he told his shipmates that the pilots were being given orders to ignore the ships continual radio calls identifying itself as an unarmed American listening post, or spy ship if you will. There was an oversize Stars and Stripes flying plus two normal sized flags for the very reason that accidents might occur but the survivor claimed that my father repeatedly said that orders were being given to continue the attack. The attacks only ceased when higher American authorities based in Egypt became aware and ordered the Israeli air force and navy to stop the attack. Strangely enough, the captain of one of our submarines that fired two torpedoes at each factory ship carrying the nuclear plant, also lost his father aboard the Liberty. As I say, communications sometimes fail; regretfully, there were no survivors from the two factory ships which were carrying the nuclear plant. Does that satisfy you Mr. Ambassador?" said Bud, thrusting his head forward and glaring at the startled official. There was a long silence and then Bud addressed his own Ambassador,

"Sir, I tendered my resignation this morning as too did the commander of our submarine, an old friend whose grand father was also a Russian Jewish refugee who was given sanctuary by the USA."

The Ambassador kept silent and the silence was only broken after some time when a crestfallen Israeli Ambassador said,

"I will report the discussion we have just had to my Government." He paused and stood up and facing Bud, bowed slightly and said "Shalom,"

The Israeli delegation excused themselves and left the room.

"That was a reprehensible act, Bud, and I hope it has purged your soul of the anger you have been living with. Our government is relieved that the nuclear plant has been destroyed which, had it been installed in Israel would have caused much trouble in the future and maybe even a breach between two friends. I intercepted your resignation and destroyed it, as too, did my old friend Admiral Perkins with the commander of the submarines resignation. David, our thanks for all your help, but tell me, how did you manage to neutralize all nine of those mafia thugs on your own?" asked the Ambassador.

"The original founder of the banking dynasty was known to have never attended a meeting of his senior executives, yet always knew what had gone on during those meetings. Some people thought that one or two of the participants in the meetings would spy for him, but that was not so. The old man designed and built this house and many laughed at him for building some of the walls over six feet thick "for old English Authenticity" he declared. But, he was a banker, whose success, like all bankers, was good intelligence; crouching down in the grass listening to the grasshoppers. Well within those walls were a labyrinth of secret passages and chambers and most rooms have spy slits where everything can be heard and seen. There are even cough boxes, boxes with face sized holes in the top where a cough or a sneeze can be suppressed. This gave me a powerful tool, when I discovered the secret that not even Lord Montdrago knew about. For example, my three former comrades who worked for His Lordship received their orders, in this very room, to execute me and Dr. Cohen, the following morning. I heard that from up behind there," said David pointing above the large desk, "This enabled me to come back later at night and hide my silenced 45 in the foliage of that plant next to you, Sir, and when we were ordered to come and sign some papers, Dr. Cohen's small pistol was detected by the metal detector at the door, the men who were about to kill us dropped their guard and while Dr. Cohen was attending to the documents, I shot them. I was forewarned about the three Russians who were waiting in here with the English Lord and again hid the 45 in the foliage with splendid results. Yesterday, I went from room to room with the silenced 45 and neutralized every one of them," David walked to the secret door, entered and closed it behind him and quickly reappeared and using his fore finger simulated five quick shots.

"They were all watching the entrance door and had their backs to me and their weapons concealed so that I could use the gunfighters of the old west's favorite shot; a shot in the back."

The Ambassador laughed heartily and asked,

"Why are you giving your secret and source of power away now?"

"Yesterday, as I entered each room and started firing I was observed by most of the security guards and others, but that is not why the secret rooms are going to be sealed, it is because genetically I have the inclination to become a peeping Tom; extreme voyeurism will forever tempt me and it must be suppressed." They all laughed.

"So now you know Dr. Cohen. You were a member of the estate staff and a participant in some of the action, what did you think at the time?" asked the Ambassador.

"I was nonplussed Sir. All I know is, and complained about at the time, was that I, a member of the chosen race and a qualified Medical man, was treated as a lowly serf, forever crawling around on my hands and knees searching for and picking up spent cartridges to protect my lord and master from suspicion. I thank the good lord that I missed yesterday as I would still be groveling around for that ninth cartridge."

They all laughed again as the Ambassador said,

"Don't get involved unless the man with the gun is dressed like a genuine gunslinger from the old west that only used a single action revolver that doesn't eject its empty cases all over the place."

"How would I recognize him?" Bernie asked,

"He will be dressed like a genuine gunfighter with a big hat, two low slung colts and wearing a Jockstrap and spurs," said David and they all laughed

The Ambassador rose to leave and held out his hand to David,

"If ever I or my staff can be of assistance, call me. We sincerely hope that if we ever need your services you will accommodate us. Fare you well, Gunsmith."